Calling on the Reaper

The Reapers Book One

Haley Tyler

For the people who like being choked,
this one's for you.

Calling on the Reaper Playlist

LISTEN TO THE FULL PLAYLIST HERE

Dying Is Absolutely Safe – Architects
Roses – Awaken I Am
If I'm There – Bad Omens
Nightmare – Besomorph, RIELL
Expiration Date – Dead Eyes
Black Rose – Deep As Ocean
Reaper – Fit For A King
Resurrection – GANK
skins – The Haunting
(Don't Fear) The Reaper (Metal Cover) – Leo
MIDDLE OF THE NIGHT – Loveless
Something In The Way – Nirvana
Man or a Monster (feat. Zayde Wolf) – Sam Tinnesz
A Thousand Years – Valiant Hearts
til the end – Witchz

Stay Connected!

JOIN MY NEWSLETTER!
JOIN MY FACEBOOK GROUP!

Stay up to date on cover reveals, preorder announcements, merch drops, giveaways, ARC sign-ups, newsletters, and more!!

Author's Note

Author's Note

I never want to trigger or offend anyone with my books, but I didn't hold back on this one.

This is an intense story with **heavy** kink and dark themes.

This is a *dark* romance.
Please read with caution.

GRIM

FIFTEEN YEARS AGO

I'd just clocked into my shift when I got called right back out. That's how it always goes, right? No chance for a breather, to ease into work—you're thrown into it headfirst.

It was the blaring siren, the one telling me I had a fifty-fifty shot of bringing home a soul. I quickly threw on my cloak, grabbed my scythe, and headed out.

I hated calls like this. I wanted to know that I was definitely bringing someone across. I didn't want to watch them die—or almost die. Just because I was a Reaper, didn't mean I was heartless—well, technically, I was, but I wasn't an asshole. Well, actually, I was that, too.

Standing in the shadows of a large tree, I watched as a young girl ran frightened from a nasty-looking man. She couldn't have been older than ten, and he was massive compared to her, although he was nothing compared to me.

His feet pounded and crunched against the gravel as he picked up speed, his eyes narrowed and mouth tight. She looked terrible—bloody and swollen, her clothes ratty and torn, her feet bared and shredded. Her black hair flew behind her as she ran, her abused body barely moving her away from the threat at her back.

"Raven!" the threat shouted. The hair on my arms stood at the

1

malevolence in his voice. She glanced over her shoulder, her chest heaving with each pained step.

That was her undoing.

She tripped and fell, her eyes wide as she face-planted onto the gravel. Something crunched on impact and the howl she made was unlike anything I'd ever heard a mortal make. I shifted uncomfortably on my feet as the man towered above her, his breathing harsh. Blood poured from Raven's face, pooling on the ground as she pushed herself up on shaky, weak elbows.

"Serves you right for running from me," he snarled as he rammed his foot into her stomach, kicking her onto her back. She let out a whimper, and when she turned, bile rose in my throat. Her nose jutted out in different directions, and her lip sported a bloody hole where her teeth punctured through. She coughed up blood but didn't try to wipe it from her mouth and chin, letting it drip down the contours of her face.

I'd seen gruesome murder scenes and never felt sick. I never blinked twice. I wasn't surprised at the horror and violence humans inflicted on one another, so why was I feeling this way now?

"I'm sorry," she cried, her voice nasally from her broken nose. She screamed as he grabbed a handful of her thick hair. He yanked her to her knees, and her bloody hands slipped against his arm, staining his skin red.

I looked around the dark, deserted street, waiting for someone to hear her, to save her, but there was nothing except acres and acres of empty farmland and trees. The moon was the only source of light, but my eyesight was better than that of a mortal—I could clearly see the fear and pain shimmering in her wide eyes.

No one could hear her screams. No one was coming for her. No one would save her.

"I'm sorry," her assailant mocked, bringing the back of his hand down across her face and snapping her head to the side. "You should've died with your bitch mother." My eyes narrowed into slits as he pulled her hair again, her neck straining back. "You know not to run from me, Raven. It only makes things worse for you."

She sobbed, full body sobs that shook the ground, rattling me to my core. Tears poured down her dirty, bloody cheeks, her entire body trembling as he backhanded her again.

My feet moved.

I couldn't stop, and before I knew what happened, I stood beside them. They didn't know I was there, of course, and they wouldn't until I decided to make my presence known. I didn't like showing myself to mortals unless I had to. They tended to fear me, but in this moment, I had no choice.

For whatever reason, the coldness that spread through my body turned to a fiery rage as I watched him hit her again, then pull his belt through the loops of his jeans.

I wasn't certain what was about to happen, but when he folded it in half, I had a good idea. If I didn't stop this, she was going to die. He would beat her to death.

It was *her* soul I was here to reap.

With a deep breath, I willed my glamour to melt away; the moment I was visible, they froze. I didn't waste any time reaching down and forcibly removing the shocked man's hand from Raven's hair. It took his mind a moment to catch up, and when it did, he began to scream.

She didn't scream like I'd expected. She didn't fight me when I motioned her to her feet and pushed her behind me. She didn't make a sound when she fell back onto her ass as I stepped between them, the man's head barely reaching my shoulder.

"It's your lucky day, little bird. He's about to die." There was murder blazing in my eyes, I knew.

That woke her up.

"Wait," she breathed. Her warm, blood-slicked hand wrapped around my icy wrist; she gasped but didn't let go. Instead, her hold tightened. I turned my head to get a clear look at her, finding her shadowed eyes the size of saucers as she stared up at me. Those haunting eyes found mine through my mask, and I felt her searing gaze penetrate down to my core. "Don't kill him."

I paused.

Glancing back at the man—the blubbering, piece-of-shit child abuser—then back at her, I asked, "Why?" It was a simple question. I knew it was her soul I was supposed to reap tonight, but I wanted to take his instead. I wanted him to die, to take him to the In-Between and leave him there, where he'd be lost forever, never at peace.

"He's my stepfather," she answered, her eyes never leaving mine. She couldn't see my face behind the mask, but she was peering into my soul all the same. If I had one, that was. It felt like she was stripping me bare, like the centuries of protective barriers I'd built around myself were nothing. "He's the only family I have."

"You want an abusive family?" I asked, tilting my head to the side. "You want a family that hurts you?" She swallowed heavily, her eyes finally leaving mine to glance at him before returning to me, to the mask again.

"He's all I have."

I looked back at the man again, viewing him in a new light. He was a piece of shit, actual human garbage, and I didn't want to spare his life. I didn't want him to take another fucking breath, but I stepped back, shifting myself to stand beside Raven instead of in front of her.

"Thank you," she murmured, her small hand still wrapped around my wrist.

The man was still in shock, his face deathly pale and his eyes wider than should've been possible. Maybe in other circumstances, it would've been funny, but he was hurting this little girl, and all I could think about was killing him. He flicked his eyes between Raven and me, then settled on her with a look that made me bristle.

I stared at him as I contemplated what to do. I felt torn and I didn't like that. I'd never felt like this before, unsure of my next move. I always had a plan, another call to answer, another soul to accompany into the next life, but right then, I was at a loss.

"You know this monster?" the man rasped. I took a small step forward, but Raven's hand tightened again on my wrist. Her hand was a collar, her arm a leash, keeping me in check. She was holding me back, making my choice for me, and simultaneously saving us both, even if she didn't know it.

I'd get in trouble with the higher-ups if I killed someone whose time wasn't up. That was a big no-no in the Reaper world. We were only guides, helping souls cross over; we didn't interfere. It wasn't our decision if someone lived or died—but why would we have the power to take a life if we weren't supposed to use it?

The decision made, I easily shook off her little hand and stepped forward. All it would take was a surge of power to my fingertips, a small touch to this fucker, and he'd be dead. I wouldn't accompany his soul anywhere. I'd leave him to be lost forever, to never find a new vessel, to stay in the In-Between forever.

Raven reached for me again, and for the first time that night, I realized how brave she truly was. She didn't seem like a weak child, not how she had moments ago. She was brave in a way I hadn't seen from many mortals. They knew their time was limited, and if they were seeing me, they knew said time was up. She didn't care. When someone didn't care, whatever they'd endured in their lives was worse than what death would bring.

What had she endured in her young life that made her not fear me? Not fear *death*?

It made my chest ache for her, then burn with so much fucking rage, I couldn't see straight.

My leather glove-clad hand shot out from beneath my cloak and wrapped around her stepfather's throat. I towered over him, my hand easily encompassing his puny neck, my thumb overlapping my fingers.

His eyes rose to my mask, and I knew he could see my eyes. They were a soulless black that usually made mortals shit themselves. Even if we weren't the bad guys, our reputation preceded us. Sometimes, like now, I used that reputation to my advantage.

I liked to make sure the evil souls I helped cross over could see the warmth I lacked, the love and light I didn't carry, the humanity I didn't have. I fucking loved seeing them terrified, but this man's horror was extra sweet.

"Please don't kill me," he squeaked.

Raven was silent behind me, and for a moment, I wondered if she would try to sacrifice herself or bargain with me—her life for his—like so many others. She didn't. Instead, she stood behind me, her eyes boring into the back of my head.

"Give me a reason why I shouldn't," I gritted out, keeping my voice low and even. "Just one fucking reason." He flicked his eyes to Raven, and I shuffled to the side, blocking her from view. His eyes shot back to mine as the waterworks began.

He sobbed harder than before—harder than Raven had when he broke her fucking face. He shook his head, his stringy, greasy hair swaying with his movement.

"I—I'll stop," he said, his eyes dropping to the ground.

"Stop what?" I growled. I had an idea, but I wanted him to say it. I wanted to hear the words come straight from his mouth.

"Hurting her."

"Hurting her, how?" I shook him roughly, my hand tightening around his throat. He sputtered and coughed, his face turning red. It was only when a small hand calmly touched my forearm that I loosened my grip, and he inhaled a deep lungful of air.

"I—I just smack her around some," he gurgled, and I glanced over my shoulder at her.

Even though she looked completely fucked, her face swollen and dripping blood, she stood proudly. So proudly, in fact, that I wanted to bow before her. She looked like a little Queen.

"You touch her any other way?" I demanded when I looked back at him. More tears leaked down his face as his body began to violently shake. I sighed tiredly.

"No," he said quietly. "Not like that."

I glanced at her again, but she gave away nothing. He opened his mouth to say something else, but I was tired of him and his bullshit. All the power I had in my body shot to my arm and through my fingers.

He died instantly.

1
RAVEN
PRESENT

"What's a girl gotta do to get a decent cup of coffee around here?" Kali, my best friend, mumbled, her blonde brows furrowed. "I thought this was New York. Isn't this place known for good coffee?" I smiled to myself and shook my head as I wiped the counter.

"I think I make pretty good coffee," I said, and she rolled her eyes.

"No offense, but your coffee sucks." She slid her cup across the counter, and I lifted my brows at her. "I'd like a full refund and to report whoever made this shit." She pointed at the cup, her lips twitching. "Where's your manager?"

"Get the fuck out of here," I laughed as I threw my damp rag at her. She caught it easily and flipped me off before grabbing her cup. She took another small sip and grimaced as she swallowed.

"Seriously, Ray, how do you always burn it?"

"Nathan made it today," I lied, and she huffed out a hard breath.

Drama. Queen.

"Should've known," she mumbled, looking irritated. "That guy could fuck up a wet dream." I snorted but didn't disagree. She wasn't wrong. "What's on the agenda tonight? Pizza and a movie?" She took another sip then set the cup down, finally giving up on trying to drink it. Grabbing it, I dumped it down the steel sink.

"I'm heading to Staten Island," I casually mentioned.

"God," she groaned, dropping her head back. "What fuckboy are you talking to now?"

I might've been known to have a thing for fuckboys. They ran with dangerous crowds, which was exactly their appeal. There was never a dull moment with them, and I needed excitement in my life. Otherwise, I'd lose my fucking mind.

"His name is C-Dog," I chirped, and Kali's eyebrows shot into her hairline.

"You have got to be kidding me," she deadpanned. "Please tell me you're joking. C-Dog? Really?"

"I think his real name is Connor. Or Collin." I thought for a moment, my eyes trained on the ceiling. "Maybe Colton?" She groaned again, then glared at me.

"Do I want to know what *C-Dog* does for a living?"

"Probably not." I smiled broadly. "But I'll tell you anyway. He's a dealer. Nothing crazy, just weed and coke."

"Nothing crazy," she repeated sarcastically.

She closed her eyes and inhaled deeply as she tried to calm herself. I'd seen her do it a million times. Her therapist told her deep breathing and counting to a hundred would help her, but it never worked, not when I was involved. I seemed to know exactly what buttons to push to keep her permanently on edge.

"Why can't you date a nice, normal guy?" she asked as she opened her eyes. She tried to keep her voice level, but her hands were balled into fists. "You're cute. You could do so much better than—"

"Normal is boring," I said, interrupting her before she could get going on her soapbox. "Nice guys are boring. There's a reason they finish last." I smiled, waiting for her to laugh at my lame joke. She just glared at me harder.

"They're safe," she countered. "And when you get a wild hare up your ass, I have to go to those stupid fucking parties with you. I've lost track of how many times we've almost died." I grinned wolfishly at her.

A few girls in school uniforms walked in, giggling at something on their phones. It was mid-afternoon, and the store was only a block away from the closest middle school. We usually got flooded with kids around this time.

"You know we have more fun almost dying than we ever would with some banker and his friends." I shuddered dramatically, mostly to make her laugh, but the thought of ending up with some wannabe Wall Street douchebag made me want to throw up.

That would be a different kind of death—slower, more painful, and a lot less fun. At least with C-Dog, I'd go out with a smile on my face.

"I literally hate you," she ground out. "Fucking hate you, Ray."

"No, you don't," I sang, and she rolled her eyes.

She rested her hip against the counter and glanced over her shoulder at the girls inspecting the rows of snacks. When she turned toward me, she leaned forward and I mimicked her movements.

"Have you gotten anymore...you know," she lifted her brows expectantly, "*gifts*?"

"You mean roses?" I hissed, my eyes flitting to the girls then dropping back to her. I let out a hard breath and tried to ignore my rolling stomach. "I found one on my kitchen counter this morning."

"Inside your apartment?" she shouted, then winced when the girls' chatter momentarily stopped. "*In* your apartment? You need to go to the police."

"I'll be fine," I said as I leaned away from her. I rested my hands on the counter to keep them from shaking.

"He was inside your apartment," she said quietly. "He's escalating. He's getting braver. That's not good, Ray."

"I probably just forgot to lock my door—"

"Raven," she snapped. "Some lunatic is stalking you. You need to go to the police."

"And say what, Kal?" I demanded, throwing my arms out wide. "That I'm finding black roses on my doorstep? That's hardly enough to investigate."

"At least tell them—"

"Kal," I sighed, rubbing my forehead. "Please just drop it. I'm fine."

She stared at me like she didn't believe me, and rightfully so.

I was scared out of my fucking mind.

Five months ago, a single black rose appeared on my welcome mat every night. The first few times, I thought nothing of it. I thought it was a prank, or maybe someone leaving them for everyone in the building. When they started appearing every single night for weeks with no notes, however, I began to feel uneasy. I asked my elderly neighbor if she'd received any roses, but she'd said no and slammed her door in my face.

It wasn't until two dozen black roses were waiting for me one night that I really started to freak out.

They'd always been left outside my door. Until this morning.

This morning, there was one on my kitchen counter, right in the middle so I couldn't miss it. Seeing it made my hackles rise. I spent an hour searching my tiny old apartment, but couldn't find any signs of the intruder or how they could've gotten in.

My door was still locked with a deadbolt and two chains, and my windows were nailed shut. Yeah, I was paranoid. Sue me.

There was no way anyone could've gotten in, but somehow, this guy did.

"What time should I meet you tonight?" Kali asked, pulling me from my thoughts. I shook my head slightly, then blinked a few times to refocus on her.

"Ten. On the corner."

"Ten? I have to work in the morning."

"Ten," I insisted.

"Fine," she grumbled. "See you at ten, bitch." She flipped me off over her shoulder as she walked out onto the bustling sidewalk.

I rolled my eyes at her dramatics and turned my attention to the girls as they strolled to the counter. That sinking feeling I'd felt in my stomach since I'd found the rose this morning began to melt away as I rang them up, and, by the end of my shift, it had vanished completely.

2

GRIM

SIX MONTHS AGO

"There he is!" Brody cheered, lifting his thick arms in the air. "The one and only—"

"Fuck off," I grumbled as I pushed past him, my shoulder knocking into his. A familiar wood-smoke scent hit me, and I glanced over my shoulder, finding Rage leaning against the wall, as always.

"Hey, wait." Brody grabbed my arm, stopping me. "Don't you want to celebrate your newfound freedom with your favorite brothers?"

"You're my only brothers," I said dryly as I turned toward him. "And not by choice."

"Nice to have you back," Caden laughed, moving to clap me on the shoulder. "I'm glad to see prison didn't dull your shine."

"Fuck you," I snarled, baring my teeth at him.

Caden and Brody were Irish twins, Rage was the youngest, and I was the oldest. While the twins weren't *literal* twins, they were still exactly the same—fucking annoying. Rage and I seemed to make up for their lack of sensibility.

"I wasn't in prison," I said as I slumped onto the black leather sofa, folding my arms over my chest.

Our house looked the same as it had fifteen years ago when I was

11

forced to leave. Exposed pipes mazed across the ceiling, black, industrial-looking rods hanging down with single light bulbs on the ends, and dark cherry hardwood floors ran throughout. The stairs had a black metal railing, and the walls were dark, exposed brick. The walls that weren't brick were painted matte black.

My brothers and I had lived here for decades, and as the trends in the Mortal Realm shifted, so did this place. It was mostly Brody's doing. He liked to stay close with the mortals, missing being one himself. His soul was the last of us to go, and when he found himself a Reaper instead of in a new vessel, he didn't take it well.

But we were all together again, and that was what mattered.

"Prison. The In-Between. Whatever." Caden waved me off dismissively. "It's all the same."

"It's not," I sighed. "Not even close."

The In-Between was like Purgatory. It was where lost souls went to live for the rest of eternity, never finding peace, or another vessel or realm. It was also where Reapers were sent to babysit said souls as punishment for breaking Reaper Law. It was bullshit and boring; it felt like you were living one long, endless day.

You never slept. You never did anything except walk your route and keep an eye on the souls that resided there. It was where I'd been since the night I killed that abuser.

Since I'd saved Raven's life.

Just the thought of *her* made my blood hum. I'd given up fifteen years of my life for some kid, and for what? So she could throw hers away partying and fucking everything with a dick?

Call me bitter.

I'd kept tabs on her throughout the years, wanting to see what she'd gotten up to. It was nothing good. She repaid my sacrifice by living dangerously and recklessly. Was she *trying* to die? That's what it seemed like to me, and it pissed me the fuck off.

I'd given up everything—my standing in the Reaper Council, the respect of my peers, my position as leader of my own crew. For what? For her to play and taunt Death every weekend?

It was bullshit.

I wanted to pay her a visit and reap the soul I should've taken all those years ago.

"Ready to start back at work?" Rage asked from across the room, his voice its usual deep rumble. His arms were folded over his thick chest, his black hair slicked back against his head, dark eyes slightly narrowed as he watched me. He looked the same as the last time I saw him, but he had more ink, and his beard was longer now.

"Not really," I admitted as I leaned forward, resting my forearms on my knees. I'd just taken that mask off and wasn't ready to put it back on. "I don't want to deal with everyone right now."

"It's only gotten more political since you left," Caden said.

"Figured it would." I scrubbed my hand over my face. "I have shit to do tonight."

"It's your first night back. What could you possibly have to do?" Brody laughed. "You never left the house before. I don't think I ever saw you with anyone—are you a virgin?"

"Fuck. You. I'm not a fucking virgin and you know it, asshole." I glowered at him, but he just grinned back at me.

"Are you sure? Your hand doesn't count." I threw a couch pillow at him as he and Caden bellowed with laughter. Even Rage grinned, the traitor.

Getting to my feet, I swiped my hands down the front of my black jeans. "I'll see you in the morning. Don't wait up." I ignored their protests as I made my way upstairs to my room.

It was strange being back here. *Home.*

As I opened the door, red lights flickered on immediately. A thin strip of colored light ran around the perimeter of the ceiling, illuminating my room as soon as I entered. Everything was exactly the same, untouched. Even my bed was still unmade.

It was me who was different.

There was something foreign, something wrong, about being home. I stood in the doorway and stared at the room that was once my sanctuary. Could it be that way again? It was where I felt safest. Where I felt most comfortable. Where I could bare my darkest desires.

Now, I didn't know what I felt.

My cloak from that night was crumpled on the floor by the closet, my scythe leaning against the wall in the corner. I squeezed my eyes shut, trying to force memories of the Reaper Police out of my mind.

Their booted feet thundered through the house, their voices booming their barked orders at my brothers. I'd rushed from my room, not caring about myself or my safety—only theirs. All I knew was that I needed to protect them.

They had my brothers face down, their knees pressed into the center of their backs. I saw fucking red, attacking Reapers left and right, not caring who I hurt. They were touching my brothers, hurting them, kneeling on them, and if I could've killed them for it, I would've.

Then one of them pinned me to the wall, and Seth, the cockiest of them all, made his way to me. He told me he was my escort to the In-Between, his sneer mocking me. He'd kept that smug expression on his face the entire time I was questioned. He stayed pleased during my entire tenure in that cell. After that, when he took me to the In-Between and left me there, bloody and broken, he looked the happiest I'd ever seen anyone.

Fucking psycho.

I stepped into my room and shut the door firmly behind me. The room felt too big and too small at the same time, like the walls were closing in, like I needed to breathe, but someone was squeezing my lungs.

Out.

I needed out.

Flinging the door open, I rushed into the hallway, and my lungs immediately opened. I leaned against the wall, my hands on my knees as I focused on my breathing.

This was new. It was something I'd developed in the last fifteen years.

Coincidence?

Definitely not.

As much as I fucking hated her, it brought me comfort knowing Raven suffered like I did. She couldn't breathe sometimes, too. She had panic attacks, but she froze. She looked normal on the outside, but on the inside? I could feel it. The fear. The panic. The way her lungs seized, how she couldn't breathe or think.

14

During my time in the In-Between, we were allowed to venture out of the realm once a year. So, every year, instead of coming home, I'd check on her. At first, I told myself I was just making sure the kid was alright and hadn't been reaped after all. As she got older and I found myself thinking about her between visits, I knew I was fucked.

She was more beautiful every year, and more often than not, I found myself staring up at the starless void wishing I was with her instead.

It wasn't her I wanted—not her vessel.

It was her soul.

Her entire being.

It was her.

It was fucking ridiculous.

It wasn't until she became a teenager that I started to hate her. And it wasn't until she turned eighteen and moved to New York City that I began to despise her. That's when the partying, the drugs, the sex—everything ramped up.

She'd been reckless in her youth, but she was outright suicidal as an adult. If I'd gleaned all that during my short yearly visits, how dangerous did she live the other three-hundred-sixty-four days?

Every year, I watched as she spiraled deeper and deeper. I wanted to fucking reap her soul and send her to the In-Between, just to punish her the way I'd been punished. It wasn't fair she was throwing her life away while I was stuck in my own personal hell for doing the right thing—for protecting her. Saving her.

I'd do it all over again.

Would I?

Fuck. I didn't know anymore.

All I knew was that I wanted to see her, feel her soul. What I did after that...well, that was yet to be decided.

I just needed to get over this bullshit anxiety first.

3

RAVEN

PRESENT

Was it a good idea to be at a trap house with wannabe drug dealers at midnight on a Wednesday? Probably not. Was it a good idea to be drunk at said trap house? Also, probably not.

Did I care? No.

Kali clutched tighter to my side, her green eyes wide as she looked around the room. Everyone was under the influence of *something*, and if they weren't already passed out, they were either fast on their way to it or fucking someone before passing out. The room was sticky and nasty, reeking of a nauseating mix of sweat, sex, vomit, and drugs.

You got used to it after a while.

C-Dog -- I still couldn't remember his real name -- ditched me almost immediately. I don't think he even remembered inviting me, which was totally fine. I'd rather be forgotten. It was for the best. I'd dealt with crazy men before, and the ones who forgot about me were far safer than those genuinely interested in me.

Which begged the question: which of those *interested* guys were leaving me roses?

"I can't believe I let you drag me here," Kali muttered under her breath. I looked down at her and nearly laughed. "How much longer do we have to stay?" She was overdramatic at the best of times, but right then, she was bordering on hysterical.

It wasn't like the party was all that bad. There hadn't even been a knife-fight and we were well past that stage now. Everyone was too faded to hold a conversation, much less a knife.

"You're not having fun?" I teased, and she shot daggers at me. "Just a while longer." I scanned the room, looking for a fuckbuddy for the night. My eyes latched onto a dark pair, and I paused. He looked familiar, but the longer I stared at him, the less I could pinpoint where I knew him from. Maybe he just had one of those faces. "Hey, that guy's kinda cute, right?" I jerked my chin to the guy in the corner.

He wasn't really that cute. He was okay. Passable...kind of.

But I felt like getting laid, and he looked promising enough. His hair was long and dark, a little greasy, but it was hot in the house. Dark stubble peppered his jaw, and his eyes tracked me animalistically. They were glazed enough to know he wasn't sober.

He would've been handsome if he'd scrubbed with some industrial-strength soap and got a haircut. A change of clothes wouldn't hurt either, seeing as his were stained with god only knew what.

"No," she scowled, not trying to hide her disgust. "Not even in the slightest. He's not cute and doesn't look nice. Remember how you said nice was boring? Well, maybe you could aim for not gross? Raise your standards a bit, babe."

I shrugged and looked away from her to lock eyes with him again. He grinned around his beer bottle but didn't make his way over to me like I'd expected. Alright, so he wanted me to chase him. I could play that game.

"I'm going to talk to him," I said, standing straighter. Kali's hand latched around my wrist.

"Absolutely not," she hissed. "Have you lost your fucking mind? He looks like a serial killer."

"Let me go," I muttered as I smiled at the guy. He was watching us with his head cocked, his hair falling to the side, amusement clear on his face.

"No," she said stubbornly. "As your best friend, it's my job to tell you when you're being a fucking idiot and risking your life needlessly.

And guess what, bitch? You're being a fucking idiot and risking your life needlessly!"

I laughed, and her face shifted from anger to genuine concern, like she was worried I'd really lost my mind. And maybe I had.

Maybe I'd lost it a long time ago on an old, deserted farm road.

I shook that night from my thoughts and rolled my shoulders, readying myself. Now was not the time to go down memory lane.

With a deep breath, I extracted my arm from Kali's death grip and put some extra swing in my hips as I traipsed across the room, dodging unconscious bodies as I went. It was hard to look sexy when I had to walk over people sprawled across the floor, but I managed.

"Hi," I said when I stopped in front of him. He wasn't much taller than me, but then again, most people weren't. I wasn't small and petite like Kali. I was tall and lanky, towering over most people—men included. So, the fact that he was a few inches taller than me was a point in his favor.

His grin turned wicked as he flicked his eyes behind me, humor filling his face before looking back at me. "Your friend looks like she's about to pass out," he said.

"Oh, she's fine." I waved dismissively in Kali's direction. "She's just dramatic." He ran his teeth across his chapped lower lip as he scanned my body, then slowly, he met my eye again.

"And you?"

"And me, what?" I laughed.

"Are you dramatic?"

"I don't think so," I said, glancing back at Kali. She had her hands wrapped around the strap of her cross-body purse, her eyes even wider than before. She looked painfully out of place. "I'm Raven." I turned back to him, finding him watching me intently.

"Eddy." He tilted his chin down, and I smiled sweetly. "You come to parties like this often, Raven?"

"Sometimes."

"I haven't seen you before." He studied me again, his eyes lingering on my chest. Something scratched the back of my mind, but I couldn't place him. His eyes...they were so familiar. "I would've remembered someone as gorgeous as you." I gave a breathy laugh and barely managed to not roll my eyes. *Laying it on a bit thick there, buddy.*

"I would've remembered you, too."

"That so?" He looked amused, and for some reason, it annoyed me. "You wanna go somewhere else?" He tilted his head toward the front door, and I glanced at Kali again. He wasn't wasting any time. But that's what I wanted him for, right? A release. A quick fuck. A stress-reliever.

"Yeah, sure." I grinned up at him.

"You can come back to my place," he said as he downed the rest of his beer and tossed it to the floor. "You from around here?"

"Brooklyn." I kept looking over my shoulder, making sure Kali was okay. No one was sober enough to mess with her, but she looked like she was five seconds away from having a massive panic attack.

"Me too." His eyes heated, and his smile turned feral.

"Perfect," I said, even though I was starting to have second thoughts. I wasn't totally feeling Eddy anymore. There was just something about him, the way he leered at me or the creepy way he smiled, that made me bristle.

This was a one-time thing. This wasn't a get-to-know-each-other night. This was a fuck-me-and-leave-me-alone-forever kind of night.

I turned my back and made my way back across the room, expecting him to follow. I was pleasantly unsurprised when I looked over my shoulder and found him right behind me, looking like a creepy, eager puppy.

"You ready to leave?" I asked Kali.

"Yes," she said before the words were fully out of my mouth. She looked at Eddy, her eyes narrowing. Kali may be small, but she was fierce and protective of those she loved. "Who's your new friend?"

"Eddy, this is my best friend, Kali." I waved my hand between them. "Kali, Eddy."

"Hey," he said, sounding disinterested. "You ready?" He slipped his arm around my waist and roughly yanked me into his side. His hold felt possessive, and I immediately hated it. "You got a ride or something?" He looked at Kali dismissively. I didn't like his tone.

"We'll take a cab," I gritted out.

"I got a bike, babe." He looked down at me, his eyes glazed. "Can only take one of you, and I only let girls I'm about to fuck on the back of it." He laughed at his own joke and squeezed my waist, shaking me slightly.

Kali and I exchanged a look. C-Dog was a fuckboy through and through. Eddy was something else entirely.

She silently dared me to leave her alone—like I'd ever actually do that. Finally, I sighed dramatically and slumped my shoulders, making a show of looking disappointed when I wasn't in the least. She let out a relieved breath and took a step closer to me.

"We'll take a cab," I said again, shoving at his hand. He didn't let go. His body tensed, then his hand tightened painfully on my waist.

"Where do you live?" he gritted out. "I'll meet you there."

"I'll just see you around." He continued squeezing me, his face losing all humor. I twisted in his hold and pulled myself free from his vice-like grip. When I met his eyes, they were angry. Cold. They narrowed, and I took an instinctive step away, bumping into Kali.

"Come on, Ray," she muttered, gently tugging on my arm. My gaze stayed locked with Eddy's as I backed away from him, every one of my senses frozen.

"See you around, Raven," he threatened with a smirk.

4

GRIM

SIX MONTHS AGO

Nerves knotted my stomach as I paced my bedroom. Was I really doing this? Going to go to her apartment and reap her? I'd just gotten home tonight. Did I want to risk going back?

She had a pull on me, and I knew it was her soul I should've taken all those years ago. Maybe if I took it now, I'd sever whatever connection we had, and I could have my fucking life back.

Fuck it.

I appeared in her apartment, my glamour in place, and immediately, I knew I'd made a mistake. My chest ached like someone had pierced it with an ax, cracking it wide open. A burn I'd never felt before, something so sad, so dark and depressing, was opening and all I wanted was for it to close.

The worst of it was the sound.

Her crying.

She was curled in a tight ball on her bed, her black hair stuck to her damp face as she sobbed, hugging her knees to her chest. I hadn't heard her cry since the night I saved her, but it wasn't like this. The way she sounded now cracked my chest even wider. She looked so fragile and small lying there, and I found myself wanting to comfort her in any way

21

I could. I wanted to make it all better, take her pain away, kill whoever made her feel like this.

It was fucking ridiculous.

I was here to reap her.

Instead of doing anything, I stood dumbfounded at the end of her bed and watched as she sobbed herself sick. What was I supposed to do? I couldn't take my glamour off. I'd give her a fucking heart attack. But I couldn't let her keep crying like this.

This is why I hated her.

She had a way of creeping under my skin and forcing herself into the empty cavity where my soul should've been. She was a manipulator. She'd manipulated me the night I saved her, and she was manipulating me now.

No more.

I couldn't allow her to do this to me anymore.

Moving to her side, I stared down at her. My chest felt too tight; I rubbed at my collarbone, wanting to claw it open. What the fuck was wrong with me? I was tougher than this. I should be able to reap some girl without a second thought, so why was she making me doubt myself?

I put my hand on her arm and she gasped, her body tensing under my touch. I immediately snapped my hand back, my eyes wide and breathing ragged.

Could she feel me?

No.

There was no way.

She sat up and looked frantically around her tiny room as she wrapped her hand around where I'd just touched her.

"H-hello?" she stammered, her voice shaky. Her cheeks were swollen and red, soaked with tears, but there was more bravery in her little toe than most mortals had in their entire bodies. Most people would've screamed and run out of the room if they felt someone invisible touch them.

Not my little bird.

She had the same expression on her face she'd had that night—resigned, like she knew whatever was about to happen was for the best, like she'd already come to terms with it. Did she know Death was near?

22

ispiderisp)

I crouched beside her to get a closer look, and fuck, she was gorgeous. There was no denying it. But she was...evil. Fuck. No, she wasn't, I just wanted her to be.

She couldn't keep doing this. She couldn't keep fucking with my head.

The longer I stared at her, and the closer I got, the more I breathed in her scent, the more my cock hardened, and the more my chest loosened. The more I felt the need to claim her as mine. The more I felt like I was finally coming home.

"Little bird," I murmured, my voice raspy and deep in the quiet. Her spine stiffened and she looked around the room again, her hazel eyes wider than before. Had she heard me?

This could be fun.

Reaching over, I knocked her phone off her beside table. She snapped her head toward it and stared down in horror.

"Ghosts aren't real," she breathed. "Ghosts are not real."

At least she wasn't crying anymore.

Wrapping my hand around her wrist, I gently jerked on her arm. She let out a startled yelped and looked around the room again. For the first time in fifteen years, I wanted to smile. More than that, I wanted to laugh.

Fuck. This. Girl.

She was making me feel better. She was the reason I'd felt so fucking low in the first place, and she was the cure for it, too? Bullshit.

"Fuck this." She jumped off her bed and bolted for the door. I followed after her, slamming it shut behind me. She screamed and put her hand on her heaving chest.

I could feel her fear, and fuck, if it wasn't turning me on.

Frantically, she looked around the apartment. I didn't know if she was looking for a way out or for a weapon, so I leaned against the wall to watch the show.

"Salt," she muttered to herself. "Salt is supposed to repel ghosts, right?" I snorted.

She flung cabinet doors open and began rummaging around. I'd never seen anyone look so relieved to have found salt. She poured it on the floor in front of her and I laughed. She really thought that would protect her from a spirit? Idiot.

With a sigh, I pushed off the wall and stalked toward her. Slowly, I dragged my boot through the line of salt she'd made. She stared at it, her eyes nearly falling from her head. Crouching, I rubbed my hand over the salt, laying it in a flat layer. Then I wrote two words.

Little bird.

She gasped and stumbled back a few steps before falling on her ass. She couldn't tear her eyes away from the words I'd written.

Fuck. Why did I do that? Why did I want her to know it was me? Why did I want to lessen her fear?

"Grim?" she whispered. Her eyes darted around the room, her full, scarred lips parting as her chest heaved.

Grim? That's what she called me? Hm. I think I liked it. I usually hated when mortals called me The Grim Reaper, but her dubbing me Grim, like she knew me, like it was my name? I liked it.

Fuck.

I needed to sever this connection. It was fucking with my head.

But now that I was close to her, now that she knew I was back, the thought of breaking whatever tie we had filled my body with a murderous rage I'd never felt before. I wanted to keep her for myself. Even if a part of me still hated her, I wanted her to stick around for a bit longer.

I wouldn't reap her tonight, but maybe I would tomorrow.

5
RAVEN
PRESENT

I rolled over and something squished under my cheek. My eyes snapped open. The early morning sun streamed in through my window, and I groaned. I was still in my clothes from last night, my hair stuck to my face.

Not my finest moment.

Had I really almost gone home with a guy named Eddy?

Gross.

I blindly patted my face, expecting to find anything but the rose stuck to it. I shot up, the room spinning around me, and I stared down at the rose in my hand. My heart began to race.

He was getting braver.

He'd never left a rose in my bedroom before. On my kitchen table, or that one time in a vase on my coffee table, but never my bedroom. Never my bed. Never when I was home.

I was positive it wasn't there when I came home last night. Even though I was drunk, I would've remembered seeing it. Unless it was on my doormat, and I brought it in...but why would I have brought it to bed with me?

I continued staring at it.

As usual, there were no thorns, no leaves, nothing but a full, lively black rose at the top of a vibrant, green stem. None of the other roses had wilted, even though I hadn't put them in water. My oldest one was five months old. I didn't know how it hadn't died yet, how it was *possible*.

Could he be breaking in and replacing them all? That was a possibility but unlikely. At first, I thought they were hyper-realistic fake flowers, but they were real. I cut one in half and inspected, going as far as to buy a cheap microscope from a pawn shop to look at the plant cells. It was very much an actual plant.

But *how*?

How could it be real and never die?

If I knew who it was, maybe I could figure out how they were preserving the flowers. I'd thought about it for months, even staking out my apartment with Kali, to no avail. The roses just appeared, but the person leaving them had never been seen.

I was starting to wonder if I'd gone crazy. Maybe I was buying them myself and forgot, leaving them on my doorstep, scaring myself into thinking I had a stalker when I was really just losing my mind.

I threw myself back onto my bed and stared at the spinning ceiling. Wouldn't that be nice? To only have to worry about my crazy ass and not a fucking stalker? I lifted the rose above my face and twirled it between my fingers before bringing it to my nose and inhaling deeply.

The other strange thing about these roses was their scent—they were more fragrant than other roses. Sweeter. Their scent was intoxicating. Addicting. I couldn't get enough of it.

How had my stalker come into my bedroom and left one on my bed, right beside me, without me knowing? I should've known someone was in my room, right?

I tossed the rose down as I slid out of bed and stumbled to the bathroom. I didn't bother looking at myself in the mirror. I knew I looked as awful as I felt.

Turning the shower on, I stepped out of my clothes and waited for the water to warm. My apartment was old and sucked, so there was a small window of opportunity for hot water. If I wasn't paying attention, I'd miss it. The water began to turn warm, and I didn't hesitate as I stepped into the tiny stall.

The bathroom was small. Your knees nearly touched the door if you sat on the toilet. I could barely lift my arms to wash my hair in the shower stall, and I had to dry off in the kitchen.

If I didn't love this city so fucking much, I would've moved away years ago.

I didn't waste time as I washed my body and hair. It wasn't like I had much of a choice. A shower was never a leisure activity, as much as I wanted it to be. I had to treat it like a sprint.

Get in. Get out.

Even though the shower head was detachable, I couldn't enjoy it because the water would turn to ice in seconds. I'd tried it a few times but it always went cold right when I was about to come and ruined the moment. So, the shower was strictly a chore, never a fun time.

A floorboard creaked outside the bathroom, and I froze, my fingers tangled in my wet, soapy hair. I stared at the thin shower curtain with bated breath.

Was it my imagination? It had to be. It was an old apartment. The building was probably just settling...

Then why did I feel like someone was watching me?

"Kali?" I called out, my voice shaky. I hated how scared I sounded.

Another floorboard creaked closer to the bathroom, and I inhaled sharply. The showerhead began pelting ice, but I couldn't feel it, not with the massive shadow forming on the other side of the curtain.

It was larger than almost anyone I'd ever seen: seven feet tall with a broad frame and heavy footsteps. The shadow slowly approached, just the cheap, too-thin curtain separating us.

I stared at him, my eyes lifting to where his face should've been. The gauzy, black hood of his cloak was visible over the shower rod. He looked too big in my tiny bathroom, but he'd look too big in any room.

Between the icy water and the fear coursing through my body, I could hardly breathe.

A familiar, sweet smell hit me moments before a giant hand snaked into the shower, a black rose held tightly in it. He held it patiently, but I couldn't move.

Not when my stalker was handing me a rose.

My mouth was dry, my heart was beating too fast.

Was I hallucinating? Or still dreaming? Maybe it was some kind of alcohol-induced psychosis.

I pulled a trembling hand from my hair and rinsed the soap off before grabbing the flower. My fingers brushed against his skin, and I expected to feel warmth, but I didn't. He was colder than the water. His hand hovered in mid-air for a moment, then slowly disappeared behind the curtain.

"Thank you," I breathed.

I didn't know why I thanked him. I should've been screaming, not that my neighbors would've given a shit or called the cops. I could've tried running to my phone and calling them myself, or at least tried calling Kali to let her know my fucking stalker was in my apartment.

Instead, I thanked him.

Maybe I really had fucking lost it.

"You're welcome, little bird." He stood still for a moment, his shoulders rising and falling with his labored breaths. "Don't see him again. He's dangerous."

I opened my mouth to ask who he was talking about, but his silhouette began to retreat. Before he was fully through the door, he disappeared. Just...evaporated.

It dawned on me then who it was, but I didn't want to let myself think his name. I didn't want to get my hopes up in case it wasn't really him.

But if it was...

I held the rose a little tighter and smelled it a little deeper, smiling softly to myself.

Grim was my stalker.

6

GRIM

FIVE MONTHS AGO

I stood in the shadows of the living room, waiting. It was nearly three in the morning. Where the fuck was she? She should've been home by now. She was always home. It was a weekday. Who the fuck partied and stayed out this late on a fucking weekday?

I'd been watching her for a month, and her routine was...sad. She partied nearly every night, and on the nights she didn't go out, she made a disgusting-looking microwaved dinner and drank a few cheap bottles of beer before turning in for the night.

No one came to her place. She hardly called anyone. She barely watched TV. She just existed.

Fuck.

How was she always able to make me feel bad for her?

I shuffled my feet and let out an irritated breath—not the first of the evening. Then I heard a key slide into the lock and the door slowly swung open. I turned toward the sound and watched as Raven entered her apartment.

She paused before she scanned the room. Her eyes lingered on the dark corners, and when she got to me, they lingered a moment longer. She couldn't see me, could she? My glamour was still in place. There was no way she should be able to see or sense me. I should be totally invisible to her.

Then why did I feel stripped bare with her eyes on mine?

After the night I'd first messed with her, I hadn't done it again. I'd been careful to not touch her, speak, or move anything. Not so I didn't scare her again, but because it was freaking me the fuck out that she knew I was around. That she sensed me.

She shook herself slightly, then flipped the light on and tossed her keys on the counter. She didn't look drunk, which I supposed was a good thing, but she did look disheveled. Going to her fridge, she opened it and grabbed a beer. At this time of night? Or would it be morning?

Popping the top, she leaned her hip on the counter and stared blankly at the wall as she took a long drink. Her hands trembled slightly, and I wondered why. What happened tonight to make her look like this? Feel like this?

I took a deep breath and stepped closer to her. My chest ached, right where my heart was—or should've been. It was like a giant black hole was opening up and swallowing everything inside, leaving only numbness behind.

It was what she was feeling.

Why?

I stood in front of her, but she had no idea. She stared through me, still fixated on the wall. I wanted to hold her, just so this pain would stop. Reaching up, I hovered my hand an inch from her face, nearly touching her. I traced her features—her full, scarred lips, her shadowed hazel eyes, her slightly crooked and scarred nose.

My fingertip accidentally brushed over her high cheekbone, and she gasped. She looked around the room again, her eyes slowly scanning the apartment, looking more alert than she had moments before. Then her eyes traveled up, up, up, and settled on mine.

Anxiety twisted my chest, and I yanked my hand away. She could *not* see me. It was impossible. But she slowly reached her hand out toward me, her dark brows bunching slightly as she lifted it.

I stepped back before she reached me, and when her hand touched nothing but air, she looked even more confused. Disappointed, even.

She touched her cheek, right where I had, then folded her lips between her teeth as she shook herself.

"Stupid," she muttered.

Quickly, she downed the rest of her beer and tossed it in the trash before stripping her clothes off. My mouth went dry as she slid off her skin-tight black jeans, kicking her boots off as she went. Her shirt was next, then she walked toward her room in just her bra and panties.

I followed her, helpless to do anything else.

I shuffled into the corner of the room and watched as she flung herself onto her bed, then rolled onto her stomach. Her dark hair shifted to the side, exposing her pale back and showing off the scythe tattooed down her spine. I inhaled sharply, my eyes trailing down the intricate design. *Fuck*. She was killing me.

My gaze dropped to her full ass as she opened her nightstand drawer. She rummaged around inside, her hips swaying side to side. My cock hardened painfully in my jeans, and I clenched my jaw tighter.

She pulled out a purple vibrator and flipped onto her back again with a small smile. The buzz was loud in the otherwise silent room. My breathing was too harsh, my cock too fucking hard, but I couldn't look away.

Dragging the rounded tip of the vibrator over her peaked nipple, she gasped as she circled it. Her breasts were still hidden under her thin black bra, but her nipples were hard as diamonds.

I wanted to suck on them, to bite them until she was screaming my name and begging me to fuck her.

Reaching behind her, she unclasped her bra and threw it to the floor. She slowly dragged the vibrator down her taut stomach to the band of her black panties and teased herself with it. Her other hand came up to cup her breast as she roughly pinched and twisted her nipple. The moan that ripped from her throat nearly made me come down my leg.

"Holy fuck," I breathed as I shifted on my feet.

I'd never seen this before. As many times as I'd stood in the shadows of mortals' bedrooms, I'd never seen this—felt this. I'd seen them at the end of their climaxes, usually when their hearts gave out and they died.

But this? Never.

She lifted her hips and dragged her panties off, tossing them to the floor beside her bra. Her legs fell apart, and the rounded tip of her vibrator lightly circled her clit. She arched her back, her eyes fluttered closed, her lips parted on a silent moan.

I moved around the room and stood above her to get a better view. I needed to see her when she came. I needed to feel her, be close to her.

Slowly, she slid her hand up her body to her throat. She wrapped it tightly around her long neck and began to squeeze. She shoved the vibrator into her pussy and cried out as her hips lifted off the bed. Mindlessly, I rubbed my hand over my cock in my jeans.

She fucked herself hard and fast, her hand on her throat tightening as her body began to tense. She was screaming and moaning, her eyes rolling back in her head as she thrust her hips up, meeting her hand.

Her body went taut, and she held her breath. I found myself holding mine, too, waiting to watch her explode, but she dropped back to the bed, opening her eyes as she let out a frustrated growl. Shutting the vibrator off, she tossed it beside her and stared up at the ceiling, looking upset.

"What the fuck is wrong with me?" she whispered.

The words felt heavy—too heavy for whatever she'd just done. They were guilt-filled, and her question didn't sound entirely rhetorical. It was like she was asking the universe and expecting an answer.

With another soft groan, she slid off the bed to her knees to look underneath. Her ass was in the air, wiggling around temptingly. I wanted to bury myself inside her and split her wide fucking open.

She pulled a shoebox out and laughed to herself as she opened it, looking giddy, most of her previous sadness disappearing. I peered over her shoulder, wanting to see what it was. When I saw it, I groaned low in my throat.

Killing me. She was fucking killing me.

It was a huge dildo. Fucking massive. Long and thick, veiny, looked eerily like my dick. Her hands couldn't wrap around it as she held it in front of her. It dwarfed her hands and body, making her look more petite, which, in comparison to most mortals, she was not.

There was a suction cup at the base, and she stuck it to the floor in front of her closet door. She quickly went inside and emerged with a black scarf. I sat on an empty chair in the opposite corner of the room to watch the show.

She looked excited as she tied the scarf around the doorknob of the closet door, then she kneeled and tied the other end around her neck. I couldn't hold back anymore. I unzipped my jeans and pulled my aching cock out, fisting it as she tightened the scarf until the fabric bit into her skin.

Grabbing a bottle of lube from the shoe box, she poured a generous amount into her hand before brushing it all over her little pussy. She rubbed more between her hands and stroked the cock suctioned to the floor between her legs.

Her face was turning red, and as she began to lower her hips, I began stroking myself. She moved her hips in a circle, enticing the tip of the cock into her entrance. I could only imagine how fucking tight that cunt was, and I gripped my cock tighter.

She rubbed her hands, still slick with lube, over her breasts, making them shiny. I groaned as she roughly pinched her nipples, pulling at them, lifting her breasts away from her body as she pushed her hips down, taking more of the cock inside her.

"Oh, fuck," she moaned, her eyes rolling back as she rode the dildo. My cock was throbbing with the need to come. I hadn't felt like coming in years, but right then, all I wanted was to cover her face in my cum. Mark her. Claim her as mine.

The further down on the cock she went, the tighter the scarf around her neck became. It took her a few moments, but she finally got it all inside her.

Then she started fucking it.

Planting her hands on her thighs, she rested her head against the door as she rode that cock for all she was worth. My hand moved in time with her hard, fast movements. I had to force my orgasm back several times so I could come with her—I was feeling too fucking good to stop.

Her face was beginning to turn a dangerous shade of reddish-purple, and a sick part of me was more turned on by that. What if she passed out with it still inside her, then woke up and finished riding it until she came?

What if I slipped it out of her and replaced it with my cock, fucked her as hard as I wanted, then filled her with my cum? I'd shove the dildo back into her used-up cunt and watch my cum overflow. When she woke, she'd be full of someone's cum with no memory of who it was or how they'd used her.

Just the thought of using her pliable, unconscious body made my toes curl in my boots. I grunted as she slammed herself down, taking it all. She cried out, her voice barely audible from the scarf squeezing her throat. Her eyes were red and watery, and her nails dug into the tops of her thighs, but she didn't stop riding.

Finally, she moved her hand to her clit, and it was like fireworks going off.

She threw her head back, her body arching deeply making the scarf tighten. Furiously, she rubbed herself as I stroked myself faster. Together, we worked ourselves closer and closer to the edge.

"Grim!" she shouted, and my hand faltered. A bolt of excited panic shot through me. Was my glamour still in place? "Oh, fuck! Grim!"

Her hand was a blur and my body tensed as I gripped my too-sensitive cockhead. Cum spurted out as I loudly groaned, catching it in my other hand. I forced myself to keep my eyes open to watch her explode.

"Grim," she whimpered over and over.

She was moaning my name as she came.

My fucking name.

Even if it wasn't my real name, it's what she called me—it was what all mortals called me.

Grim.

The Grim Reaper.

She was screaming for me—calling for me.

Her body slumped forward, and she worked her fingers under the tight band of fabric, then took in a huge lungful of air. She looked perfectly sated. She winced slightly as she slid off the dildo, then fell limply to the floor beside it. Sighing contentedly, she nestled her head into her bent arm and closed her eyes. She couldn't be going to sleep on the floor, could she?

I quickly cleaned my hands, and when I returned to her bedroom, she was still curled up on the floor. I didn't know what else to do. I

34

couldn't just leave her on the fucking floor. So, I quickly melted my glamour, scooped her into my arms, and carried her to bed.

"I knew you'd come back," she slurred as she rubbed her cheek against the pillow, her eyes still closed. My hands clutching the blanket I was tucking around her froze. "I knew you'd come back for me."

I stared down at her. She was asleep. She didn't know I was there, but her words still made me feel panicky. Then, a warmth I didn't fully understand and didn't want to examine too closely bloomed through my chest.

She knew I'd come back for her, that I hadn't left her.

Hesitating, I brushed her black hair away from her face, and she sighed, her lips curving into a small smile. I tucked the blanket under her chin, and she grabbed hold of it, nestling deeper into her little cocoon.

Fuck, she was weaseling her way inside me. It wasn't hard for her to do—I wasn't trying to keep her out.

I forced myself to step away and willed my glamour back into place. Still staring at her, I walked backward out of her bedroom, shaking my head at myself.

I didn't know what hold she had on me or why I allowed it, but I needed to break it. Whatever was tethering us to each other, I needed to sever it and forget about her forever, before things got to the point of no return.

The thought of that made my chest ache. The thought of never seeing her again made me *ache*. I rubbed my chest as I silently moved through the apartment. As I left, my eyes caught something outside her front door. I stared down at it, my chest aching further.

I shifted my glamour back and made a split-second decision that shifted our lives forever.

I conjured a single black rose and left it on her doorstep, right above The Grim Reaper printed on her welcome mat.

7

RAVEN

FOUR MONTHS AGO

My dress billowed around me, tangling in my legs. It was my favorite dress, the one I'd been saving for a special occasion. Tonight was *the* special occasion.

I was going to see him again.

The last time I saw him was fifteen years ago, but it hadn't been from a lack of trying.

He saved me the night my stepfather was going to kill me—I saw it in his eyes. It hadn't been the first time he'd beaten me, but it was the first time I'd feared for my life. So, I ran. I ran and ran and ran until he caught me.

Then *he* saved me.

Grim.

My stepfather's body fell limply to the ground, his eyes rolling back in his head, his mouth wide open in an eternal scream. It should've scared me, or maybe scarred me, but it didn't. *He* didn't.

I'd stared up at my savior, but he only stared down at my stepfather. I wish I could've seen his face, but his mask covered it. I wanted to know what he was thinking, if he'd felt as free as I had in that moment, but he never even looked at me.

He kept his back to me as he lifted his head, as if he was waiting for

36

something. Then, when I opened my mouth to say something, thank him maybe, or ask what happened next, he vanished.

He just...disappeared.

I searched for him all night. When I couldn't find him, I began to think I'd gone insane and killed my stepfather myself. But I knew what I saw—who I saw—and I hadn't killed him, even if I'd wanted to.

It took me years to figure out who my savior was, and when I did, I hardly believed it. It was The Reaper. Like, The Grim Reaper. The actual Grim fucking Reaper had saved my life. I searched for years, trying to figure out why.

Why me? Why would he choose to save me? Had he saved others like me? Was he a good guy after all?

I found nothing. There was lore, of course, but nothing interesting. No answers. So, I did the only thing I could think of—die. I just wanted to see him again. No, I needed to see him again, if only to thank him.

Maybe it was all in my head, but I felt a pull toward him. A deep, aching need I didn't understand, but I knew I needed him to fill it. I'd felt it the moment our eyes met through his mask, scorching my soul and leaving his mark on me forever. I couldn't explain the feelings I had for him. I'd only been ten at the time and hadn't said more than a few words, and yet...I needed him more than I needed my heart to live or my lungs to breathe.

I needed him.

Tonight, more than any other night in my life, I needed him.

I stood on the edge of the building, the full moon spotlighting me, and silently begged him to come to me. I could barely see the ground from where I was. The cars and trees looked like toys, and the people looked like ants. I was so high, I could've reached up and ran my fingers through Heaven.

Shuffling closer, I let my toes hang over the cement edge. My stomach flipped and my world spun as I stared down. I was going to do this. I *needed* to do this.

This was so I could see him again. I would end everything just to see him.

With that reminder, I took a deep breath and let one foot hover in front of me. I stretched my arms out on either side for balance. The cold wind pricked my skin and whipped around me, tangling my gauzy dress more around my legs.

I dropped my foot back to the ledge and ran my clammy hands down my stomach to ease my nerves. When my body flattened against the sidewalk, would that be how I went into the afterlife? Would he see me like that? Broken and bloody? Unrecognizable?

Would he remember me when we finally met again? Would he hold me in his arms and tell me how much he'd missed me? Would he have missed me as much as I'd missed him?

Stretching my arms out again, I wobbled as I reached my foot back out, ready to let myself fall. My eyes slowly closed, and I let myself smell the city I'd never smell again, hear the chatter, the sirens and honking cars I'd never hear again.

I was going to miss New York. It had always been my dream to live here, and I'd made it happen. At eighteen and fresh out of the system, I moved here with nothing.

I was going to miss the people, my job, my friends. I was really, really going to miss Kali.

The thought of my best friend made tears pool in my eyes. What was she going to think when she found out? We were supposed to go out tonight to celebrate my twenty-fifth birthday. Instead, I was here, about to fall to my death to meet Death again.

Would she hate me?

I'd hate me if I was her.

I was going to miss her more than anything else, but if I didn't do this, I knew I'd miss him more.

My foot shifted on the rough concrete, inching closer to the edge. With a deep breath, I readied myself for the fall. Suddenly, huge, cold hands wrapped around my waist and yanked me back, throwing me back onto the dirty rooftop. I skidded back, a scream lodged in my throat as I blinked up at the cloaked figure towering above me. His broad shoulders were rising and falling with his angry, rapid breaths.

"What the fuck do you think you're doing?" he shouted. His deep, familiar voice echoed around the surrounding buildings, then bounced around in my skull before finally penetrating my heart.

"Grim?" I rasped, tears finally flowing freely from my eyes. "You came." He paused and tilted his head to the side. "You really came."

"What—" He shook his head, his black eyes closing behind his mask. "What the fuck were you doing?" I rubbed my lips together, then wiped my face as I sat straighter.

"I was trying to see you again," I said. He stepped back, away from me, and it was like a blow to the chest.

I pushed myself to my feet and straightened my dress, smoothing my hands down the back to brush off any debris. I needed to look my absolute best for him.

"You were trying to see me again," he slowly repeated. I didn't remember his voice being so rough and raspy. So dark. But it was, and it made my skin tight. I stepped toward him, and he stepped back again, his cloak billowing in the wind behind him. "You—"

"Don't you remember me?" I asked, smiling softly. "I'm Raven." I put my hand to my chest, my brows pushing together. "You remember me, don't you, Grim?"

"No," he said curtly, and my stomach bottomed out.

I was going to be sick.

I was going to throw my heart up right there in front of him.

Wrapping my arms around myself, I stared up at him. He was bigger than I remembered, broader, more intimidating. His mask was dirtier and more scuffed. It looked like candle wax had been dripped down the front, his eyes hidden behind it. There was no mouth, no nose, nothing remotely human about it. But those eyes...they were so cold, but something burned behind them. Something that wasn't cold at all. Something that was anything but inhuman.

"You saved me once," I said quietly. He inhaled sharply, his shoulders bunching tightly. "You really don't remember." There was a long pause, then he cleared his throat.

"No."

I didn't believe him—I didn't *want* to believe him, rather. He had to remember me. He just had to. He'd left such an impact on me and I was sure I'd made one on him. He had to think of me daily, just as I'd thought of him. He had to dream about me, get off to me, live his life just so he could see me again.

39

I stared at him and shook my head. No, I didn't believe him. I didn't know why, but I didn't. Even if he was telling the truth and he really didn't remember me, he would. I'd make him remember me.

"You need to go home," he said. "Stop trying to kill yourself." I perked up at his words.

"So, you do know me." I took a step closer. This time, he didn't retreat, but his gloved hands clenched into tight fists at his sides.

"I know you're a stupid little girl who tries to die every other day," he snapped. "I know that next time you pull a stunt like this," he threw his arm toward the ledge, "I won't be there to save you."

"I didn't want you to save me." I rubbed my hands up and down my bare arms, ignoring the goosebumps and dew that had settled over my skin. His eyes narrowed slightly, then roamed over my body.

I straightened, showing him my dress. It was my favorite. I'd spent more money than I wanted to admit on it, but it was my death dress—the dress I saved to wear for when I met Death again. I'd gone into slight debt over it, but I didn't care. I loved it.

It was a sleeveless, black, gauzy gown. It flowed around my feet, barely dragging along the ground. It was beautiful, but I mostly chose it because it reminded me of his cloak. I wanted to match him. I wanted to look like him. I wanted to show him that I was his.

"You might not want to be saved, but you need to be," he sighed. "Go home, Raven."

"How do I go with you?" I asked, taking another step toward him. His head tilted to the side again, his dark eyes shadowed.

"Go with me?" He shook his head. "You don't go with me."

"Unless I'm dead, right?" I asked, and he shook his head again.

"You do not go with me." He emphasized his words slowly.

"But if I'm dead—"

"You don't fucking go with me!" His voice rattled the windows of the buildings around us. I didn't shy away from him, though, and I wouldn't. My savior wouldn't hurt me.

He stooped and grabbed his discarded scythe, gripping it tightly in his trembling hand. My breath hitched when his eyes met mine again, hard and angry, but there was something...else in the inky blackness. Something more. Something I couldn't decipher.

"Go home. I won't tell you again."

"Grim—"

"That's not my name," he growled. "Raven, go home. I mean it."

The words barely left his mouth before he began to disappear, blending in with the night around us. We stared at each other until he was fully gone, the outlines of his massive body turning invisible.

Then I was totally alone again.

The rooftop seemed so small when he was there with me. The world seemed so small when I was next to him. Now, I felt lost and cold in this big city, in the even bigger world, in the infinite universe, without him.

8

RAVEN

PRESENT

K ali sat across from me, the chatter in the small café loud around us. She leaned forward, resting her arms on the edge of the table as I looked around, feeling eyes on me. After this morning, I'd felt more and more unnerved.

It was Grim. It had to be. But *why*? After seeing him on the rooftop on my birthday, I hadn't tried to call on him again, and he hadn't come for me. So why was he here now, breaking into my apartment, giving me roses? Stalking me? I didn't know the rules of being a Reaper, but surely there was something against stalking someone you weren't going to kill.

Unless he was planning on killing me.

My blood ran cold at the thought.

"Are you listening to me?" Kali snapped. I blinked a few times and shook my head, giving her an apologetic smile.

"Sorry, Kal," I sighed. "Still hungover. What were you saying?"

"I was saying," she said, drawing the word out as she glared at me. "Did you hear about the murder last night?" I scrunched my brows together, and she sighed again, sharper. "You really should pay more attention to the shit that happens in your neighborhood."

"It happened in my neighborhood?" I took a sip of water as I glanced out the window at the people on the sidewalk. I scanned the busy street, expecting—hoping—to find a pair of dark eyes trained on me, but there was nothing. No one.

"Yes," she said. "It was a girl in her mid-twenties, black hair, green eyes—she looked like you." I looked back at her and shrugged.

"A lot of girls look like me," I said. "I'm an emo white girl. We all look the same." She shook her head as she leaned back in her chair.

"No, she *really* looked like you." She pulled her phone from her purse and began to scroll. "Like, eerily like you. So much so, I thought she *was* you." She laid her phone on the table and spun it around, sliding it to me.

I hesitated, my gaze lingering on hers before I grabbed it. My hand shook slightly as I brought it to my face. Sure enough, the girl in the photo looked like me.

Her hair was long, pin-straight, and black. Her skin was too-pale, and even her hazel-green eyes had a haunted, faraway look to them. A shiver snaked down my spine, and an uneasy feeling began to swirl in the pit of my stomach.

"She doesn't look like me," I lied, and tossed the phone back on the table. Kali stared at me for a moment, her lips tightening. She snatched the phone up and stared at it, then lifted her eyes.

"She does." I shook my head and looked out the window again. "Just because you don't want to admit it—"

"Admit what?" I snapped, glaring back at her. "Admit some girl kind of resembles me?"

"Admit that a girl who looks like your twin was fucking killed in your neighborhood," she said. "Admit that your stalker could've done this. He could've mistaken her for you and killed her."

"That's a reach, even for you." I rolled my eyes. "We don't even know if I'm being stalked."

"Raven!" she hissed. "What do you call it then? A secret admirer? A totally safe, not-creepy guy trying to work up the courage to ask you on a fucking date? Come on, you're smarter than this."

I huffed out a breath and looked around the café. I still couldn't shake the feeling of being watched, and I hadn't been able to shake it since the roses started. Truthfully, it was probably before that, but that's when I noticed it more.

Was Grim here?

I looked behind me, fully expecting to see him standing over me. But he wasn't there, and a weird pang of disappointment stabbed at my chest. I didn't want him to be stalking me, did I?

Who was I kidding? Of course, I did.

"Maybe it's Mason," I suggested.

"Mason?" She laughed mockingly. "He hasn't texted you in months. You think he's leaving you roses?" I shrugged, and she laughed again. The sound grated down my nerves. "It's not Mason, Ray. It's some dangerous psycho—"

"You don't know that."

"Fine," she said, throwing her hand at me, looking irritated. "Text him. Ask him if he's been leaving them."

"Like he'd tell me the truth," I snorted.

"Ask him," she challenged.

With a small huff, I yanked my phone from my jeans and made a show of scrolling through my messages to Mason's name. It was from four months ago. There was only one message—an outgoing one from me telling him I'd had a good time with him. I'd never heard back, and I got the hint.

I lifted my eyes to her, glaring at her with furrowed brows, but she just glared back. I didn't give myself a chance to overthink it as I tapped out a quick message.

Hey.

It's Raven

"There," I said, showing her my screen. She rolled her eyes and reached for my phone, but I pulled it away.

"That's the worst text I've ever seen," she said dryly.

"You wanted me to text him!" I locked my phone and flipped it screen-side down on the table. "You didn't tell me what to say, so deal with it." My leg bounced wildly under the table as I waited for a reply. I couldn't help it. My gaze kept traveling back to the phone, waiting.

"Let me see it," she said, reaching for it again. I slapped my hand over it and glared at her.

"No." I scooted it away. "He's not even going to repl—" The phone vibrated, and my eyes went wide.

No fucking way.

She grinned broadly at me. *Bitch.*

"What did he say?"

With a deep breath, I flipped the phone over and unlocked it. My heart was in my throat as I stared at the message.

HEY, RAVEN. HAVEN'T HEARD FROM YOU IN A WHILE

"TYPICAL," SHE SCOFFED AFTER I READ IT TO HER. "SAY, 'Yeah, you ghosted me after we fucked'."

"I'm not telling him that," I said mindlessly. I tapped on the screen as I scooted down in my chair, a slight grin curving my lips. "Should I ask him about the roses? Or lead up to it?"

"Rip it off like a band-aid."

Before I could send anything, he sent another text.

I'D LIKE TO SEE YOU AGAIN

I STARED AT IT FOR A MOMENT. I WAS PRETTY SURE MY HEART stopped beating. He wanted to see me again? Did that mean he wanted to hook up again? It *had* been really hot, and the second time...I shook my head. Kali didn't know about that time, and she could never know. She'd kill me.

SURE.

. . .

"Sure?" Kali read the text and lifted her eyes to mine. "Seriously?"

"I don't want to seem too eager." I shrugged. "He needs to chase me a bit." She shook her head, her lips twitching.

"Since when have you ever played hard to get?" she laughed. "You're as easy as they come." I bit my lip. Yeah, she really had no fucking idea.

The phone vibrated, and I lurched forward to grab it from her, but she pulled it away. As she quickly read the text, her smile fell. "Maybe I'll break in again—Raven, what the fuck!" She snapped her head up, her eyes blazing.

"It was a roleplay," I explained quickly. "The night we hooked up." It was a lie, and I knew she saw right through it.

"No," she said slowly. "You told me you two did some freak-shit that night, but an intruder roleplay was not something you mentioned." She reread the text. "This is him saying he's broken into your apartment. Go to the police."

I groaned and scrubbed my hand over my face, then held it out. This was why I didn't tell her about the second hook-up. "Give it back."

"He might be your stalker," she said, sounding way too fucking excited.

"Mason is not my stalker." I felt sure of that after this morning. After seeing my *stalker* evaporate into thin air, I knew who it was. Or, I assumed I knew who it was. "Give it back, Kal."

"Are you sure—"

"I'm positive." I wiggled my fingers impatiently. "He was a one-night-stand with a kinky fantasy. That's all." Her lips tightened further. "Please." She hesitantly dropped my phone into my palm.

"If he comes around, call me immediately," she said seriously, and I nodded as I typed a message back to him. "I'm serious. I don't want yours to be the next body they find." I looked up at her, finding her uncharacteristically serious.

"I'll be fine," I said. "I'm not going to die."

9
GRIM
FOUR MONTHS AGO

Storming into my room, I slammed the door behind me. I couldn't believe she'd done that, tried to jump off a fucking building. For what? To fucking die? To *go* with me?

What did that even mean, go with me? She knew who I was, obviously—a fucking Reaper. She knew she had to die to come with me. So why would she want to?

It made me irrationally angry. Maybe it wasn't irrational at all. Maybe it was a perfectly normal response to a mortal girl trying to die.

I ran my fingers roughly through my hair and shoved my cloak off, letting it fall to the floor. It was too heavy these days. There was a bass coming from Caden's room that made the floor throb; the music seeped in through the walls, vibrating them. I swallowed my building rage and panic and squeezed my eyes shut.

This wasn't fucking happening.

I wasn't about to have a panic attack about watching Raven nearly turn herself into a fucking pancake.

Grabbing my leather jacket on the way from the room, I shrugged it on and headed for the stairs. Something we occasionally did was walk with mortals. We, meaning all Reapers. It wasn't something I did often —or ever—but tonight, I needed out. The Reaper Realm was too stuffy and suffocating, with more and more Reapers coming to me daily, begging me to run for Council again.

I didn't want that life. I couldn't live it again.

I needed to get away from these soulless soul-eaters.

"Hey," Rage barked, his voice gruff as he stomped toward me. I glanced at him, biting my tongue. "Where are you going?"

"Out," I grumbled as I shoved past him, knocking into his shoulder as I headed for the front door.

"You're kidding," he deadpanned. "Tonight?" I paused and looked over my shoulder at him, finding him glaring at me with his arms crossed over his thick chest.

"What's tonight?" He stared silently at me, his eyes hard. I knew the moment he saw me remember. I let out a long breath as I turned toward him. "Brody."

"Brody," he confirmed.

"Shit." I scrubbed my hand over my face as I sighed. "Let's take him to the Mortal Realm."

"What?" he scoffed. "Not tonight. Not when he's like this."

"Come on," I moaned. "It'll be good for him to get out."

"He'll reap someone and get sent to the In-Between. Or worse." He leveled me with a look, and I sighed.

"He'll be fine."

"Why?" He narrowed his eyes into slits as he assessed me. "Why do you want to go? You never want to go to the Mortal Realm." I cleared my throat and shifted from one foot to the other.

"Just wanted to do something different," I said. "Needed to get out." He continued eyeing me, then looked over his shoulder at the stairs. I followed his gaze, seeing past the brick walls and wooden doors to Brody's room, where I knew it was dark, quiet, cold. Lifeless.

The opposite of him.

"Fine," Rage ground out.

I followed as he stormed up the steps and banged on Caden's door, but his knock was drowned out by the blaring music. We pounded on it for a few minutes before he yanked it open, his face full of fury and annoyance.

"What?" he snapped. He was shirtless and sweaty, clearly in the middle of a workout, irritated at being interrupted. Under his calm, cocky, laid-back exterior, Caden was as full of rage as the rest of us.

He was the tallest of the four of us, but Rage was the biggest and broadest. Brody was the leanest, and I was somewhere in the middle of everyone.

"Clean yourself up. We're going to the Mortal Realm," Rage said.

"No," Caden scoffed. Rage's hand slapped the door, stopping it as Caden tried to close it in our faces. They glared at each other for a long moment, and I wrung my hands together, feeling antsy.

"Yes," Rage growled. "We're going."

"Did you forget—"

"That's why we're going," I said. They both turned toward me.

"You're going?" Caden asked incredulously. "Since when do you go to the Mortal Realm? If you're not working, you don't leave the house."

"I leave the house," I said defensively. I couldn't think of places I went other than Raven's apartment, but I left the fucking house. He snorted and folded his arms over his chest. His tattoos were on full display, shiny with sweat.

"Where do you go?" he challenged.

"Places." I glanced at Brody's door. "Just get dressed, fuckface." He laughed, thinking he won, and Rage let him shut the door before we moved on to Brody's room.

"You're sure?" Rage asked me in a low voice.

No. I wasn't sure at all.

I swallowed heavily, then nodded. "He needs this."

I didn't know what the fuck he needed—I hadn't been home in fifteen years. I needed this, though, and I was feeling selfish.

"Brody! We're coming in, whether you want us to or not!" Rage shouted as he banged on the door. "You have five seconds!" We glanced at each other, and I counted to ten in my head before nodding. He shoved the door open.

As expected, the room was pitch black and ice cold. It was like walking into a cave. We glanced around, and even with my enhanced eyesight, I couldn't see a damn thing.

"Brody," I said in a low voice. "I'm turning the light on."

"No," he rasped, sounding defeated. "I don't want it on."

"Too bad," Rage snapped.

Sometimes, I wondered if Rage was trying to live up to his name, or if he really was that angry all the time. I could never tell. He always seemed so genuinely pissed but had the softest heart of anyone I knew—including Brody.

I flipped the light on, and the three of us hissed in unison as it burned our eyes. I squeezed them shut, covering them with my forearm as they adjusted to the light. My stomach dropped when I saw Brody.

He was lying on his bed, curled on his side, his dark hair matted and stuck to his face. His face was swollen and red, his eyes glassy. They looked shattered. *He* looked shattered. It fucking wrecked me.

"Hey," I murmured as I drifted toward him. "Being a Reaper isn't all that bad." He slowly opened his eyes and slid them to me. The look he gave me could kill.

"It's the single worst thing to happen to a soul," he muttered.

"I'd say the single worst thing to happen to a soul is to be exterminated, not become a Reaper."

"We're the ones who exterminate them," he said and closed his eyes. My stomach twisted further, and I glanced at Rage. He shook his head slightly, telling me not to argue.

Brody had shown signs of being an Exterminator since he'd become a Reaper. It had gotten worse in the fifteen years I'd been gone. Rage told me about his episodes when I got home. If it were true, if Brody was an Exterminator, the Reaper Council would collect him if they found out. Exterminators were rare, coveted for their powers.

They were the most powerful Reapers, the only ones able to kill another Reaper. It was a burden for those who held the power, and for someone like Brody, it would weigh heavier on him than most. He hadn't tried to bring his power out, and we didn't encourage him to.

I knew better than the three of them how much being a Reaper sucked, but more than that, how much of a fucking joke it was. We helped souls cross and find new vessels, a new home for their new lives, and it was exhausting.

No one was ever happy to see us. We weren't welcomed. We were feared and hated. We were the boogeymen of the Mortal Realm.

In the Reaper Realm, it was all a game, how much you were willing to sacrifice your beliefs and morals to get ahead. When I was on the Council, they were all holier-than-thou, fake-righteous Reapers who pretended to know what was best for the Realm, when in reality, they were so far removed, they didn't know what was really happening. They created rules and laws that went against the very nature of being a Reaper, like taking away the right to reap someone.

Centuries ago, we could decide which souls we wanted to take and which ones we wanted to spare. Now, when we get the call, we have no choice but to take the soul. Before I'd been sent to the In-Between, it had been my mission to remove that rule and give Reapers their natural abilities back. I wanted us to have a choice again.

Now that I was home, everyone seemed to think I should pick up where I left off, but I couldn't. I wasn't the same person I was fifteen years ago. Even if I was, things were too different now. The game was different. More rules and regulations had been passed to make it both easier and harder to reap.

I knew I had a target on my back, and in turn, so did my brothers. Raven might, too. I needed to protect them, and I couldn't do that if my head was clouded with legislation.

Brody glared up at me, but I could handle it. If it meant getting him out of his room and his head, I was fine with him hating me tonight.

"Get the fuck up." I gripped his shirt and ripped him out of the bed, suddenly angry at how he was behaving. He couldn't hide away because things were hard. He needed to face them head-on, like the rest of us. He crashed to the floor and sat frozen for a moment, shocked. Then, he shot to his feet and swung at me.

I easily dodged his fist, then grabbed his wrist and pinned it to his side before shoving him toward the closet. Rage stood by the door, watching us with his usual blank face.

"Get dressed," I growled, shoving him again. "We're leaving in ten minutes."

10

RAVEN

PRESENT

I was fucking exhausted.

I couldn't sleep last night, not when every creaking floorboard and howl of wind made me think someone was in my apartment. Not just any someone—Grim.

It didn't make any sense. Why would he be leaving me roses? Why would he be my stalker?

He knew I remembered him. He knew I wasn't afraid of him. He knew I wanted him. What game was he playing?

Unless it wasn't him.

I'd done enough research over the years to learn that demons could mimic other people, especially if it was the person you desired most. Could it be a demon messing with me? Could Grim be out there, still not remembering or caring about me? Was I being stalked and haunted by a fucking demon?

My mind wasn't on work all day, so I continually fucked up orders and rang people up wrong. If you know anything about New Yorkers, it's that they have no time for fuck ups. So, I'd been yelled at all day and nearly sent home by my boss. I convinced him to let me stay since I couldn't afford not to work, but I knew I was on thin ice.

Now, I was on the subway. I'd left my headphones at home, so I was stuck listening to the chatter around me, which was honestly fine. Sometimes, eavesdropping on people and learning about their lives was far more entertaining than whatever I could listen to on my own.

Tonight, the topic of conversation was murder.

A new girl had been found dead this afternoon. I scooted slightly closer to the girls beside me, straining to hear their hushed conversation. The redhead leaned toward her friend, showing her phone to the other girl.

"It's the second one this week," she said. "The cops are saying that young women should stay inside after dark."

"They're putting us on a curfew instead of finding the guy?" the other girl scoffed. "Typical. It's always our responsibility to not get killed, right?"

"I think it's just a safety precaution," the redhead replied warily. "They're trying to minimize the number of victims."

I drowned out the rest of their conversation as I grabbed my phone and did a quick search. Sure enough, the first link was to an article posted an hour ago. Another girl—black hair, pale skin, green eyes—had been found dead in Brookyln. The street was closer to my apartment than the first.

Was it my stalker?

If Grim was my stalker, there'd be no reason for him to murder these girls, not like this. He could reap them, but he wouldn't slaughter them. Why would he? From how they'd been described, these murders were gruesome. The girls were assaulted, their throats slit, their bodies mutilated.

It didn't sound like Grim.

It couldn't be him.

I tapped out a quick text to Kali, wanting her to know. She needed to be just as aware as me. She was worried it was my stalker, but I wasn't. I was worried it was just a psychopath picking girls at random, and she could be next.

After sending her a text, I stared at my phone for a long time, but she didn't respond right away. She was probably looking it up for herself. I would've done the same thing. Finally, three dots appeared, then disappeared, and reappeared.

. . .

HOLY SHIT.

I SNORTED AND ROLLED MY EYES AT HER REPLY. PEOPLE began gathering around the exits, indicating the train was nearing its next stop. My stop. I put my phone away, slung my purse over my shoulder, and moved toward one of the less crowded doors at the back.

My back was aching, my feet were killing me, and right then, more than any other time in my adult life, I was asking myself why I'd decided to live in a city where I couldn't have my own car or a tub to take a hot bubble bath when I got home.

The train lurched to a stop, and I stumbled back a step before righting myself. As the doors slid open, people began rushing in and out. I stepped onto the landing, keeping my head down and trying to make myself as small as possible. It didn't help, of course, and I knocked into someone.

"Shit," I muttered, barely glancing up. "Sorry—" I paused, my throat going dry when Eddy's eyes met mine.

"Raven?" He pushed his brows together, looking just as confused as I felt. "It's Eddy." He pointed to himself. He looked different. Cleaner and less disgusting, for one, but he was wearing a suit. "We met at that party the other night."

"Yeah," I said, nodding slightly. "Yeah, I remember."

"We were both pretty gone." He laughed as he rubbed the back of his neck, and red crept into his face. "I was just getting off work and was heading out to grab some drinks with a few friends." I nodded again and looked over his shoulder at the stairs leading to the sidewalk. I needed to get to them so I could go home. "You wanna come with?"

I returned my gaze to his and blinked a few times. "I'm sorry, what?" He laughed, his throat bobbing under his short stubble.

"I asked if you wanted to grab a drink with me," he said as he scanned my body. "If you're not busy."

"Actually, I'm just getting off work, and I'm exhausted," I said, trying to sound apologetic. "Maybe another time." He nodded a few times and tried to look sympathetic, but his lips tightened into a thin line, his eyes flashing with irritation. I'd seen that look a million times—a man trying to keep his composure in public.

"Let me get your number since I didn't get it the other night." It wasn't a question. He pulled his phone out, and I shifted on my feet, glancing at the stairs behind him again. I rattled off my number, wanting this interaction to be over as quickly as possible. "I'll text you, so you have mine, too."

"Okie-dokie," I said, sidestepping him.

I felt slimier in his presence than the other night, probably because I was sober and in my right mind. His eyes stabbed into my back as I hurried across the floor and up the steps.

I could still feel his gaze—or *a* gaze—my entire walk home.

11

GRIM

FOUR MONTHS AGO

I was still riled tight with pent-up rage as we walked into the club. Every head in the fucking place turned our direction. That tended to happen when four, seven-foot men appeared. Some glared at us, some eye-fucked us, but mostly, everyone had the overwhelming sense to back the fuck up.

We looked like mortals without our glamour. If it weren't for our height, ice-cold skin, soulless eyes, and non-beating hearts, you'd never know we weren't human.

Caden sauntered to the bar and rested his hip against it. The bartender craned his head back and swiveled his eyes between us as we approached. His throat bobbed exaggeratedly as he swallowed, and Rage scoffed as he looked away. He had no patience for cowards.

"Wh-what can I get you guys?" His voice was shaky and breathless. *Scared.*

Oh right, our presence seemed to let mortals know we were danger-ous, too. I didn't know how they knew Death walked with them, but they *always* fucking knew.

"I'll have a vodka martini, extra dirty." Caden turned his head toward us, his eyebrows raised expectantly.

"Scotch. Neat," Rage barked, still not looking at the bartender.

56

"Same," I said mindlessly.

"Just get me five tequila shots," Brody grumbled. We all turned to look at him, but he was just glaring down at the bartender, waiting for him to say something.

"Right away," the kid stammered, then tripped over his feet and scurried away to make our drinks.

Caden bobbed his head in time with the music, and I knew as soon as he got his drink, he was heading to the floor to dance. If it was any other night, Brody would be out there with him. They'd wing-man for each other while Rage and I would sit at the bar, have a few drinks, and ignore everyone around us, including each other, for the most part. The twins would end up going home with girls while Rage and I waited around until they were done. Then, we'd all head back to the Reaper Realm together.

I turned and folded my arms over my chest as I scanned the club. It wasn't huge, but it was crowded. There was a DJ booth set up on a low stage, and people swarmed around the front, dancing and grinding on each other. Rage made a disgusted sound, and I grunted in agreement.

As I did a final sweep through the crowd, my heart lurched into my throat, and time stopped around me. A girl, much taller than everyone else, with raven-black hair and moonlight pale skin, was dancing with a much smaller blonde girl. They were laughing and smiling, and I was so fucking confused.

Only a few hours ago, she was ready to jump off a fucking building, and now she was here, dancing with her friend?

She paused and looked around, her eyes taking everything in. I had the urge to duck and hide. As if I could fucking hide from her. She turned in a small circle, and when she got to me, to my brothers, she paused again. She looked at them, but her eyes returned to me, and she gave me the slightest smirk.

It went straight to my fucking dick.

Then she turned around and started dancing again. There was no fucking reason for her to be here. There was no reason for *me* to be here. But here we both here, in this sweaty, dark, too-loud club on a random night. Was it a coincidence, or something more?

"Who is that?" Caden asked as he handed me my drink, his eyes trained on Raven. I roughly cleared my throat and took a long sip.

"No idea," I lied. I felt his eyes on me.

"Is she why you wanted to come out tonight?" He sipped his martini as he studied her. "Didn't know she'd be your type, but I can see it. The blonde, though—" He groaned low in his throat and shifted on his feet. "I like that one. A lot."

"I don't know either of them." A half lie. I didn't know who Raven was with. He snorted as he took a longer sip.

"So you wouldn't mind me talking to them?" he asked. "Maybe buy her a drink or two? I'm sure I could convince them both to go home with me." I glared at him, my temper wringing tighter in my chest.

"Knock yourself out," I ground out, my jaw clenched. He threw his head back and laughed, drawing the attention of everyone around us. I elbowed him in the ribs, making him grunt out a breath. He didn't lose that fucking grin, though.

"Hey, Brods. You wanna dance? I found a couple girls for us." Caden threw the rest of his drink back and tossed the glass on the bar. Brody tossed back shot after shot as soon as the bartender set them down. He glanced at Caden, then out at the dancefloor, and shrugged.

"Whatever," he sighed.

I watched my brothers move onto the floor, the crowd parting for them. Caden walked right up to Raven and her friend. Brody stood off to the side, looking like he'd rather be anywhere but there. I felt his pain. Usually, that's how I felt. Right now, though, I wanted to be here and only here.

Raven laughed and shook her head, then looked my direction. She waved at me, her smile bright. Too bright for a girl who was so ready to die. I awkwardly lifted my hand, and she smiled broader, then tilted her head, inviting me to the floor. I shook my head, telling her no. She made an exaggerated pouting face, sticking her full bottom lip out. *Brat.*

"Who's the girl?" Rage asked. Her eyes left mine to look at him, and I'd never wanted to kill my brother so fucking much in my life.

"Don't know," I said. She looked at me, smiled sweetly, then looked back at Caden.

His charm was in full swing with her friend, who was eating it up.

She had her hand resting on his forearm, seemingly for balance, and if I knew Caden—which I fucking did—he was loving it.

"Where's Brody?" There was a hint of panic in Rage's tone that had my spine stiffening.

I looked around the room, searching for the only other big fucker here, but couldn't find him. He should be easy to spot, but he was gone. Rage and I glanced at each other, and I swore under my breath before throwing my drink back, not feeling the burn as it went down.

He tossed money onto the bar, and we stormed through the crowd, ready to search for him.

We didn't have to look far.

Outside, he was leaning against the side of the building, his head resting on the wall and his eyes closed. His chest was heaving, his hair plastered to his forehead. Rage began to storm toward him, but I grabbed his arm and shook my head.

"Leave him," I muttered. "He needs to do this by himself." Rage glared at me.

Brody was the baby, and we all treated him as such, but it was time we treated him like the man—the Reaper—he was. He wasn't a baby and he needed to work this shit out on his own. He couldn't rely on us to do it for him. He couldn't go off the rails every year and fall into a depression when this day came around.

No one liked turning into a Reaper. It was a scary, painful process. It happened one of two ways: your soul forced you to become one, or a Reaper turned you. We were all chosen to become Reapers, one way or another.

A Reaper turned our parents, and as we died, they turned us. I was the first, then Rage. Our parents were Exterminated before we could turn Caden and Body, and a part of me felt like they secretly hated us for the extra time we had with them.

Being a Reaper was something Brody had never come to terms with. He hated himself for it. I understood why.

Why him? Why any of us? Why were we dealt this shitty hand? Why did we have to reap mortals and choose where their souls went? Why were we the bad guys when we'd done nothing? We didn't want this any more than they did.

59

He took it harder than any of us, though. I struggled for centuries with it, but he was still a baby in Reaper years. But it was time for him to learn to deal with it, too. He could be coddled, but he couldn't avoid his job. He couldn't avoid who he was just because he didn't like it. He needed to figure out how to cope with it, just like we all had.

Turning on my heel, I left Rage and Brody outside and went back into the club. They could be mad at me all they wanted. They could hate what the In-Between did to me. They could hate me. I didn't care. The shit Brody was fighting in his head and his heart was something only he could slay. I couldn't do it for him—no one could.

The sooner he realized that, the sooner he could save himself.

I searched for Raven as soon as I entered the club. I found Caden grinding with her friend, then felt my blood hum when I looked down, watching some fucker dancing with Raven. She looked uncomfortable but wasn't pushing him away. I didn't like him touching her.

Maybe I should've been more methodical in the way I approached them. Maybe I should've let her dance with the asshole all night. Maybe I should've let her go home with him, too.

But I didn't.

No. Instead, I found myself hauling him away from her. He fell to his ass, then shot to his feet, ready to fight, but as soon as he saw me, he immediately ran with his tail tucked.

Raven and her friend stared up at me with wide eyes, Raven's red lips parted. There was a tense silence around us, like a bubble had formed as everyone held their breath, waiting to see what would happen. The bass rattled in my chest as Raven and I stared at each other, her eyes holding me more captive than they ever had.

I was so fucked.

Then Caden threw his head back and laughed. Just like that, the bubble popped.

Raven's shoulders slumped slightly and she let out a breathy laugh of her own. She smiled softly, her white teeth gleaming in the neon lights. Her eyes searched mine, and, just for a moment, her smile fell.

I realized she had no idea who I was.

She'd never seen me without the mask. She didn't know what I looked like. But my eyes—she'd seen my eyes. She couldn't know me from them alone, could she?

"I'm Mason," I said, leaning down. Her breath hitched slightly, and she dropped her eyes to my lips, then lifted them to my eyes again.

"Raven," she said. Her friend nudged her with her elbow, and Raven rolled her eyes. "And my best friend, Kali."

"Nice to meet you," I said, then quickly tacked on, "Both." I could feel Caden's eyes on me, and I knew I'd have to explain this—explain her —later. Right then, though, being close to her as me, as Mason, was giving me a head rush.

"So, you're brothers?" Kali asked over the music, looking between Caden and me.

"Yeah," I said gruffly.

"Unfortunately," Caden sighed at the same time, and she laughed. "I got all the looks. The brains. The brawn. The humor. What did you get again?"

"Oh, I don't know," Raven said, eyeing me, then him. "He looks like he could kick your ass." Caden snorted.

"Could not," he said. "He's tried for years. He can't."

"Time and place, Cade," I said as I folded my arms over my chest, planting my feet apart. "Time and place."

"I'd pay money to see that," Raven laughed.

"Would you both be shirtless, by chance?" Kali asked. The girls looked at each other, then erupted in giggles.

I couldn't help but smile down at Raven. I'd never seen her like...like this. Carefree. Almost happy. She'd always been scared, always on the brink of death when we interacted. In her apartment, she was alone and always seemed so sad.

Right then, the way she was acting was a far cry from the girl she was earlier. She wasn't the girl who choked herself with a scarf a month ago, or the one begging me to reap her a few hours ago. This was someone else entirely.

"Do you want us with our shirts off?" Caden asked, lifting his brow.

"Oh, I think she wants you with more than just your shirt off," Raven said, laughing as she wiped her eyes. Kali swatted at her but laughed again.

"That could be arranged," he said. "But not with him." He jerked his chin at me. "Only you and me." Kali's face flushed red, and I rolled my eyes. Raven made a gagging sound and I snorted. "Can I get you a drink?" Kali nodded eagerly up at him, and off they went, leaving us alone.

Raven stared after them, a soft smile on her face. It slowly fell, then she looked up at me. We stared at each other for a moment, and again, her eyes narrowed slightly as she flicked them between mine. I felt like I was naked, like she was stripping me bare right there in the middle of the club. Then she shook her head, that suspicious look gone.

"Do you want a drink?" I asked, not nearly as smoothly as Caden. She grinned, then shook her head.

"I better not," she sighed. "I have to work in the morning and being hungover while dealing with assholes is the worst combo." I nodded sympathetically. "Where do you work?" I cleared my throat as I looked around, pretending I hadn't heard her question. I couldn't exactly tell her I was a Reaper. *Her* Reaper. "You know, yeah, maybe I will have that drink." I glanced down, finding her watching me again.

I didn't say anything. I just tilted my head to the side and let her step in front of me. I followed her as she walked through the crowd, then stood behind her as she leaned over the bar to wait for the bartender, her ass just as tempting as it had been a few weeks ago when she wiggled around on the floor, looking under the bed for her giant fucking dildo.

I roughly cleared my throat at the memory and looked around. Now was not the time to get a hard-on, especially when she kept brushing up against me. Fuck. I cleared my throat again. She leaned over more, and this time, I watched her do it on purpose—she kneeled on the barstool and pressed her ass against my growing cock.

Maybe I shouldn't have done it, opened this door with her, but I couldn't help it. I moved my hand to her hip and squeezed it in warning. She looked over her shoulder at me, her eyes hooded and a teasing smirk on her lips.

Any restraint I had snapped, and I wrapped my arm around her waist, yanking her off the barstool. She yelped, then laughed as I carried her through the crowd toward the exit.

"I can walk," she laughed when we got outside. I ignored her and hauled her up, keeping her back pinned to my chest. "Mason, put me down."

"No." I stomped my way down the street, then paused. I knew exactly where she lived, but she couldn't know that. "Where's your place?"

"Let's go to a hotel," she said, and I squeezed her tighter.

"That wasn't the question," I growled. "I'm fucking you in your bed. I want you to think about me every night when you're lying in it, trying to fall asleep." She inhaled sharply, then glanced at me over her shoulder again, her eyes reflecting the moonlight.

"Who said I'm going to let you fuck me?"

"You did, when you were grinding your ass into me," I said low in her ear.

"Maybe I was just having fun," she countered, breathless. "Maybe that wasn't an invite."

"Maybe I don't care." I squeezed her again. "You're mine to claim tonight, and I'm going to fuck you senseless. You're telling me you don't want that?" She flicked her eyes between mine, and again, I had the overwhelming feeling that I should hide.

"Do I know you?" she whispered. "I swear—" She shook her head. "Never mind."

"No, you don't know me," I said. Another half lie. She didn't know Mason. "But tonight, you will. Tonight, you'll know me better than anyone else ever has, and I'm going to know you." I ran my hand up her bare leg, under the short hem of her dress, and she gasped. "I'm going to ruin all other men for you. You're mine now, little—" I stopped myself before I could say *little bird*. Her breath hitched as I trailed my fingers higher but stopped before I reached her hip. "Tell me you want me to fuck you." My lips were pressed against her ear, my voice low. "Say it, Raven. Say you want me."

I put her on the ground but kept my hand wrapped around her arm. She stared at me, her chest heaving with each breath. I wanted to know what she was thinking. Had I given myself away? Did she know it was me?

"I want you."

12

RAVEN

PRESENT

*I*t's our anniversary in two days, little bird. Meet me where it began.

I STARED DOWN AT THE NOTE, MY BLOOD TURNING TO ICE. It was typed on a small piece of cardstock. It wasn't signed, but it didn't need to be. I knew who it was from. *Him*.

Grim.

My Reaper.

Dozens and dozens of roses surrounded it. I had to shove my door open since so many roses were piled in my small apartment. It would've been a sweet and romantic gesture if it had been for any other reason than celebrating the death of my stepfather.

Even though he was abusive and terrible, he was the only person I had. After Grim killed him and left me behind, I had no one. I was sent to foster care, already too old to be adopted. Not that I *wanted* to be adopted. I bounced from home to home, never settling enough to make a connection with those I lived with, let alone make a friend.

I was totally on my own, alone in the world. For years, I hated him for it. I hated Grim for taking away the only source of stability I had. Sure, it was chaotic, abusive stability, but it was stability nonetheless.

Maybe, if he hadn't left immediately afterward, it wouldn't have been so bad. Maybe, if he would've helped me figure out what to do, or let me go with him, or...if he just wouldn't have abandoned me that night, I wouldn't have ended up like *this*.

I stomped through the apartment, crushing the roses under my feet. My interaction with Eddy was still fresh in my mind. It was weird, and I needed to wash away the creepy, slimy way he'd looked at me, but I couldn't. Not with all these fucking roses everywhere.

Grumbling to myself, I grabbed them by the handful and shoved them into a garbage bag. I didn't care about keeping them anymore. These were weird fucking mementos anyway, and I didn't need to keep them. If Grim thought I was going to meet him on that road again, he was fucking delusional.

My phone buzzed in my pocket, and I dropped the bag to fish it out. I didn't know why I felt so irritated, but everything was setting me off. Maybe it was the serial killer on the loose, running into Eddy, or these fucking roses. Maybe it was just the reminder of what day was coming up.

I remembered this day vividly every year. I always wondered what it would've been like to spend it with Grim, but every year—for fifteen fucking years—he was gone. It was like I hadn't even existed. Now...*now* he wants to meet me where it all began?

YOU LOOKED PRETTY TONIGHT

I GROANED. FUCKING EDDY. I WANTED TO THROW MY PHONE at the wall, smash it into a million pieces. Did he not get the hint that I wasn't interested in him? Why would I be? He was a creepy, greasy weirdo, and I didn't want anything to do with him. I'd never been so fucking glad I hadn't hooked up with someone as I was in that moment. If I'd slept with him, he would've fallen in love.

I could *not* have that.

I ignored the text and went back to cleaning up the roses. I was positive it was Grim leaving them in my apartment, but it was just so weird. Roses meant nothing to me, to us. They held no secret or deeper meaning, so why was he leaving them? My phone buzzed again, and I let out a louder, frustrated sound as I looked at the screen.

I WISH WE COULD'VE HAD THAT DRINK

I TOSSED MY PHONE ON THE COUNTER. SERIOUSLY, COULD HE not take a fucking hint? I was not interested. I didn't even know why I'd given him my number. Maybe I could change it tomorrow. It vibrated again, and I snatched it up.

MAYBE WE CAN HANG OUT TOMORROW NIGHT

HOW COULD I GET RID OF HIM? I NIBBLED MY BOTTOM LIP. I could just be a bitch and hope he got the hint, or I could continue to ignore him.

OR I COULD COME OVER TONIGHT

OH, FUCK IT.

I'M NOT INTERESTED. SORRY.

THE TYPING BUBBLES IMMEDIATELY APPEARED, AND I WAITED with bated breath, the roses filling my apartment momentarily forgotten.

. . .

I JUST WANT TO BE FRIENDS

I ROLLED MY EYES. SURE, HE DID.

I tossed my phone back on the counter. I told him I wasn't interested, he could take it or leave it, but I'd made myself clear. Looking around at the roses, I got annoyed all over again. What was it with men? Could Grim even be considered a man as a Reaper? He was definitely masculine, but did that mean he was a *man*? He certainly had the audacity of one.

Annoyed, I threw the trash bag down, ignoring my buzzing phone, and stomped my way to my bedroom. The roses crushed under my feet, the petals leaking juice and soaking into the hardwood. I'd deal with them later.

I grabbed clothes and stomped over the roses again as I went to the bathroom. Maybe I was just annoyed he thought he had the right to come into my apartment and do this. He didn't. Maybe I was still annoyed that I'd reached out to Mason, only for him to go right back to ghosting me again.

Maybe I'd just swear men off forever; it was clear the ones I wanted were either Reapers, stalking me, or not interested in anything other than a kinky hookup. Plus, the ones I didn't want were the biggest fucking creeps on the planet.

I stood in the shower and squeezed my eyes shut, letting the warm water wash over me. When I opened them again, I screamed.

A towering figure loomed on the opposite side of the bathroom, just like he had the other day, the shower curtain between us. He was further away than last time, but no less imposing. He'd just appeared from nothing. I hadn't heard him approach or any doors or windows open. One moment he wasn't there, and the next, he was.

"You don't like your surprise?" His voice was raspier than I remembered, and, despite the warm water, goosebumps rippled over my skin.

"It was a lot," I answered truthfully. "I've had a long day." He was silent for a moment, then took a step forward.

"I told you to stay away from him." He dropped his voice, and my toes curled at the command it carried.

"Who?" I asked. I wanted to rip the curtain back and see him, but something kept me from doing it. Was it the false sense of protection I felt from it?

"I'll see you in two days."

"I can't—"

"I'll see you in two days."

"Grim." My voice broke, and he paused. "I can't go back there. Please." There was another long pause before he cleared his throat.

"I'll see you in two days." Then he was gone. Again.

13

RAVEN

FOUR MONTHS AGO

When you're eager to hookup with someone for the first time, you can't keep your hands off each other. Your lips hardly separate, and you're lucky if you make it through the door before clothes come off. The anticipation of them being inside of you, or you inside them, is too much. The commute is the longest, cruelest foreplay of your life.

It wasn't like that with Mason.

He kept his giant hand wrapped around my neck as we walked. Not my hand or my arm, not my waist, but my neck. It was a possessive hold, and every time I tried to free myself, his grip tightened.

It should've scared me. *He* should've scared me, but there was something in his eyes that kept me grounded. There was a promise of safety in them I didn't understand. Maybe my head was just too fucked up from Grim earlier, or maybe I was looking for something that wasn't there, but Mason made me feel *something*. An instant connection. A spark.

As I unlocked my door, his hand never left its place on my neck. My hands trembled slightly as I pushed it open, and I mentally went over everything I'd done before leaving for the club. Had I cleaned up? I hadn't been expecting to bring anyone home. I didn't want him to think I lived like a pig.

As we entered, he stepped into my apartment like he owned it, like he'd been there a million times. He didn't look around or take in his surroundings. He just pressed me against the door as he locked it, his dark eyes gleaming from the moonlight shining through the window. My breath caught, and, not for the first time that night, I thought I saw Grim.

He was on my mind, and since Mason was just as big as Grim, it was my mind playing tricks on me. I knew that. But when he looked at me like that, completely unguarded, I felt like I was falling down the rabbit hole and Grim would be at the bottom, ready to catch me.

His hand ran along the wall until he found the light switch, and he flipped it on. The light momentarily blinded me, and I blinked a few times, letting my eyes adjust. Once they did, the look on his face was predatory. He was staring at my mouth like he wanted to ravage it. God, I wanted him to.

I wanted to give him everything.

I held my breath as I waited for him to kiss me. Time moved slowly as he rested his hand on the door by my head, the other on the wall, caging me in. As he lowered his mouth to mine, my heart began to gallop. It was happening. The tip of his cold nose touched the tip of mine, and electricity shot through my body.

As I pushed onto my toes, ready to take the reins if he wasn't, he pulled away. His body wasn't overly warm, but I missed his presence, the feel of him pressed against me.

"Let me see you," he rasped. His eyes trailed over my body, and lava burned beneath my skin. With shaky fingers, I reached for the hem of my dress. "Slowly."

I revealed my body to him, inch by agonizingly slow inch. His eyes darkened, his attention rapt as he watched. He was deathly still, barely breathing, and it gave me an odd sense of power to know I was having this effect on him. He was helpless to do anything but watch me.

I dropped my dress to the floor, the fabric pooling around my feet. Subtly, I shifted, trying not to fidget and hide myself with my arms. He didn't react, his eyes just stayed fixed on mine. They didn't immediately roam over my body like I expected. The room was thick with tension as the silent seconds ticked by.

Then his eyes slowly dropped, and the way he looked at me, like he was ravenous and I was his favorite meal, made my core tighten. He sucked his bottom lip between his teeth, his eyes still slowly traveling down the long length of my body.

"Come here." He held his hand out. His command startled me, his voice too loud in the silent room, but I moved to him without hesitation. My hand slid easily into his, and he spun me in a slow circle. His eyes scorched every inch of me. I could barely breathe. "Your tattoo." He ran his cool finger lightly up my spine, and I shuddered. "What is it?"

"A reminder," I whispered.

"It's a scythe," he said. "A reminder of what?" I didn't answer him immediately.

"Of who I lost," is all I said. His breath hitched, and I glanced over my shoulder, finding his eyes still trained on my back.

"You'll find them again." His breath ghosted along my skin as he brushed my hair to one side. "Or they'll find you." His fingers lightly trailed down my arm until he got to my hand, and he interlaced our fingers tightly together. I gasped when his full, soft lips pressed against my shoulder. "They never should've lost you." He kissed up my neck, his other hand wrapped around my waist, his fingers teasing the hem of my panties. "They never should've left you."

My heart was hammering in my chest. He was making my mind swim with a million emotions, and I wanted him to stop, but I also never wanted this to end. He didn't know what he was talking about, but his words hit home, making my heart swell with sadness.

I ignored everything I felt and focused on his hands, on the way his lips felt against my skin, how his cock pressed against my back, and my mind quieted. His fingers dipped under the lace of my panties, and his booted foot slid between mine to gently nudge my legs further apart.

His thick fingers skimmed my pussy, and I gasped, letting my head fall back against his chest. He lifted our hands and rested mine on my breast, squeezing until I moaned. I hadn't realized my eyes were closed until he nibbled my earlobe, then ran his tongue along my pulse before pressing his lips to my ear and whispering, "Eyes on me."

I opened them and stared at him upside down. He looked imposing like this, but something about it turned me on more. Knowing he was this giant man who could use me, abuse me, take anything he wanted from me made me press my thighs together. The slightest hint of a smirk teased his lips.

"Something wrong?" he murmured before dipping his head to my neck again. "Do you need me to do something for you?"

"Touch me," I whimpered.

"I *am* touching you." The hand holding mine squeezed my breast again while the other ran up and down my pussy, never touching me where I needed him to.

"Please." I tried to look at him, but his head was buried in my neck. I couldn't turn my head, but I felt him grin against my skin.

"I like the way it sounds when you beg," he muttered, his voice vibrating through me. I groaned and pushed my head harder against his shoulder. He chuckled darkly as he moved our hands to my other breast. "Can I get you to beg me some more?"

I'd never been with someone like this, someone who wanted fore-play and talked like this. It was always a blur of clothes and bodies, and after he came and we parted ways, I finished myself off at home. This, the way Mason was, this was new.

"I asked you a question." His voice was firmer, and his hold on my breast tightened almost to the point of pain. "Can my little slut beg more?" My pussy clenched at his words, and I whimpered.

"Please, please, touch me." I angled my legs further apart. He laughed softly as he stood straight, pulling his hands from me. My head spun from how quickly he'd stopped touching me and how much I needed his hands back on me. "Was that not good?" I turned to face him, panic filling my chest that I'd disappointed him.

"Oh, little Raven," he breathed as he gripped my chin. He tipped my head back, forcing me to look into his depthless black eyes. "We're going to have so much fun, aren't we?" I nodded, completely lost to him. "Get on your knees for me."

Without thinking, I dropped to my knees. We'd barely made it into my apartment, only a few feet from the front door, and somehow, it made me wetter knowing he couldn't wait. I waited for him to tell me what he wanted, but he stayed quiet as he stared down at me.

"Crawl to your room," he finally said as he stepped to the side. My brows bunched slightly, but I dropped to my hands and began to crawl. His hand landed on my ass, and I yelped then looked up at him in question. "No one told you to stop." I swallowed hard as I started to crawl again. He spanked me, harder this time, and I bit my lip to keep my whimper in. "Let me hear you." He spanked me again, and I didn't hold back the groan.

He laughed as he stepped around me and flipped the light on. He stood at the foot of the bed and folded his arms over his chest. He was muscular, but not grossly so. I couldn't wait to see what he was hiding under his shirt. His black hair was short, his tan skin golden, and a short black beard covered his square jaw. But his eyes—they were so dark, so black; they were endless.

"Get on the bed." He took a step back, his biceps flexing as he watched me crawl onto my bed, then roll onto my back. I stared at him as I slowly spread my legs apart. His jaw flexed as his eyes dropped, then slowly, he lifted them. "You have any toys?"

I paused. Had I heard him correctly? He asked if I had any toys? I'd never had a guy ask if I had toys.

"Yeah," I said hesitantly, eyeing him. He smirked, his eyes gleaming.

"How many?" I hesitated again. I had my regular vibrator, the one that probably wouldn't scare him away, and I had my monster under the bed. His brow lifted. "It's not a hard question," he said. "How many toys?"

"Two," I blurted, then mentally slapped myself. I hadn't meant to tell him that. I'd meant to only tell him about the vibrator. His grin turned evil as he moved toward the bed.

"Where are they?" I rolled over and reached into my nightstand, pulling out my vibrator. This was so fucking awkward. No one knew I had these, let alone had seen them, and now this literal stranger was asking me about them. "The other one?"

"Under the bed," I mumbled. I moved to slide to the floor, but he held his hand up as he kneeled. He barely rummaged around before he grabbed the box. He held it up, his brows raised in question. I nodded and laid back down.

My stomach swirled with anxiety as I watched him open the box. I lifted my eyes to his face, carefully gauging his reaction, but he gave nothing away as he pulled the dildo and the bottle of lube out. He tossed them on the bed beside me, then sat at my feet.

"That fits inside you?" he asked, his voice low. I swallowed hard as I nodded. "It stretches your little pussy?" I nodded again. "Show me." I knew this was coming. Why else would he ask if I had toys? I still felt a bolt of shock and embarrassment at his words.

He rested his hands on either side of me and leaned forward until his body hovered over mine. I couldn't breathe. I couldn't think. All I could do was stare at him, breathe him in, focus solely on him.

"Show me, Raven," he growled. "Let me watch you fuck yourself." I clenched my blanket at my sides, my chest heaving. He dipped his head, his eyes still raised and locked on mine, as he kissed the center of my chest. Slowly, he moved to one breast and gently tugged the soft cup of my bra down. "Unless you want me to fuck you with it."

I couldn't speak: my throat was too dry and my heart was beating too fast. His tongue slowly circled my nipple, then his teeth clamped down. My back arched, a small gasp leaving me as he bit harder.

"Tell me what you want," he demanded. He moved to the other breast, giving it the same treatment.

"You," I breathed. "I want you to fuck me." He grinned around my nipple, and I groaned, the sight ungodly.

"You know what I want to hear from you," he said. He licked between my breasts, down my stomach to my panties. He grabbed the band of my panties with his teeth and pulled it slightly away from my body before letting it pop back against my abdomen.

"Please," I begged. "Please fuck me with it." He grinned, then in one motion, grabbed my panties and yanked. The fabric tore effortlessly away, and he shoved them in his pocket before winking at me.

He grabbed my legs and pushed them wide, forcing me to recline back. I stared up at the ceiling. I couldn't believe this was happening. I was about to let him fuck me with my dildo. What the fuck was wrong with me?

His fingers dug into my thighs as he pushed them further apart, then his tongue tapped my clit, and my hips lifted off the bed. I snapped my eyes to him, finding him laying between my legs, his arm banded across my hips, his eyes boring into mine. Slowly, he ran his tongue along my entire seam, and I bunched the fabric tighter in my fists.

"So wet already," he said, his voice muffled. He pressed his lips against my clit and gently sucked. My back arched, and I pushed against his mouth, wanting more. He laughed softly before flicking my clit faster with his tongue, coaxing my pleasure higher.

I spread my legs as far as I could and moved my hand to the back of his head as I lifted my hips, pressing his face harder against my pussy. He growled, his eyes locked with mine as he lost control. He was relentless. His tongue, his fingers, his lips and teeth, everything was pushing me to the edge. I ground hard against his mouth and gripped his hair tighter, my moans growing louder and louder.

"Fuck, please, please," I moaned over and over. He wanted me to beg, and if that's what it took to come, I'd never stop. "Please don't stop." I rolled my hips again, and his tongue moved faster. I couldn't hold back. It was right there. I shamelessly used his face for my pleasure as I rode the wave higher and higher.

Finally, I threw my head back, my back arching off the bed, and screamed as I came. He didn't stop. His tongue lashed against my sensitive clit, then down to my entrance, drinking everything I had to give him. He didn't stop until my body fell limply to the bed, entirely spent.

"That was the best thing I've ever seen," he said. "You're the best thing I've ever fucking tasted." He licked his lips, savoring what I gave him. "I think you're going to be the best thing I've ever felt." He hovered over me again, propping himself up on his forearms by my head. "Taste yourself."

I ran my tongue along his lips, and his eyes rolled back. I gently pushed inside, then kissed him fervently. He pressed me into the bed, sinking his weight onto me as he ravished my mouth with his. I couldn't escape him. He was everywhere, all-consuming.

Slowly, he peeled himself away. I nearly forgot about the dildo until he kneeled between my legs and grabbed it. He grinned at me as he aimed it at my pussy. I spread my legs even wider, watching as he rubbed the rounded tip against my sensitive clit.

"Take your bra off, then put your hands above your head," he commanded. I did as he said, removing my bra and tossing it to the floor, then raising my arms above my head. He whipped his belt off in a fluid motion before wrapping it around my wrists, then around the post on my headboard. His hands slid down my arms until he reached my breasts, and he roughly cupped them before pinching my nipples until I cried out at the bite of pain.

He moved the dildo back to my pussy and slowly stroked the tip through me. I whimpered and writhed against the bindings, wanting him to fuck me but not wanting him to stop teasing me. Everything he was doing felt so good, but I needed more.

Slowly, he pushed the tip inside, and I cried out. His eyes were on my face: not where he was pushing inside me, but watching my reaction —the mixture of pleasure and pain *he* was creating. He shoved it in more, then finally dropped his eyes, his jaw flexing as he watched himself fuck me.

"Do you like being tied up and helpless?" he rasped. "Do you like knowing I could fuck you anyway I wanted, and you couldn't stop me? I could choke you until you passed out or fucked your ass while I fucked your cunt with this cock," he shoved the dildo in more, emphasizing his words, "or shove my cock down your throat until you couldn't breathe. You'd be totally helpless."

I twisted in the bindings again, then jerked on them. They were secured tightly to the headboard; my arms weren't going anywhere until he let them. He pressed more inside of me, then groaned when the dildo bottomed out. Slowly, he dragged it out, letting me feel every bumpy ridge and artificial vein.

"Do you want me to fill both your little holes?" He lifted his eyes to mine. "Your answer doesn't really matter. I'm going to do it regardless." I whimpered and clenched around the fake cock as he shoved it back inside me. He stopped holding back and started fucking me with it, harder and faster than before. "I'm asking you questions," he said as he gripped my jaw, "and I'm expecting answers."

I screamed as he worked me up higher, pushing me toward another orgasm. Then, he shoved it all the way in and stopped. My chest heaved as my pussy fluttered around it.

"Answer me," he growled, gripping my jaw tighter. "Do you like being helpless?"

"Yes," I breathed. He barely pulled out, then slammed it back in, making me cry out.

"Do you want me to fuck both your holes at the same time?" He twisted the dildo, spinning it around, making my eyes roll back at the new sensation. His hand lashed out, slapping my face, and I gasped. I stared up at him, shocked. "Answer me." He slammed the dildo harder into me, and my hips lifted off the bed.

"Yes!" I screamed. "Do anything you want to me. I'm yours. Use me, abuse me, do your worst." He paused, then a slow smile spread across his face.

"Oh, little Raven. I'm not going to abuse you. Not tonight. But I will use you."

He kept the dildo shoved all the way inside my pussy as he slid off the bed and quickly undressed. His cock was massive, bigger than the dildo inside me, and my mouth went dry. There was no way I could take both of them.

He fisted his cock as he stared at me, his eyes wild. He was riding the edge of control. I'd seen it enough to know he was on the brink of losing it. Why did I want him to lose it so badly? Why did I want to see what it would look like for him to go crazy? For him to snap?

"You look so pretty," he muttered, his eyes traveling over my body. "I like when you look like this. All tied up. All mine." He crawled back onto the bed and lifted my legs, holding them over his forearms. "Ready?" He laughed as he grabbed the bottle of lube he'd discarded earlier.

He poured a generous amount on his cock, letting it flow over my body. Stroking his hand over his cock, then over my pussy down to my ass, he pressed a finger inside. A scream lodged in my throat at the sudden intrusion, but he didn't seem to notice or care. He rubbed his slick hand up my body, over my breasts, then gripped my neck.

Dropping my other leg, he gripped his cock and guided it to my ass. I couldn't believe this was happening. I was about to get fucked in the ass by a guy I met tonight, literally only hours ago. He was terrifying in all the best ways.

The thick head of his dick pressed against me, and I bit my lip hard enough to draw blood. Suddenly, he pushed inside me, his cock stretching me as I screamed.

"*Fuck.*"

His groan was long and deep, filling the room as his eyes rolled back. He tightened his hold on my neck and slowly began thrusting deeper.

I writhed against him and jerked on the belt, but it was no use. I wasn't going anywhere—not that I wanted to. He finally moved the rest of the way in, bottoming out, and I screamed again.

"Fuck, I love hearing you scream," he rasped. He gripped the base of the dildo and lifted his eyes to mine, a wicked smirk on his face. "Ready?" He asked again. I didn't answer, I couldn't, and his smirk grew wider.

Slowly, he pulled his cock out, then slammed back in before doing the same with the dildo. He quickly found a rhythm that we both liked, and soon, I felt myself clenching around him. His hold on my throat tightened until I couldn't breathe. Panic shot through me.

What if he didn't let go? What if he choked me until I passed out? What if he choked me until I died? *What if he killed me?* He fucked me harder and faster, using me for his pleasure. His grip tightened, and when I tried to take a breath this time, I couldn't.

Our eyes met, and I silently tried to tell him, but he just grunted and slammed into me harder. "I'm not letting go," he rasped between thrusts, "until you come." He moved faster. The dildo twisted up slightly and hit a spot inside me that made me see stars.

I couldn't breathe. I was running out of air. My vision was turning black, but my orgasm was building. My head began to throb, and my mouth fell open. He was serious. He wasn't going to let go.

"I'm going to cum in your ass after you pass out," he grunted. "You're a filthy fucking whore, so you'd like that, wouldn't you?" His fingers flexed on my neck, and I barely sucked in a breath. "My dirty little bird. My dirty fucking slut."

My body tightened, my legs clamping around his sides as I came harder than I ever had. He let go of my throat and I inhaled, my orgasm still shooting through my body. He yanked the dildo out and tossed it to the floor before grabbing my legs and flinging them over his shoulders, bending my body in half as he leaned over me.

I couldn't get enough air. My vision slowly began to return, the ringing in my ears barely subsiding as he slammed into me over and over again. His face dug into my neck, his tongue flicking over my pulse.

"Fuck," he growled. "Say my name." I tried to open my mouth to speak, but no words came out. His cock began to thicken, and his movements became frantic. "Say it." He lifted his head to look at me, his eyes searing through me.

"Mason," I breathed. He squeezed his eyes shut, an odd expression flitting over his face before he dropped his head back to my neck.

He slammed into me a few more times before he stilled, his body going rigid above me. He let out a long groan, and I felt him spill inside me. We breathed together for a few moments before he lifted up and kissed me gently, too gently for a man who'd just done what he did.

Without a word, he untied me from the headboard and massaged my wrists, then helped clean me with a warm washcloth from the bathroom. He was full of surprises. No one had ever done that for me. The biggest shock came when he hesitated by the bed, then curled his massive body around mine and pulled me back against his chest.

"You don't have to do this," I said, my eyes drooping.

"I know," he murmured against my hair. "Can I just hold you for a bit?" I nodded and nuzzled back against him. His arm was heavy over me, and I sighed as he pressed a kiss to the back of my head. His final words drifted to me on a wave of unconsciousness.

"What have you done to me, little bird?"

14

RAVEN

PRESENT

I was restless.

I had twenty-four hours until I needed to meet Grim *where it all began*, and I desperately needed a distraction. I couldn't go back there, could I? Anxiety twisted itself around my stomach and hadn't let go since I read his note. There was a part of me that wished I could just ignore him, not give him power over me, but that was impossible.

Grim always had a hold on me. I didn't know what it was about him that made me stupid, but when he was involved, my brain turned off. I was weak. I always had been. I'd always tried to tell myself that I was a strong and independent woman, but I knew if he told me to kneel for him, I'd drop to my knees without a second thought.

Kali, unsurprisingly, didn't want to go out. Not with a killer on the loose, plus my track record for finding sketchy guys and sketchier parties. Okay, maybe I should've been more careful with my life and cared about my safety more, but I didn't care. So what if I died? What was the worst that would happen? I wouldn't have to work at the store anymore, and I'd get to see Grim. It was a no-lose scenario.

I tousled my hair, letting my eyes roam over my body in the mirror, and smirked at myself. I felt good. Sexy. I was in my favorite little black slip dress, black strappy heels, and dark, smoky makeup. It was my go-to get-laid look.

A floorboard creaked behind me, and I shifted my head to look over my shoulder at my empty apartment.

"Grim?" I said, my voice tight. "I swear to God, if you're in here—" I scanned the dark room. Something brushed against me, a barely there breath against my cheek, and goosebumps rippled over my skin. "Fuck off." I glared at nothing, feeling ridiculous, and grabbed my coat and purse to head out.

The crisp, early-autumn air assaulted me, pricking my skin as I walked down the concrete steps. I scanned the dark street, taking in the shadowed alleys and empty sidewalks. My neighborhood was becoming more and more deserted after dark since the killer appeared.

I ignored the way my hair stood on end and the chill that snaked down my spine. There was no one out. There was no reason for me to feel creeped out, and I had a sneaking suspicion that I had an invisible shadow in the form of a Reaper at my back. If a killer was going to attack me, at least Grim was with me.

Maybe.

I hoped.

Still, I couldn't shake the ominous feeling of being watched, like someone was standing too close to me, and at any moment, they'd reach out and grab me. Was it Grim? Or was it something else entirely? My imagination. Just my imagination.

I shook my head, mentally berating myself for feeling scared over nothing. I was scaring myself because Kali wouldn't stop texting me news articles about murders.

That was it. I was fine.

Pulling my phone from my purse, I scrolled through my contacts and sent a *Where's the party?* text to twenty people, hoping one of them would respond.

"Raven?"

My spine stiffened, and I slowly turned around. I smiled tightly at Eddy, dipping my head slightly.

"Hey," I said, glancing around the empty street.

"I thought that was you." He laughed as his eyes trailed over my body. "Where are you headed tonight?" When his eyes met mine again, there was a spark in them I recognized, and it sent my body into full fight or flight mode. Instead of doing either, I froze.

"Just walking home," I lied, my voice shaky. "My boyfriend is meeting me there." He cocked his head to the side, his smile wolfish.

"Boyfriend?" he asked, his voice low. "Is this a new boyfriend?"

Shit. Why did I say boyfriend?

"We're on and off," I said, waving dismissively. "We're on right now."

"Sure." He laughed, the sound mocking. "Let me walk you home. I'm sure he wouldn't want you out here all alone, not when there's a killer out there." I swallowed heavily and took a small step back.

"It's okay," I said. "I'm close. You don't—"

"Let me walk with you." His voice was stern, and his smile fell for a moment before his mask slipped back into place. My hands broke out in a clammy, cold sweat, and I slid them down my coat.

"Sure," I croaked. I tried to smile, but my lips trembled. I glanced around the street again. A couple was walking their dog on the other sidewalk. Would they come if I called for help? "Thanks."

"No problem." He rested his hand on the small of my back and pushed me forward. "I'm glad we ran into each other again. You stopped responding to my texts."

My blood ran cold, but I tried to not let my fear show. He looked different than he had at the party and different than he had at the train. He looked and smelled sober. He wasn't clean-cut like he'd been last night. He was...*off*. He was high-strung, almost vibrating. Something was bubbling under the surface, and a small grin was playing on his lips, like he was trying to hold in a laugh.

His eyes were forward as we walked, not on me, but I knew he was aware of my every movement. I couldn't escape him; he surrounded me. I quickly glanced around again, trying to figure a way out of this situation. I could text Kali, but I didn't want to get her involved in case he was dangerous. The last thing I wanted was for her to get hurt.

"I never got a chance to apologize," he said.

"Apologize? For what?" I wasn't paying attention to him, not fully. I was focusing more on my surroundings instead of the threat at my side.

"For my behavior at the party," he sighed. "I was having a bad day. Well, a bad week." He laughed, his teeth flashing in the moonlight. "I was too drunk that night, and if I scared you or was too forward, I'm sorry."

"Oh," I said mindlessly. "It's fine." I scanned the street again. How could I ditch him?

I could go to a random apartment building and hope I could get in. But then he'd have someone else's address, and I couldn't live with myself if something happened because of me. I didn't know if Eddy was dangerous, but I didn't want to find out.

"I think we're going the wrong way." I laughed dumbly and stopped abruptly. "I always get so turned around." He paused and stared down at me, his eyebrows pushed tightly together.

"You don't know the way to your place?" he asked.

"New to the area," I lied. I'd been in the same apartment for the last five years. I knew exactly where I was. He nodded a few times, then smiled.

"After you," he said, sweeping his arm out in front of us. I laughed nervously, feeling my chest tighten painfully with anxiety. Shit, shit, shit. What the fuck was I supposed to do?

As I opened my mouth, my phone dinged, and I welcomed the distraction.

LET'S HANG OUT TONIGHT.

I SLUMPED IN RELIEF AT THE RANDOM TEXT FROM MASON. I hadn't heard from him since I'd texted him the other day, and he wasn't one of the people I'd texted earlier, so whatever god was looking out for me tonight was getting a thank you note in the morning. When I looked up at Eddy, he was staring down at me, his face tight with tension.

"Change of plans," I said, relieved. "My friend invited me out." His head tilted to the side.

"Can I come?" he asked, his eyes dropping to my body again.

"I don't think you can invite yourself," I scoffed but tried to hide it with a laugh.

"If it's a hangout like last week, then I doubt it'll be considered rude to invite myself," he countered. I glanced around the empty street again.

"I don't know—"

"Come on," he said, ignoring how uncomfortable I was. "Let's stop by my place so I can change, then we can head out."

"I don't want to be late," I said.

"Five minutes," he pushed. "I've been in these clothes all day, and I live right up the street." He jerked his chin forward. I looked at his clothes, feeling my stomach twist further. Black hoodie, black jeans, black sneakers. No one dressed like that. Well, I did, but he was a creep, and when a creepy guy wore all black, it usually meant he was up to no good, right?

"Okay," I ground out. "Five minutes."

"Thanks, babe." The pet name made me bristle. No one called me babe, potential fuckbuddy or not. Eddy was definitely not a potential fuckbuddy.

A few minutes later, I followed him up old, chipped concrete steps. As we entered the decrepit building, my unease grew further. This was a stupid fucking idea. What the fuck was I doing, following a stranger into his home?

I'd done it a million times without a second thought and had planned to do this exact thing with him last week, but this felt different. This felt wrong. If I told Mason where I was, would he care enough to save me? We didn't know each other like that. He was nothing more than some random hookup.

"I'll wait for you outside," I said, jerking my thumb over my shoulder. "I need to call my boyfriend." He stopped to look down at me.

"You'll be cold," he said tightly. "Come on. I don't bite. Unless you want me to." He laughed as he winked. I tried to smile back, but I couldn't. I felt too uncomfortable.

I needed to find my damn backbone. That look in his eyes was back, the same cold look my stepfather had right before he lost his shit. Maybe it was fear, or maybe it was that I recognized the brutal truth that I'd end up on the five o'clock news if I didn't follow him.

I might end up on it either way.

"Alright," I rasped, my voice barely audible. I felt myself begin to shrink back into that ten-year-old girl running from her abuser. My mind flashed to the giant cloaked figure who'd saved me.

Grim.

My Grim.

Where was he?

I didn't know. All I knew was that he wasn't here to save me. This time, I was on my own.

15

GRIM

THREE MONTHS AGO

"Where have you been?" Caden asked. He smirked, and it made me want to punch him in the fucking face. I ignored him as I walked into the kitchen. He leaned against the counter and folded his arms over his chest. "Seeing that girl again?" I grabbed a beer from the fridge, still ignoring him. "What was her name?" I clutched it tightly in my hand. He was fishing, I knew that, but it was still annoying as fuck.

"Cade," I growled in warning.

"No, that's my name," he said, and I turned toward him. "It started with an *R*, right? Rebecca? No. River? No..."

"Raven," I gritted out. He snapped his fingers and pointed at me.

"That's it! Raven." He smiled triumphantly. "How is little Miss *Raven* these days?"

"I wouldn't know." I popped the top off my beer and took a long swig. He snorted and rolled his eyes.

"Sure," he said as he pushed himself on top of the counter. He swung his feet, letting them kick the cabinets. "And I have two dicks."

"You do?" Brody asked as he strolled toward us. "Man, I got the short end of the stick."

86

"Hey, our big bro says he's not seeing Raven," Caden said. "You buy that story?" Brody snorted.

"Not at all," he said as he rummaged through the pantry. He paused and looked over his shoulder at us. "Should we expect her for Christmas this year?"

"We're Reapers. We don't celebrate Christmas," I said dryly. My hands shook. I wanted to hit something, someone. Preferably *two* someones.

"Is there some Reaper holiday I should know about instead?" he asked, turning to look at me.

"We don't—whatever." I threw my hands up in defeat. "Do whatever you want!" Rage walked in next, and I groaned. What was this? A family fucking reunion?

"What's going on?" he asked, looking between us.

"Mase says Reapers don't celebrate Christmas," Brody said.

"We've celebrated Christmas for years," Rage scoffed.

"We've given each other gifts on a random fucking day and called it Christmas," I countered. "It's different than celebrating." He shrugged.

"We drink alcohol and open gifts. Sounds like Christmas to me," Caden said, and Brody nodded in agreement. Rage's lips twitched, and I flipped him off. Fucker was supposed to be on *my* side.

"She can't come to the Reaper Realm anyway," I said matter-of-factly.

"Who?" Rage asked, looking toward Caden.

"Mason's new girlfriend."

"Raven?" Rage looked at me. Then the asshole smiled. Wide.

I grabbed the closest thing to me, which happened to be an apple, and threw it at his head. He ducked out of the way and laughed. We didn't hear Rage laugh often, so when we did, it was always a shock. Right then, though, I was too fucking far gone with annoyance and anger to care or be shocked. I chucked another apple at him, but he caught it and threw it back, hitting me in the chest.

"Alright, enough," Brody said, laughing. "The apples are innocent in all this." I glared at Rage, but he couldn't stop laughing.

"I wasn't seeing her," I said, and Caden snorted. "I wasn't!"

"Where were you then?" Rage asked, wiping his eyes.

"The Council wanted to see me." That sobered everyone up, and their smiles fell. "Fuckers." I took another sip of my beer, glaring at the guys.

"For what?" Brody asked warily, taking a step toward me. "They're not sending you back, are they?"

"Nah." I waved dismissively. "They were checking to see how I'm handling being back."

"And?" Rage prompted. "What else?" I swallowed thickly, then looked around the kitchen before sighing.

"Some of them want me back on the Council," I said quietly. "They said things are getting bad again and—"

"Fuck." Rage scrubbed his hand over his face. "This is what got you fucked last time!"

"No," I said slowly. "Reaping someone I wasn't supposed to reap is what got me fucked last time."

"No," Caden snapped. "You were close to changing things—*really* fucking close, Mase. That was just a convenient story for them to justify sending you away." I nodded. I knew that. They didn't like that I was making waves, changing the way Reapers lived their lives and did their jobs.

"Are you thinking about going back?" Brody asked. "You can't be seriously considering it." I let my silence speak for itself. Rage groaned and dropped his head back.

"This is going to bite you in the dick, man," Caden warned.

"Bite you in the ass," Brody said, correcting him, and Caden shrugged.

"Same difference."

"It'll be fine," I said.

I didn't know if I wanted to be back on the Council or not. It was a lot of responsibility, and the attention it put on Brody wasn't great. I put my brothers in danger and got myself sent to the In-Between, but the Reapers needed someone to speak for them. They needed someone to protect them from the people abusing their power and taking their rights away.

Was that someone me? I didn't think so.

Where we were once respected creatures, we were now laughing stocks. We couldn't breathe without having a higher-up tell us we were doing it wrong. We used to have the freedom to choose who was reaped and who wasn't.

In my early days as a Reaper, I was able to protect people like Raven —victims. Sometimes, they were too far gone, and I didn't have a choice, but that night, I could've saved her without any consequences. Now, we couldn't make that choice.

We had a quota to meet each month. We couldn't save mortals from themselves or protect them from the evil ones out to get them. Our rights were stripped from us, leaving us nothing more than messengers, errand boys. We had no purpose or meaning left.

I'd already traveled down this path once. I'd already put myself and my brothers in danger, and I couldn't do it again. Especially not now that I had Raven to consider, too. This pull I felt toward her was only growing stronger, and I didn't understand it.

I couldn't be the speaker for the Reapers again. If anyone was made for that life, it was Caden. He was charismatic, and people listened to him. He had a way of carrying a conversation without making you feel like an idiot for asking questions. He should be the one leading this campaign for Reaper rights, not me. I moved through the kitchen, suddenly feeling an overwhelming need to get out. I couldn't be home anymore. The room, my brothers' gazes, the responsibility and truth of what was happening in our world, was too much. I needed air. I needed to claw my lungs out of my chest and take a breath.

"You okay?" Brody grabbed my shoulder, but I pushed his hand away. My breathing was coming too fast, and the room was beginning to spin. "Mason." I tried to take a deep breath, but my lungs wouldn't fill.

I couldn't breathe.

My chest was getting squeezed too tight. I knew I wouldn't die—I couldn't—but the fear was still there. The panic.

Raven.

Was Raven panicking? Was something wrong with her? Was this just me, something that was going on in my head?

"Mason," Brody said again. He said something else, but the whooshing in my ears drowned him out. I glanced at my brothers a final time, then slipped into Raven's bedroom.

16

RAVEN

PRESENT

Eddy's place smelled pungent, to put it kindly. It was smaller than mine, dark, the overwhelming stench making my eyes water. I could smell it from the hall. I didn't want to believe it was his place emitting the smell, but when he opened the door, it hit me like a brick wall.

"Welcome," he said proudly as he swept his arm out, gesturing for me to enter. I gave him a weak smile as I shuffled past. "Make yourself at home."

"I'll wait here," I said and watched as he flipped the deadbolt. My stomach dropped. Our gazes met, but he turned his attention away and moved toward the kitchen.

"Don't be silly," he said as he opened the fridge. More of that pungent odor hit me, and I bit the inside of my cheek to keep from gagging. "Get comfy."

"We won't be here long," I said. "You just said you needed a few minutes to change." I shuffled closer to the door.

"I need a shower too."

"You said—"

"I know what I said." His eyes flashed with anger, then his casual

90

mask slid back into place, and he smiled at me. "Do you want a drink?" He turned his attention back to the fridge. "I have wine."

"I don't like wine." I looked around his apartment. It was bare, except for a mirror by the front door and an old sofa in the living room. There wasn't a TV, a coffee table, photos on the walls—nothing remotely homey. "Did you just move in?"

"Hmm? Oh, no. I've been here a while," he said. "I have beer, too."

"You don't have any furniture." I peeked at him, and my heart lurched. The fridge light illuminated the underside of his face, giving him a sinister look. He slowly grinned, and more of the devil began to appear.

"Why do you look so scared?" he laughed. "I told you I don't bite." I tried to laugh, but it wouldn't come out. My throat was too tight. He shut the fridge door then leaned against the counter. Crossing his arms, he tilted his head as he studied me.

"Why are you so nervous?" I hadn't realized I'd been wringing my hands together, and I forced myself to stop.

"I'm not," I lied. "I'm just ready to see my friends, that's all." He watched me, *inspected* me, like he was waiting for something else. When I gave him nothing, he sighed.

"I won't be long." He pushed off the counter, and as he made his way across the small kitchen, I pressed my back against the wall, trying to avoid contact. He seemed to enjoy it—my discomfort.

He purposefully turned and brushed his body firmly against mine as he leered down at me. I swallowed hard as he grinned, pressing harder against me, and I turned my head away from him.

"You know," he said, his voice lower now. "We could just stay here." He rested his hand against the wall, caging me in. "We could pick up where we left off the other night."

"I'm okay," I said and gently shoved his chest. He didn't budge. "I'd like to leave now."

"Come on," he laughed. "We both know you don't really have a boyfriend." I looked up at him, finding his yellowed-teeth gleaming in the dim light.

"Yes, I do."

"His name?" he challenged, lifting his brows. My mind raced as I searched for a name. Why couldn't I think of a name? I knew a million of them. Why couldn't I think of one now?

"Grim." His name slipped out before I could stop it.

"Grim? What kind of name is Grim?" He pushed his brows together, that stupid, mocking smirk on his face. "That's a terrible name to make up. You could've at least made it believable. Could've said Bob, for fucks sake."

"I don't have to prove anything to you," I snapped. His face shifted, the humor melting away. Raw anger took its place, the same kind my stepfather had, and I felt myself shrink into the scared little girl I'd been all those years ago.

"You stuck-up bitches are all the same," he sneered. "Always down to fuck when you're drunk, but when you sober up—"

"We come to our senses?" I finished for him. My eyes widened, and I folded my lips between my teeth. I hadn't meant to say that out loud.

"You think you're better than me?" He lowered his face to mine, his putrid breath hitting my face, burning my nose.

"Look, Eddy, this is just a misunderstanding," I said placatingly. I patted his arm, trying to calm him down, but he was too far gone. "Let's just go to this party and forget—"

"I don't want to go to that fucking party!" Spit landed on my face, and I squeezed my eyes shut. "I want to finish what we started!" He banged his hand on the wall, and I jolted.

If Kali could see me now, she'd be screaming, *I told you so! You need to run, bitch!*"

"I'm not interested," I said as calmly as I could. Squeezing my hands together, I glanced around his sparse apartment for anything to use as a weapon.

"I don't care," he scoffed. His hand tangled in my hair, and my hands latched onto his wrist. He dragged me further into his apartment, but I would've rather died than move another inch.

I lifted my knee, hitting him between his legs, and he let me go as he sputtered out a grunt of pain. His knees buckled, and he fell to the floor, groaning as his head rolled back. I didn't wait to see if he would be alright; I turned and fled back to the door.

I reached for the doorknob, twisting it, then let out a panicked cry when it wouldn't open. My fingers fumbled with the deadbolt as I turned it. I reached for the knob again, but his hand wrapped around the collar of my coat, and he jerked me back.

I stomped down, digging my heel into the top of his foot, then lurched forward. I didn't hesitate as I brought my elbow back and smashed the mirror beside the door. It shattered, the thin, long pieces of glass falling to the floor. Blindly, I reached down, ignoring the sting of pain as the sharp edge sliced into my palm.

Whirling around, I held the glass shard in front of me. The tip gleamed in the yellow light as he crouched slightly. We stared at each other, panting as we waited for the other to pounce first.

As he shifted his feet, ready to attack, Death himself appeared beside me, fury rippling off him, his sights set on Eddy.

17
GRIM
THREE MONTHS AGO

She was fine. She wasn't panicking—she wasn't even awake. Staring at her curled up in her bed, the covers tucked tightly under her chin, some of that tightness in my chest began to loosen, and I took a deep breath.

Moving toward her, I sank onto the end of her bed. My glamour was still in place, but since I felt this pull toward her and hoped she felt it too, I thought she'd sense my presence and wake up. I thought she'd feel me , even if she couldn't see or physically feel me. Maybe I just wanted her to need me as much as I seemed to need her.

I rested my elbows on my knees and dug the heels of my palms into my eyes.

I needed to breathe. I needed to calm down. Things happening in the Reaper Realm weren't going to change overnight, and I couldn't expect them to. Still, the burden was weighing heavy on me.

Raven shifted, and I glanced at her, finding her on her stomach, her arms folded above her head. Gently, I tugged the blanket down, revealing her bare skin. A damp towel and her robe laid on the bed beside her, so I assumed she'd gotten out of the shower and slid right into bed, not bothering to get dressed.

My dick hardened at the sight, my mild panic attack subsiding. I pulled the blanket down further and watched more of her tattoo bare itself to me. I stood, then pulled the blanket off, letting it fall to the floor. Now, she was naked and asleep and totally mine to do with as I pleased.

Keeping my glamour on, I ran my hand down the slope of her back, lightly trailing my fingertips along her spine. Goosebumps rippled across her skin, barely visible in the moonlight shining in through the window. She turned her head and I paused, waiting to see if she would wake up. When she didn't, I gently moved her long hair to one side and stared down at her peaceful, sleeping face.

Her lips parted slightly, her nose barely twitching with her breaths. I ran my knuckle across her cheek, then down her neck, and down her back again. This time, when I got to her ass, I gently groped it, my eyes locked on her face to gauge her reaction. She didn't stir, so I squeezed harder. Still, nothing.

I nudged her legs apart, just enough for my fingers to slide against her pussy. Using my middle finger, I began to slowly circle her clit, then stroke back and forth. Her hips shifted up, then rolled against my finger, like even in her sleep, she was begging for my cock.

With my other hand, I undid my jeans and palmed my dick, pumping myself in time with the strokes on her clit. I moved my finger to her entrance and dipped in slightly, then moved back to her clit, using her growing wetness to help my finger drive up her pleasure.

She sighed and shifted again, spreading her legs slightly. I squeezed my dick harder, trying not to come too soon as I stroked her faster. I wanted her to come, but I didn't want to wake her up yet. I wanted her to wake up with my cock already buried in her tight cunt.

I spread her legs further and climbed between them, rubbing the head of my cock against her pussy, watching her lips wrap around me, eager to suck me in. I spread her wetness around and then slowly began to push inside. I flicked my eyes between where my cock was entering her and her face. Her brows were scrunched, her mouth more open, but she was still asleep.

She was probably having a wet dream, not realizing all the sensations she felt were real. She wouldn't be able to feel me until I melted my glamour, so I waited until I was fully seated inside her, pressing against every inch of her little pussy, before melting it away.

Slowly, I began to pull out. She moaned, and I knew she felt me now: it wasn't a dream anymore. I gripped her wrists above her head, pinning them to the pillow, and slid almost all the way out, leaving only my head before I slammed back inside.

Her eyes snapped open, and she screamed. She thrashed in my hold as I fucked her into the bed. My hand tightened around her wrists as my other wrapped around the back of her neck to keep her head pinned down.

"What the fuck!" Her voice was hoarse and full of panic, but her words ended on a moan. I fucked her harder, her pussy fluttering around my dick. I laid on top of her, resting my chest against her back, and she let out a sob.

"You like waking up with my cock inside you, little Raven?" I breathed heavy in her ear, then ran my tongue along her cheek, licking up her tears. "You like being a little cock-sleeve that I only use when I need to come?"

"Mason?" she cried. She tried to turn her head to look back at me, but I pushed harder on her neck, forcing her to stay still. "What the fuck! Get off me!"

"Why would I do that?" I slowed my pace as I pushed back up and dragged my cock out. She groaned, her eyes rolling back in her head, and I smirked. Little slut was enjoying herself, even if she wanted to pretend she wasn't.

"You can't do this," she breathed. "You can't break into my apartment and—"

"And what?" I slowly pushed back in. "Fuck you?" Her legs spread more and she pushed her ass up, letting me hit a deeper angle. She screamed as I bottomed out inside her again, filling her completely. "You love this, you little slut."

"No," she screamed. "Get off me."

"After I come inside you," I said.

"Don't—" She tried to turn again, but I didn't let her. "I'm not on the pill."

"I can't get you pregnant." I wasn't going to explain *how*, but she just needed to know I couldn't. I stopped moving, my cock half-buried inside her, and let her process it.

"You had a vasectomy?"

"I'm totally infertile." I slowly pumped my hips, barely moving. I must've been rubbing against a spot she liked, because she pushed her hips up further, arching her back and letting me hit deeper.

"Right there," she whimpered. "Fuck, please don't stop." I barely moved my cock, just an inch or two in and back out. In and out. Over and over. "Fuck, fuck!" It was driving me wild. I let go of her neck and wrists and gripped her soft hips to fuck her how she wanted. "Please, Mason!" It was torture to fuck her like this. I wanted to fuck her into the bed, slam into her so hard that she bruised and couldn't walk. I wanted her to feel pain for days after tonight. I wanted to leave my mark on her—*in* her.

But this is what she needed, and I found myself wanting to give her any and everything. Even if I had to give something up in return.

She reached above her head to wrap her hands around the metal bars of her headboard, her knuckles turning white from how tightly she squeezed. My fingers dug into her skin as her pussy clenched around me. She pressed her face into the pillow and screamed her voice raw as she came. I kept rubbing that spot, fucking her shallow and fast, just how she liked.

When her body relaxed, I couldn't take it anymore and lifted her hips higher, dragging her to her knees, then slammed back into her, pulling a scream for her again. I pushed and pulled her body, using her for my own pleasure. She tightened around me again, and her body began to shake.

"You're coming again?" I fucked her harder, our bodies slapping together with each hard thrust. The headboard slammed into the wall, the metal coils of her mattress squeaking and groaning beneath us. I slid my hand up her curved back and wove my fingers into her hair, then yanked her head roughly back, straining her neck as I rode her.

"Yes!" Her eyes were closed, her mouth open. A look of pure ecstasy covered her face, one I'd never seen before, and fuck if it didn't turn me on even more. "I've dreamed about your dick for weeks."

"Yeah?" I stared down at my cock sliding in and out of her cunt, at her stretched pussy lips, and the way they molded perfectly to my size. "You make yourself come to the thought?"

"Yes," she groaned. "Every night."

"That's my girl." Her pussy tightened again, and I gripped her hair harder. "This pussy is so fucking good."

"It's yours," she rasped. "All yours, whenever you want it."

"I know," I growled as I slapped her ass. "I already know I own you." She moaned, then dropped one hand and slid it down her body between her legs. "That's it, baby. Play with your pussy for me. Make yourself come again."

"Choke me." She pushed back against me with each thrust, taking more and more of my dick as she went. I moved my hand from her hip to her throat and lifted her, bringing her back to my chest, and tightened my grip, fucking into her faster as I squeezed her throat. She rubbed her pussy faster, and when she opened her eyes, they were bloodshot. She tried to scream, but I was squeezing too tightly for her to take a breath.

I was slightly worried she'd pass out, but I didn't let go. She needed this, for whatever reason, and I did, too. Choking her, the power of having her life and death in my hands, made my cock thicken and my orgasm build.

"Come for me," I growled in her ear. "Come for your master." Her pussy tightened around me and her mouth opened in a silent scream as her eyes rolled back. I fucked her through her orgasm, my hand still tight around her throat.

Finally, she tapped my wrist, and I let go. She inhaled deeply, and I let her fall back onto her stomach. I stroked my cock with her pussy a few more times, then let her swallow me whole as I came. I moved as deep as I could get, wanting her to feel every drop that poured into her. Her pussy clenched, milking my dick as I groaned. Finally, I stopped, staying buried inside her.

"I hope you were serious," she breathed, sounding exhausted.

"About what?"

"About being infertile." She barely glanced at me over her shoulder, but I turned my head away.

"I was," I said.

She was silent for a few moments, then I pulled my softening cock from her probably-sensitive cunt, tucked it away, and pulled her blanket back over her. I pretended to leave, and as Mason, I did. She heard me open and close the door, but I slipped my glamour back on to stay in her apartment. I watched her get up and lock the door. I watched her stare at herself in the mirror and clean my cum from between her legs.

I watched her lay back down and stare at the ceiling. I watched her smile softly to herself. And I watched her fall back asleep.

18
GRIM
TWO MONTHS AGO

It was the fourth murdered soul this month. She was a young woman, outrageously beautiful, with dark hair, long legs, and hazel eyes. The murder scene was fucking brutal. The fucker who'd done it killed her as he came, slitting her throat when he was still inside her, relishing in the feeling of taking her life while pumping what would be new life into her.

I wanted to fucking reap *him*. I wanted to kill *him*. I wanted to not only send him to the In-Between, but annihilate his fucking soul and rid him from every plane of existence.

But I couldn't do that, not with the Council breathing down my fucking neck.

So, I helped the tortured soul pass on and hoped she'd find a new vessel, one that would hopefully live a better fate than her last. I couldn't fucking stand it anymore. I was losing my mind doing this shit.

I couldn't see the point. Why couldn't I choose who to take? I could have fucking *saved* her. I knew she was the one I was there to reap, but instead, I had to stand and watch as he killed her when I could've reaped him before he'd had the chance.

After a shitty fucking day, all I'd wanted to do was go home and not deal with anyone. But as soon as I stepped through the door, I knew something was wrong. Brody was gone. He'd been taken. *Again.*

"They needed him for questioning," Caden said as he paced in the living room. "They said they had witnesses."

"Witnesses? What did he do?" I asked.

"Nothing." He stopped and stared at me. "He's being accused of being an Exterminator." The silence stretched between us, unsaid words filling the air with tension. I let out a long breath.

"He didn't kill another Reaper? You're sure?" I asked as I rubbed my forehead.

"Positive," Caden said, nodding. "I'm with him every fucking day. I would've seen it happen." I nodded a few times, having expected that answer. "Mase, they're going to fucking break him."

"I'll be back," I grumbled.

"You're going?" Caden took a step toward me. "I'll go—"

"I'll be back." I leveled him with a hard look. "You and Rage stay here." Caden hesitated, wringing his hands, but he took a breath and nodded. I had no fucking clue where Rage was, but Caden would fill him in.

Quickly, I slipped through the realm to the Council building. I stomped up the marble steps, Reapers averting their eyes when they saw it was me and not one of my brothers. I ignored them as I stormed inside, heading straight for the High Reaper's chamber. He was going to answer for this. I didn't bother knocking; I just shoved the door open.

"Sir!" his assistant called behind me. I ignored her as I headed toward his office. "Sir, you can't—" I pushed High Reaper Thomas' door open and slammed it shut behind me. He sat behind his desk, looking smug as fucking ever.

His black hair was neatly combed to the side, gray peppered across his temples. He leaned back in his chair, his black cloak falling open slightly, revealing his stupid fucking suit.

"Where's my brother? I'm taking him home," I said. I stood by the door, keeping my booted foot against it so the assistant couldn't open it.

"He's being detained," Thomas drawled. He picked invisible lint from his cloak, then lifted his eyes to mine. "You know better than anyone how long that can take."

"You have no right to keep him here," I ground out. My hands clenched into fists. "He's done nothing—"

"Ah," Thomas lifted his hand, a small grin on his face, "but he has."

"What's he being accused of?" I folded my arms over my chest. "He's done nothing."

"He's been accused of killing another Reaper," he said. "He was sent to Reap a soul, and instead, he let her live. A Reaper was sent to do his job for him, *again*, and your brother killed him."

"Bullshit," I scoffed. "I'm taking him home. Which block is he in? You have no reason to hold him here."

"A lot has changed since you've been gone," he drawled. "I don't need a reason to do anything. I can do whatever I want, whenever I want." I clenched my jaw so tight my teeth nearly cracked. Thomas smiled at me as he stood. "He's in block A. Take him home, but I'll be in touch with him soon. The things we've learned about him have been...interesting."

"No, you won't," I growled. "You're not coming near my brothers."

That patronizing smile remained on his face. "We'll see."

I glared at him a moment longer, then yanked the door open and shoved his assistant out of the way as I stormed from the office. This was fucking bullshit. He couldn't do this. That bullshit story? He couldn't expect me to believe that, could he?

These halls were once ones I walked daily. I'd wanted to be a High Reaper at one time, wanting to change the Realm for the better. Now, I knew it was all fucking pointless. It was all a game to them, and I didn't play it, *wouldn't* play it. All I fucking wanted was to protect my brothers, fuck Raven, figure out what the fuck was connecting us, and move on with my life. I didn't want to be in this building any more than I had to be.

"Mason," a voice called from behind me. I didn't turn or acknowledge him as I moved swiftly down the sterile marble hall.

The cell blocks were in the back of the building, not clean or marble or nearly as presentable as the building in the front. The cells were dark and damp. It was where I'd been held for months before being sent to the In-Between. I'm stronger than Brody, and it nearly fucking killed me. He wouldn't survive longer than the few hours he'd already been there.

"Hey, Mason, wait." I let out a breath as I stopped and whirled around.

"What?" I snapped. Wesley's eyes widened, then he cleared his throat.

"What are you doing here?" he asked, his accent thicker than I remembered, and peered over my shoulder.

"Came to get Brody," I grunted as I folded my arms over my chest. His eyebrows lifted. "He didn't do shit." He raised his hands and laughed nervously.

"Didn't think he did," he said. "But why is he here?" He looked over my shoulder again, down the hall to the cells.

"Thomas accused him of Exterminating another Reaper," I said quietly. I looked around the empty hall, making sure we were alone. "It's bullshit."

"Who'd he kill?" I opened my mouth, and he lifted his hand. "Who was he *accused* of killing?" I rubbed my forehead. Why hadn't I thought to ask that?

"I don't know," I breathed. "This isn't the first time he's been picked up, but it's the first time he's been accused of anything. All the other times, they just suspected something was different about him, but this time...." I shook my head. "He didn't do anything, Wes."

"I'll walk with you," he said, jerking his chin forward. I narrowed my eyes slightly. Wesley wasn't a bad guy. He tried to do the right thing, but the last time I'd seen him was fifteen years ago, and, as Thomas pointed out, a lot had changed.

I turned without a word toward the cells again. Wes strolled beside me, his hands shoved into his front pockets. We were silent for a few moments, the air thick with tension. He cleared his throat, and I glanced at him.

"So, I heard you've been going to the Mortal Realm a lot," he said quietly. He kept his eyes down, but I knew he knew everything.

"Where did you hear that?" I asked. He shrugged, not giving anything away. "I don't think I go more than anyone else."

"No?" He grinned. "You think everyone goes to some mortal's bedroom every night?" I froze, the blood in my body turning to ice.

"How do you know about that?" I hissed as I looked around. "About her?"

"Relax," he muttered. "Your secret is safe with me." I stared at him, waiting for him to elaborate. "How about you come by my place tonight? I have some friends coming over. I'd like you to meet them."

"Wes," I sighed.

"We have a committee," he murmured. We looked around again, and he took a step closer. "It's called Souls for Reapers. We've learned some interesting things I think you'd like to know."

"You can't just start a committee to take souls," I said, and he shook his head.

"It's not to *take* them," he whispered. "It's to get ours back." I blinked at him, then laughed. His face stayed blank, and I shook my head.

"You almost fucking had me," I said, pointing at him. "Almost. But that's fucking ridiculous. We don't have souls—"

"We do, though," he snapped. "Our souls are still inside us, but the Council has repressed them. They've made it impossible for us to feel them. But they're there." He rubbed the center of his chest and I flicked my eyes between his.

"That's impossible, Wes," I muttered. He shook his head as I spoke.

"The girl, she's the one you saved, right?" He took another step toward me, his voice dropping further. I looked around again, then nodded. "And you feel *things* for her, yeah? Things you can't explain?"

"It's because I saved her and—"

"Why did you save her?" he asked, his voice excited. "Why?" I swallowed hard and rubbed my hands down the front of my jeans.

"I don't know," I admitted. "I just felt called to." He nodded, a small smile on his face.

"Because her soul *called* to yours," he said.

"No." I shook my head. "It was because she was a scared child, and I felt bad—"

"You've reaped millions of children before. Why was she different? What was it about her specifically that made you want to save her?" He was challenging me, and I didn't like it. I didn't have an answer for him, and, honestly, I didn't want to investigate too closely.

"I was having an off night—"

"It was because she's your soulmate."

"Wesley." I squeezed my eyes shut. "That's fucking ridiculous." I took a few steps away from him. "I might feel something toward her, but that's only because I saved her and—"

"You saved her because your souls are connected," he said, nodding.

"I'm not talking about this." I took a few more steps away. "I'm not entertaining this bullshit theory. I have enough shit to worry about with Brody. I don't need this."

"Just think about it," he said. "Bring her. We have ways of testing it—"

"I'm not bringing her here," I growled. "She'll never step foot in this fucking realm."

"We can go to her," he offered, a sly grin on his face.

"No." I turned my back. "Drop it. I don't want to hear about this again."

19

RAVEN

PRESENT

We froze.

Our eyes were locked on Grim. His fury rippled off of him in waves as he glared at Eddy. I waited for him to attack, for him to do something, *anything*, but he just stood there, staring.

"Who the fuck are you?" Eddy snarled. He didn't sound nearly as scared as he should've.

"Grim," I said, and Eddy's eyes flicked to me. I couldn't help the cocky grin that spread across my face. It wasn't a name I'd made up, and he saw that now. He knew Grim was a real...*thing*. "This is Grim."

Eddy laughed. It was mocking and unhinged as he looked between us. Grim was massive and intimidating, terrifying, and the way he was watching Eddy should've made him wither, but it didn't.

I shuffled closer to Grim, and still, he didn't move to attack Eddy. He didn't do anything. He just stood totally still and let me move to him. I wasn't sure he was breathing. His hands were balled into tight, shaky fists at his sides, but otherwise, he wasn't moving.

Eddy stepped toward me, a smirk on his face when Grim didn't react. The shard of glass shook in my hand, slicing my palm open. Blood dripped from the tip onto the dirty floor, but I didn't take my eyes off

106

Eddy. With each step, I could see his confidence grow. What the fuck was Grim doing? *Not* doing? Why didn't he kill him?

"Grim," I whimpered. His shoulders bunched, but my voice seemed to wake him up. He wrapped his arm around my waist, and I tipped my head back to look up at him. He was still staring at Eddy, watching him like prey.

Then the world began to fade.

Slowly, the apartment began to fall away, then my body lit on fire as my limbs and skin and bones shredded. I screamed, the pain agonizing as blackness enveloped me completely. Wind whirled around me, whipping my face and stealing the breath from my lungs. I was stretched too far, too thin, my body contorting into painful positions.

Then red light glowed around me as I fell to my hands and knees, carpet cushioning my fall. My hair hung around my face as I dry-heaved. I was terrified to look at myself, positive all that would be left would be ribbons of flesh, but I opened my eyes and forced myself to look.

I was fine. Untouched.

I fell to my side as I stared down at the rest of my body. Even hidden under my coat, it was whole. I wasn't bloody or hurt. I wasn't shredded. With each passing second, the pain was subsiding, and I was beginning to forget how badly it hurt.

Suddenly, his boots came into view. I wasn't prepared for his deep, rumbling voice as he demanded, "Let me see your hand." I slowly rolled onto my back as he towered above me, the red glow making him look devilish. "Raven, let me see your hand." He held his hand out impatiently.

"I'm fine," I rasped. My throat felt raw. He let out a hard breath, then crouched beside me and roughly grabbed my hand. I was too weak to fight him, so I didn't even try. Wet blood stained my palm as he inspected it closely, tilting it in the low light. I lifted my head to watch, trying to see his eyes past the mask, but he was as mysterious and hidden as ever.

"I told you to stay away from him," he muttered.

"You never said his name," I said. "How was I supposed to know who you were talking about?" I laid my head back down, staring at the ceiling. We weren't at my apartment. "Where are we?"

"My place." I looked at him again, but he wouldn't look back. "I'll get something to clean your hand." He dropped my hand unceremoniously and pushed to his feet. Our eyes locked for a moment, but he shook his head slightly and left the room.

I took the chance to look around again. Knowing it was his place, I felt...*strange*; not safe like I thought I would, but not unsafe either. Something was off, like at any moment, something would jump out at me. A shiver snaked down my spine, and my chest tightened.

Did he bring me here to kill me? I quickly sat up. Where did he even live? How was I supposed to get home? I got to my feet, swaying slightly, and tried to steady my breathing. Had I just gone from one dangerous man to another?

This was Grim. He wouldn't hurt me, right? He'd been stalking me for the last four months, and I didn't know why. He pretended he didn't know who I was on my birthday, but he obviously did. I rubbed the center of my chest, trying to loosen the building panic.

The door banged opened and I let out a startled cry, whirling around to find Grim in the doorway, his chest heaving. "What is it?" he demanded as he looked around the room again. "What's wrong? Did something scare you?"

I let out a small, manic laugh, and he paused, slowly turning his head toward me.

I wanted to see his face behind the mask. Did he even have a face? All these years, I assumed he looked human, but he was a Reaper. What if he was faceless, and he wore a mask to not scare humans further?

"You did," I said, throwing my hand at him. I rubbed my chest again. The panic was subsiding, and in its place came a pain like I'd never felt, like my heart was aching but deeper. My *soul*. My soul was aching. "You scared me." The words tumbled from my mouth, but I didn't know if I fully believed them.

"I scared you," he repeated slowly, his voice muffled.

The ache bloomed more, and my throat threatened to close. I felt sad, like I wanted to cry and scream and punch something all at once. It didn't make any fucking sense. Why was I feeling like this? It was like someone was hijacking my emotions, forcing me to feel something I didn't want to.

"Why am I here?" I asked. I pressed my hand harder to my chest, wanting to push it through my sternum to grab my heart. I wanted to squeeze it until it stopped hurting. "Why didn't you take me home?"

"You're safer here," he said, then quietly added, "With me."

"Right," I breathed. I looked around his room again, that feeling in my chest growing. Loneliness and regret, that's what it felt like. I didn't understand why. I glanced at him, finding his head bowed and hands in tight fists at his sides.

"Just—get some rest." He took a step back and gripped the door-knob. "There's clothes in the closet; take whatever you want. Don't leave this room."

Without another word, he left me alone. I tried to ignore the swirl of emotions inside me, warring with each other. There was nothing in this room that told me anything about Grim, not that I could see right away. So, I quickly yanked a shirt from his closet to wear before laying on his ridiculously large bed.

I stared at the ceiling and strained to hear the muffled, far away male voices from somewhere outside the room. I wanted to find out what was going on, who those voices belonged to, but part of me was terrified at what I would find.

So, I stayed put. Not because I wanted to obey Grim, but because I'd already gone through too much that night. I wanted to sleep for a while and pretend that everything was normal, if just for a little bit.

20

GRIM

ONE MONTH AGO

"You've got to be fucking kidding me," I mumbled. Wes strolled toward me, a smile on his face.

"Hey, Mase," he said, jerking his chin in my direction. His hair was longer, brushing his shoulders, and his beard was shaggier than it had been a month ago. I took a deep breath as I stepped my feet apart.

"What?" I barked, not wanting to deal with any small talk. I wanted to get this over with as soon as fucking possible.

"You get shit figured out with Brody?" he asked. I looked around the Council building, nodding at a passing Reaper, then glared back at Wes.

"Yep," I said with a nod. I wasn't going to tell him Brody was gone. I didn't know where the fuck he was, and it was stressing me the fuck out. The morning after he got home, we woke up to find him gone. Just fucking gone.

At first, we thought he'd been picked up again. We quickly figured out that he hadn't, so we searched the Mortal Realm, but we couldn't find him. Caden checked their usual haunts, but he wasn't there. We were worried fucking sick, but I had to admit it was probably the best

110

thing for him. The Council couldn't get him if he wasn't in the realm. If they couldn't get him, he would be safe.

Wesley stared at me for a moment, then cleared his throat. "Good," he said. I waited for him to continue, keeping my face blank. "Look, I know you said you didn't want to talk about it—"

"I meant it." I walked past him. I knew exactly what he was talking about, and I didn't want to hear it. It was bullshit, but the more I thought about it, the more it made sense. I didn't want to admit it. I didn't want to admit that he could be right—that we could have souls.

"Wait." He grabbed my arm, and I paused. Glaring at him over my shoulder, I lifted my brows impatiently. "Just come to my place tonight. Let me explain everything."

"How did you even know about her? How did you know I was going to the Mortal Realm?" I spat as I turned back toward him. I'd been careful. Of course, everyone knew why I'd been sent away, but no one knew who I'd saved. They didn't know about Raven. I'd been careful when I went to the Mortal Realm. I left from my place. I never left from public, so there was no way I could've been followed. He scrubbed his hand over his mouth, then shrugged.

"We've been keeping an eye on you," he said, and my head reared back.

"What the fuck?" I growled as I stepped toward him. He moved back and lifted his hands up placatingly.

"Not like that," he said quickly. "After everything happened, I wanted to look into it more, and that's when I figured out that we still have souls." He whispered the last few words and looked around. Reapers walked past us, seemingly unbothered by our presence.

"That's fucking crazy," I hissed.

"Come to my place—"

"No," I snapped, shaking my head. "I meant it when I said I wasn't interested, Wes."

"Bring your girl," he added, hoping that would change my mind.

"No," I said again. "Drop it. I don't want anything to do with this bullshit. Leave me alone." He stared at me for a moment, then took another step back and nodded a few times.

"Fine," he said quietly. "Alright. My door is always open." I jerked my chin at him and spun on my heel. I was done listening to his crazy talk.

WHAT THE FUCK WAS I DOING?

I told Wes I didn't want anything to do with his stupid fucking committee, so why was I here, pacing in front of his door? I wrung my hands together, my palms slick.

I couldn't stop thinking about it. All afternoon—truthfully, all fucking month—I couldn't stop thinking about what he'd said. We had souls. Reapers had souls. It made fucking sense; I didn't want to admit it, but it did.

The way Brody felt things on a deeper level, the connection we still felt toward mortals, the connection I felt toward Raven, the ache we felt when we lost another Reaper or when we had to help a soul pass...

It all made sense.

I didn't want it to. I didn't want to admit that Wes, or whoever else he had in there with him, could be right. If he was right, then everything we'd ever known about ourselves would be a lie. That would mean asking questions I wasn't sure we were ready to answer.

With a deep breath, I turned toward the door. It was a massive black wooden door with a brass Reaper knocker. It was ominous, but maybe it was just in my head, knowing that whatever lay on the other side held the answers I didn't want.

Before I could knock, it swung open, and Wes' smug face greeted me. "Knew you'd come." He stepped aside, and I stared into his home. I'd been there before, but this time, it felt different. We weren't shooting the shit; this was serious. I glanced at him as I rubbed my hands down the front of my jeans and stepped inside.

The click of the door behind me had me steeling my spine. The hall was dark, black-painted walls closing in around me. Gold light fixtures hung low from the ceiling, emitting a dim yellow glow. Wes pushed past me and I followed, our footsteps muffled on the long Persian rug.

"The guys are already here," he threw over his shoulder. I tensed as I wrung my hands again.

"Who?" I asked, my voice low. He grinned as he walked into the sunken living room. I looked around, surprised as fuck to find three of the most respected High Reapers on the Council sitting in Wesley's living room.

Wolfe, Malik, and Damen quieted as I entered. They looked between Wes and me, their shoulders tense. "What's he doing here?" Wolfe asked, his raspy voice darker than I remembered.

"Mason's joining us," Wesley casually said as he strolled toward the bar cart at the back of the room.

"He's joining us?" Damen repeated incredulously, his eyes tracking Wes as he grabbed a bottle of something amber. Malik and Wolfe silently assessed me, waiting to see what I had to say.

"He's the reason we started this group, wasn't he?" Wes asked, his back to us. "I thought it fitting that he joined us." Glasses clinked as he prepared a drink. I cleared my throat uncomfortably: he could've given me more of a heads up. I didn't know I was the sole fucking reason their little group had formed. *Fucking hell.*

"Wes invited me," I said dumbly, squeezing my hands even tighter.

"Did he?" Wolfe turned his attention to Wes, but his back was still to us.

"You still drink scotch, don't you, Mase?" Wes asked, ignoring everyone's growing tension.

"Yeah," I said gruffly. I scanned the room, then moved to the chair furthest from the group. Their eyes were on me, but I tried to ignore them as I sank onto the edge of the chair, resting my forearms on my knees as I stared out the window. "Your, um...your garden looks nice." Wes snorted.

"Thanks." He moved toward me, holding out a glass. I took it and finally risked a glance at the other guys. They were watching me carefully.

"Tell us about the girl," Wes said as he sat on the couch. He folded one long leg over the other, his black, shoulder-length hair swaying as he took a sip of his drink.

"Girl?" I repeated.

"The one you saved," Malik gritted out. I turned my eyes to him, folding my lips between my teeth as I nodded. I told them the story of the night I saved Raven. I told them about her stepfather chasing her, how I knew I was supposed to reap her but chose to take him instead, how since that night—since the moment I saw her—I'd felt a connection to her that was unexplainable.

"I've been seeing her the last few months," I admitted quietly. This could get me fucked, but I was choosing to trust Wes and, in turn, these men. They stared at me with less suspicion and more curiosity.

"Seeing her?" Wesley leaned forward, his dark blue eyes narrowed. "What do you mean?" I let out a hard breath and threw back the rest of my drink before setting the glass on the floor.

"At first, I would spend an hour or two in her apartment. I had my glamour on so she couldn't see me, but I think she felt me. I don't know how to explain it. One night, she tried to jump off a fucking building and—fuck, I don't know. Something snapped." I ran my fingers through my hair as I pushed to my feet. "I hated the thought of her dying, but I couldn't ignore the part of me that wanted to reap her soul and turn her. I wanted her to become one of us. How sick is that? To wish for her to become a fucking monster for my own selfishness?"

"It's not selfish to want to be with your soulmate forever," Wesley said reasonably. I leveled him with a look before pacing in front of the chair.

"How do I even know she's my fucking soulmate? How do I know this is even real? How can I even be sure I have a soul?" I asked, my mind racing.

"I had one," Wes said, and I paused. Slowly, I turned to stare at him.

"What?" I breathed. "A soul?"

"A soulmate," he explained. The guys shifted uncomfortably as they shared a look. I sank back to the chair and stared at Wes, waiting for him to continue. He let out a long sigh. "Around the time you left, I met a mortal. I'd been in the Mortal Realm one night, and we started talking, and, I don't know, we just hit it off. I thought I was just falling in love with her, but that was still a shock to me. I didn't even know we could love." He looked at the guys, but they weren't looking at him, clearly avoiding eye contact.

"Anyway," he continued. "It was around the time I started figuring out that we might have souls. I stumbled upon this old book—" He stood and moved to the bookshelf lining the wall behind the couch. "It explained everything. I took it to Malik, and at first—"

"At first, I thought he was fucking crazy," Malik finished. "I thought it was bullshit. Reapers having souls? A conspiracy that we've been kept in the dark? Bullshit, right? We would've known. We would've felt them. But the more I looked into it, the more I realized Wes was onto something."

"They came to me," Damen said, "and asked if I could find any records of Reapers with souls. I scoffed at the idea, as we all did, but looked into it anyways. What I found was...interesting." I stared at Damen, my chest tight with excitement, with fear. I felt so many different emotions, I felt sick. "I found the records for every single Reaper who'd ever been turned, and nowhere did it say anything about them losing their souls." I scrunched my brows together.

"That doesn't mean—"

"That doesn't mean shit, I know," he said, holding his hand up. "So I looked into it further. I went as far back as I could until I finally found the first Reaper on record." I sat back in the chair, my breath leaving me in a hard whoosh. "They still had their soul."

"Did it say that?" I asked, and he nodded. Wes handed me a little book already open to a page. I set it in my lap and peered down at the yellow, fragile pages.

Reapers are living, breathing creatures cursed with helping souls pass from one realm to another. We're cursed with choosing which mortals live and die, which souls will be Exterminated completely. We're in charge of keeping the balance, ensuring there aren't too many souls on any plane at any given time. There can't be too many in the Mortal Realm, or it risks being overrun with madmen, but if there are too few, it won't survive. The Soul Realm must thrive to create more souls and find more vessels in the Mortal Realm, and the In-Between must stay open for the lost souls who can't find a home in any other. Reapers have both the responsibility and curse of being in charge.

A Reaper, once fully changed, will have their soul repressed. Otherwise, it will be impossible for them to do what must be done. They will feel everything, and the choices they must make—the choice to Exterminate a soul, change one into a Reaper, or kill a mortal and rip their soul from their vessel—would be an impossible decision.

A Reaper mustn't feel sympathy for mortals or their fellow Reapers.

A Reaper mustn't let emotions get in the way of their duties.

A Reaper mustn't forget what needs to be done.

I BLINKED A FEW TIMES, THEN LOOKED UP AT WESLEY. HE was staring at me cautiously, his lips tight. "Do you understand?" he asked quietly.

"We've been repressed," I muttered. I looked to Wolfe as he nodded a few times. "What happened to your mortal? Your mate?" I looked to Wes: his jaw tensed and he turned his back.

"She died." He rested his hand on the wall and hung his head. "I was too late to save her soul, too late to turn her into a Reaper. Another Reaper Exterminated her. She's gone forever."

My chest tightened. The thought of losing Raven forever made me want to fucking die. I wanted to rush to her, make sure she was okay. I couldn't imagine my life without her. Even if I'd only been seeing her with my glamour on or as Mason, I wouldn't survive it if she was Exterminated. If my brothers were gone, I could get through it, but her...I rubbed the center of my chest.

"I'm sorry, Wes." Emotion burned in the back of my nose. He waved his hand dismissively. "You've found your...mates?" I asked the others. They shook their heads and Wolfe cleared his throat.

"I haven't looked, and I have no interest in finding them," he said. "Just because I know I have a soul doesn't change anything. I'm still a Reaper." I nodded a few times and looked at the others, but they stayed silent.

"Bring her here," Wes said, his voice thick. "We test on you both, see if you're actually mated."

"And if we're not?" I breathed, even though the words gutted me.

"Then she's not your mate, but it changes nothing. You still have a soul."

What Wes said didn't matter. I didn't care about having a soul if she wasn't my mate. If she wasn't my soulmate, it changed everything.

21
RAVEN
PRESENT

I paced the bedroom, my thumb in my mouth as I gnawed on my nail. I'd fallen asleep; I didn't know for how long, but when I woke up and tried to open the door, it was locked. Panic shot through me, then guilt. The guilt warring with the panic confused me—why was I feeling guilty? What did I even have to feel guilty about?

There was a knock, and I paused in the center of the room and stared at the door. I didn't answer, but the door slowly opened, and Grim hesitantly entered, holding a plate and a bottle of water.

"You have food?" I blurted. There was a beat of silence, then a breathy, dark chuckle as he dropped his head forward.

"Yeah, little bird, Reapers eat and drink, too," he said. "How else would we have the strength to put up with you mortals?"

"Is that what you call us?" I turned fully to face him. "Mortals?"

"Isn't that what you call us?" he countered. "Reapers?"

"That's what you are."

"And you're a mortal."

I blinked at him, and he stared back. We waited for the other to speak first, to break the tension, but when it was clear he wasn't going to, I sighed and dropped my hands to my sides. He shifted a few times, seeming uncomfortable as he looked around the room. I wanted to rip that stupid mask off his face.

"Take your mask off," I said, and his head snapped to me.

"I can't." He set the plate and bottle down on the desk by the door and gestured to it. "Eat."

"I want to go home." I folded my arms over my chest, and he sighed.

"It's not safe," he said.

"Why not?" I chewed on my lip, peeling off the skin. "Was he—were you there to reap me?" My words were barely audible.

"No," he said quickly. "No, you weren't going to die. I was there to save you."

"But you didn't kill him." I didn't know why it upset me so much that he didn't kill Eddy, that he didn't protect me, but it did. It wasn't like he had any obligation to do so, but it still made me feel...betrayed.

"I couldn't," he answered. "If I did, I would've been taken from you again and—"

"Again?" I pushed my brows together. "What are you talking about?" He shook his head a few times.

"Nothing," he muttered. "Eat, little bird. I'll check on you in a bit." He stepped into the hall, and I felt a surge of panic at the thought of being left alone again.

"Wait," I said, stretching my arm out toward him. "Where are you going?" I hated how vulnerable my voice sounded.

"I need to talk to some people," he said. "I'll be back later."

"Can I leave the room?" I asked. He looked around, and when he looked back at me, I felt the word before he said it.

"No," he said quietly.

I nodded a few times, blinking back tears, and sank onto the bed. We stared at each other as he slowly shut the door, the lock clicking loudly into place.

I DIDN'T KNOW WHAT ELSE TO DO TO PASS THE TIME OTHER than snoop. I'd already gone through his dresser, finding nothing but clothes, and looked through his bookshelf and desk. Who didn't have their dirty secrets hidden in their drawers?

Floating shelves hung above the bed, filled with random things. I stood on the bed to get a closer look, hoping to find something interesting. There was a journal with a pen stuck in the middle, random coins, a folded colorful cloth that looked like a flag of some kind, books propped against each other, and a framed photo. I shuffled closer, squinting to see the picture in the dim red lighting.

Was it weird for a Reaper to have a photo of people in his room? Who were they to him? They must've been important if he had them above his bed.

Four men stood together, the two in the middle smiling with their arms slung over each other, the one on the far left stone-faced, and the one on the far right with his arms folded over his chest, a slight smirk on his face. I moved closer, smiling to myself as I scanned the photo again. My eyes lingered on the one on the far right, and my blood ran cold.

I snatched the photo off the shelf and held it an inch from my face. That couldn't be him. It didn't make any sense.

Why would Grim have a photo of Mason in his room? I scanned the others again, my stomach twisting more. That was Caden, and...what was the other's name? I'd only talked to him for a moment at the club before he left. Why does Grim have this photo?

Real fear jolted through me. I knew Grim had been stalking me, but I hadn't thought anything of it. I hadn't been afraid of him or the fact that he'd been breaking into my apartment. I didn't think twice about it. I didn't think he'd ever hurt me. Had he done something to Mason and his brothers? Is that why I hadn't heard from him in so long? Had Grim caught Mason in my bedroom last month? Sure, he'd texted me tonight, but anyone could've used his phone.

My hands began to tremble as I stared at the photo. Was it even Mason? I stared at him, my stomach rolling. It was him. I'd stared into his eyes long enough to recognize them. It was Mason.

The door opened, but I didn't turn around. I could feel Grim's eyes on the back of my head, but I couldn't force myself to move. I could barely force myself to breathe. This didn't make any sense. Was Mason even alive? Was it my fault he was dead?

"Raven?" Grim said cautiously. Anxiety overwhelmed me, hitting me like a brick in the center of my chest.

"Why do you have this photo?" I murmured, my back still to him. My body began to shake, my hands turning to ice as I stared at the photo. That smirk, the one that looked like he had a secret, the one that made my knees weak, stared back at me.

"Little bird—"

"Don't," I breathed. "Just answer me. Is he alive?" He let out a hard breath, and I squeezed my eyes shut, tears pricking them. I readied myself for his answer.

"Yes," he said, "and no." My brows bunched tightly together.

"What does that mean?" Finally, I turned toward him. He wrung his hands tightly as he watched me, his eyes hidden behind the mask. "What—"

Something banged downstairs, and Grim's shoulders straightened. "Get in the closet." He moved toward me, reaching his hand out for me.

"What?" My heart jumped into my throat as shouting floated up from beneath us. "Who's here? What's going on?" Stomping sounded somewhere nearby, getting closer to us. "Grim?" Fear bolted through me.

"Please trust me to keep you safe," he rushed out. "Get in the closet and don't come out. No matter what." He yanked me off the bed and shoved me inside his closet, and I peered through the slats as four masked men entered the room. Grim stood at his full height as he turned toward them, and I held my breath.

22

GRIM

PRESENT

"Where's Brody?" Seth demanded, his three buddies tight on his heels. If Raven heard that, then she definitely knew who I was now. I felt her confusion, her panic, then her fear before I saw her with the photo. I didn't think she'd figured out who I was, but I wasn't a fucking idiot. I knew I couldn't keep it from her forever. It's why I wanted to meet with her on our anniversary, which happened to be today. I was going to take the mask off and give her the big reveal—ta-da! I'm Mason *and* Grim.

"Don't fucking know," I snarled. "Get the fuck out of my house." Seth stepped forward, and I bunched my hands into fists.

He could exterminate me. He could end me right there in front of Raven, and I couldn't let her see that. More than that, if I was gone, I couldn't protect her; the thought of them finding her and—I didn't know what the fuck they'd do to her. Whatever it would be, I knew it wouldn't be good, and I couldn't allow it to happen.

"Do you think I'm a fucking idiot?" he snapped.

"Well—"

"You think I believe you don't know where he is?" He took another step forward. I needed to de-escalate this before it got out of hand.

"Seth, I really don't know," I said seriously, my voice even. "If I did—"

"Don't even say you'd tell me," he said. "We both know you wouldn't." I shrugged unapologetically. Raven's panic was thick in my chest, and I tried to send a flood of calmness through my body, hopefully to her. I didn't know if she could even feel my emotions like I could feel hers, but I needed her to calm the fuck down before they heard her hyperventilate.

"Look—"

"Come with me." The men began to move toward me, and I let out a breath. I didn't want to go with them. I'd end up in a cell, I knew that, and I wouldn't fucking survive it again.

"Let's talk here," I said, throwing my arm toward the door. "We can talk downstairs. I'll answer whatever questions—"

"Thomas wants to see you," he gritted out. There was something off about his tone, and it gave me pause.

"Why?" I asked, narrowing my eyes.

"He wouldn't tell me why." Ah, that was it. He was upset Thomas wouldn't give him details about what he wanted.

I could talk with Thomas. I'd have to make sure Seth and his fucking cronies were out of the house and away from Raven before I agreed to anything, though. I didn't want her here with them without me.

"Alright," I said, stepping toward them. "But I want you all out of my fucking house. Leave my brothers alone."

"Caden is coming with you," Seth informed me. "Rage is—"

"You can't control Rage," I said, smiling behind my mask. "He'll do what he wants." Seth let out a breath. He knew I was right. He'd tried to force Rage to do what he wanted the entire time I was gone, but Rage didn't budge. Stubborn was too mild a word for my brother.

"Yeah," he breathed. "Rage stays. Caden comes." I nodded and waited for them to retreat. They backed out a few steps but kept their eyes trained on me. There was no way to discreetly say anything to Raven, to reassure her I'd be back. Fuck, *I* didn't even know if I'd be back, but if they weren't forcing Rage to come with us, it couldn't be as bad as I was anticipating. Surely it meant we were coming home.

"I'll be home tonight, yeah?" I said at the door, loud enough for her to hopefully hear and understand the question was really meant for her.

"Yeah," Seth snapped. "Let's go."

———

CADEN AND I STEPPED INTO THOMAS' OFFICE. I STOOD BY the door again, not wanting to get too comfortable. Caden sunk into the leather chair across from Thomas without shaking his hand, and I smirked at my brother's blatant disrespect toward our elder High Reaper. I didn't blame him.

"What?" Caden asked, sounding bored, though I knew he was anything but. Thomas' face tightened as he slowly sat in his chair.

"Won't you sit, Mason?" He gestured to the chair beside Caden, but I leaned harder against the door, folding my arms over my chest, and leveled him with a look.

"I'm fine right here."

"Fine," he breathed as he rubbed his forehead. "I understand you've been in contact with some...." He trailed off as he looked out the window overlooking the courtyard. A giant bronze statue of a Reaper stood tall and proud in the center. It used to be something I respected, but now, with everything I'd learned from Wes and our meetings, all I wanted to do was rip it from the ground. "Interesting people."

Caden and I stayed silent. Thomas wanted us to give ourselves away, and we wouldn't fucking do it. I didn't know what 'interesting people' he was referring to, but if I had to guess, I'd assume he was talking about Wes and the guys. Thomas let out a breathy laugh and looked back at us, his eyes scanning Caden first, then lifting to me.

"You're both successful, respected Reapers," he said. "Well, you can be again." He jerked his chin at me, and I clenched my jaw. "I'd hate to see you throw your positions away over a silly group, for protecting your fugitive brother."

"Our brother—"

"Cade," I warned, my voice even.

I understood why they didn't want Rage here now. They knew Caden was quick to fly off the handle and to react without thinking first. They knew I'd have a hard time keeping him in check. With Rage here, he could control us both, remind us of what's important. They wanted us to slip up and say something to give Brody away.

"We don't know what you're talking about," I said. "We're leaving. Cade, come on." Caden looked at me over his shoulder, his dark brows bunched over his eyes. He hesitated for a moment before he got to his feet. I knew he was pissed; I could feel it filling the room, but I'd deal with his anger after we were well away from the Council and eavesdropping ears. I wrapped my hand around the golden doorknob as Thomas cleared his throat.

"When we find Brody, we're going to Exterminate him," he said casually. "You both know that, don't you?" Caden stopped dead, his eyes on mine. I barely shook my head. He was baiting us, I knew that. Caden had to know that. I also knew it was working: Caden was about to explode. "And if we find out either of you know anything about his current whereabouts, I'm afraid you'll be Exterminated along with him."

"Is that supposed to scare me?" Caden snarled as he turned around. "Am I supposed to be fucking scared? I'd die a million times over for my brother." Thomas smiled smugly at him, then lifted his eyes to mine.

"Cade," I growled. "Stop talking."

"If you think even for a fucking second," Caden took a step forward until just the desk separated them, "that I won't make your life a living fucking hell, Tom, then you've lost your mind. I will destroy you. You come after my family again, I'll rip your fucking head off and mount it on that stupid fucking statue." He pointed at the window. "Threaten us again, and I promise it will be the last thing you ever fucking do."

"Caden." I grabbed him by the collar of his shirt and yanked him back.

"You hear me, you old fuck?" he shouted. Thomas smiled at us, his hands clasped in his lap as he watched me yank the door open and shove Caden into the hall.

As soon as we made it into the lobby, I slapped the back of his head. He didn't care. He fumed as he paced, his hands clenching into fists. He was muttering to himself, his face turning red as his anger rose.

"You can't threaten him," I hissed. "They're going to think you're an Exterminator and—"

"And what?" he shouted, throwing his arms out wide as he stopped in front of me. "Come get me? Take me to a fucking cell? Let them, Mase! Fucking let them!" I took a deep breath. He needed me level-headed right now, not screaming back at him. It was hard as shit, though.

"I won't let that happen," I said quietly.

"Like you wouldn't let anything happen to Brody?" He shoved my shoulders, but his voice broke. "He's gone, Mase. I don't know where the fuck he is. He hasn't been home in a month and—"

"I know," I said, dropping my head.

"Yeah, you know," he nodded a few times, "but you don't care." I snapped my head up.

"What?"

"You're too busy worrying about that fucking girl—"

"Caden," I groaned. "Now is not the time."

"You're too busy with her to look for him!" Tears welled in his eyes, his voice shaky as he glared at me. "She's more important to you than we are!" I squeezed my eyes shut as I took a deep breath.

"That's not true," I said. "I can love you all."

"You love her?" he croaked and stumbled back a step. "You—you can't love her." I looked around the lobby, at the passing Reapers giving us strange looks, then grabbed his arm and hauled him from the building. It was time Caden knew.

23

GRIM
PRESENT

"Sit." I jerked my chin at the couch, and Caden and Rage hesitantly sat as they glanced at each other. "I think it's time we talk about—" I let out a long, hard breath, "Her." I flicked my eyes up to the ceiling, and they looked at each other again.

"Okay," Rage drawled out hesitantly.

I paced in front of them, unsure of what to say. Where the fuck did I even start? She was my soulmate? That we still had our souls? I shoved my fingers through my hair. They were going to think I was nuts, I knew that, but they had to know the truth. Then, maybe they could find their mates and—that was fucking stupid. Rage with a soulmate? Poor fucking soul.

"She's my soulmate," I blurted, then winced. That wasn't how I wanted it to come out. "She's the girl I saved and the reason—"

"The reason you were sent away," Caden finished, his voice low. "You're saying she's your soulmate." He was staring at me like I'd lost my mind. I didn't totally blame him. "You do realize we're Reapers, right? Like, we *reap* souls? We don't have them."

"We do," I insisted. "Wes found out—"

"Wait." Rage held his hand up. "Wes? As in *Wesley*? The Reaper

127

from the Council?" I nodded, and he let out a breath, then nodded for me to continue.

"He found out we have souls."

"Oookay." Caden drew the word out and shared a look with Rage. "Is this why you're holding the girl hostage in your bedroom?"

"I'm not holding her hostage." I squeezed my eyes shut. "I'm fucking this up. Fuck."

"Start from the beginning," Rage grumbled. "Wes found out we have souls. How?"

I explained everything. From saving Raven, to Wes finding the book, to starting the group with the guys, to how Wes showed me everything. I told them about Raven, how I'd been seeing her for the last few months and already knew who she was when we went home together after the club.

Rage didn't look happy, but when did he ever? Caden looked...a bit shell-shocked. He stared at me, his mouth open, eyes wide. "Brody is going to lose his shit when he hears about this," was the first thing he said. Then, "Holy shit, we have souls. I have a soul. And a soulmate."

He got to his feet and began to pace around the room. I didn't know what to do. Comfort him? How the fuck was I supposed to do that? I watched as he had a mini breakdown, then stared at the stairs that lead to the second floor.

"Does she know?" he asked, his hands on his hips.

"No," I said. "She doesn't—" I scrubbed my hand over my face. This was the part I wasn't looking forward to. "She doesn't know I'm Mason." They snapped their heads to me.

"What?" Rage said. "How the fuck doesn't she know that?"

"She's only seen Grim with his mask on, and Mason was always in mortal clothes." I shrugged and ran my hands down the front of my jeans. "I've never told her we're the same person, but I think she's figured it out."

"Well, I'd fucking hope so," Caden deadpanned. "How many seven-foot fucks does she know?" I bit back a laugh. He had a point. Had she known this entire time? No, surely she hadn't. If she had, she would've made it known the last time I saw her. She would've called me Mason, not Grim.

"You need to tell her," Rage said. "*Everything.*"

"I know," I sighed.

"Why is she here?" Caden walked toward me, his brows tight. "I know she's your...whatever, but why is she *here*? Why did you bring her here?"

"There's a serial killer in the Mortal Realm," I explained. "I've been reaping his victim's souls. Last night, Raven was in his apartment with him. She has no idea he's the killer and that she's in fucking danger." They blinked at me.

"If the Council catches wind that you saved her again—"

"He wasn't going to kill her," I said quickly. "I wasn't called to reap her. I was already following her—"

"And you saved her," Rage finished with a groan. "Fuck."

"I can't take her back to the Mortal Realm until I'm sure she's safe," I concluded, looking between my brothers. Caden nodded in understanding, while Rage just grunted.

"Are you going to kill the guy?" Caden asked. I groaned.

"I can't," I said. "Not with the Council watching me. Not with Brody missing. They're watching all of us." They nodded a few times.

"She can't stay here forever," he said warily. "You know that, right?"

"Yeah," I muttered as I ran a hand through my hair. A pang of sadness shot through me at the thought of taking her home, even though she didn't know who I was or who we were to each other, not yet. She would though, and when she did...what? She'd still be a mortal. "I'll talk to her."

"You might wanna do that now," Caden said, nodding toward the stairs. I followed his gaze, finding Raven standing at the top, her eyes wide as she stared down at me. I was barely breathing as I waited for her to say or do something, anything, but she didn't. She just stared. That was somehow worse than if she screamed and hit me.

Finally, I took a step forward, and it shook her out of her daze. She turned on her heel and retreated back into my bedroom. I glanced at Rage and Caden, who quickly averted their attention to the floor. The betrayal I felt burning in my chest was coming from her, and it hurt knowing that's what she was feeling. Toward me. Fuck.

"Try to keep it down," Caden said with a small laugh. "You know, make-up sex is always—"

"Shut up," Rage snapped, slapping the back of his head. "Do you ever think before you open your fucking mouth?" I shook my head as I climbed the stairs, the sound of them bickering fading as I slowly approached the cracked-open bedroom door.

My stomach twisted with anxiety as I stopped a few feet away. I didn't have my mask or cloak on. I was going to talk to her as Mason, not Grim. I fucking loved when she called me Grim, but I needed her to know we were the same guy, that I didn't deceive her. It was just a mask. I was the same, with or without it.

Taking a deep breath, I pushed the door open and stepped inside.

24

RAVEN

PRESENT

I sat in the center of the bed and watched as he leaned against the closed door. Mason folded his arms over his chest, our eyes locked. Or was it Grim? What was I even supposed to call him? Who *was* he? I rubbed the center of my chest as more emotion bubbled to the surface. I didn't want to believe it.

"Little bird," he murmured. Tears stung my eyes, and my chin wobbled. He pushed off the door and took a step toward me, then stopped. "Can I sit?" He gestured toward the bed, and I clutched my knees to my chest as I nodded. He sat in front of me and rested his hands on either side of my knees as he brought his face closer to mine.

"Mason?" I whispered. He nodded a few times, his eyes locked on mine. "Or Grim?"

"Both," he answered immediately. "I'm not one without the other." He brought his hand to my face and gently wiped a stray tear from my cheek with his thumb. "Don't cry. I don't like seeing you cry."

"Yes, you do," I said with a small laugh. The corner of his mouth tucked up, and he slid his hand to the back of my neck.

"Only when I'm inside you," he muttered. "I only ever want to see your tears when I'm fucking you." My stomach tightened at his words, and I dropped my eyes to his mouth. "You can't look at me like that. I

131

came in here to talk to you." I lifted my eyes to his, and they were *blazing*. "Stop it."

"I'm not doing anything," I breathed. His grip on my neck tightened, and I lowered my eyes to his lips again.

"Raven," he warned.

I needed to be stronger than this, but something about his presence was grounding. All day I'd been out of sorts, anxious and scared, and even though I was angry and betrayed, feeling him touch me, looking into his eyes, I felt calmer. Safer. Even as Grim, I knew I was safe with him. Even when I'd been scared and questioned why he'd brought me here, a part of me knew he wouldn't hurt me. Not physically. And Mason—even though we'd only had two brief interactions that were purely sexual, I felt a deep connection to him that I couldn't explain, one that told me I could trust him with my life. Now, I understood why. I wasn't trusting Mason with my life. I was trusting Grim.

"Mason—"

"Grim," he corrected. "I like when you call me Grim."

"More than Master?" I smirked when his grip on my nape tightened.

"You need to stop," he growled, moving closer.

"Make me, *Master*."

His other hand lashed out and wrapped around my jaw. I gasped as he squeezed my face, puckering my lips until they opened. My eyes widened as he brought his face closer to mine, terrifying in the red light.

"You do not control me, little bird," he growled. "I control you. You can't manipulate me into getting what you want, even if I want it, too. Right now, we have shit to figure out. Afterward, I'll fuck you until you can't breathe, but for now, stop trying to make me lose control."

"I want you to lose control," I mumbled as he squeezed my face harder.

"I don't care what you want," he said. "Stop being a brat." He harshly let me go, shoving me back until I hit the headboard. I inhaled deeply as he pushed to his feet and moved to the center of the room. He rubbed his hands down the front of his jeans as he stared at me, his eyes slowly roaming down my body. Roughly, he shook his head and turned his back to me. "We need to talk about this."

"I don't want to talk," I whined.

It took me a moment to realize what I was doing. I was trying to ignore what was happening between us. I was trying to prolong the inevitable and pretend like he was still just Mason, that we were in my apartment doing some weird role-play.

Just for a little longer, I wanted to pretend everything was normal, that I wasn't in a house full of Reapers, that I hadn't been attacked by Eddy. I wanted to pretend Grim hadn't lied to me. I didn't want to know whatever he had to say, because I knew whatever it was would change my life forever, and I wasn't ready.

He didn't care.

He was going to barrel his way into my life and force it to change whether I wanted it to or not. He ignored my whining as he paced the bedroom. He mumbled to himself, then paused and stared at me.

"Come on," he said, holding his hand out. "I have people I want you to meet."

"What?" My head reared back. "I can't leave." I looked down at myself. I was wearing one of his t-shirts I'd stolen from his closet. While it looked like a giant dress on me, I couldn't meet anyone looking like that. "Will you just tell me what's going on?"

"They can explain it better than I can."

"Why did you lie to me?" I murmured. His shoulders slumped slightly. "Can they explain *that* better?"

"The night you were going to jump off that building—"

"It was my birthday," I said, and his head snapped to me.

"Your birthday," he repeated. "Why the fuck—" He shook his head as he let out a breath. "Why were you trying to die on your birthday?"

"I didn't want to die," I said. "I wanted you." He inhaled sharply, then squeezed his eyes shut.

"You got me, didn't you?" he said, and my heart sank.

"Not the way I wanted," I muttered. "I got Mason, not Grim."

"We're the same," he groaned. "You're acting like we're two different people."

"Because in my head, you are!" I pushed to my feet and glared up at him. I wasn't used to people taller than me. I was usually one of the tallest in the room, so having Grim tower over me was intimidating and new. Still, I wouldn't back down. "You—" I jabbed my finger in the center of his chest, "are Mason. When you have the mask on, you're Grim."

"That's it?" he scoffed. "A fucking mask?"

"You act differently when it's on," I snapped. "You carry yourself differently. Even your voice sounds different. Everything about you is different."

"That's who you want?" he said, his eyes flicking between mine. "You want that cold, heartless bastard? Not me?" He banged his fist against his chest. "Not Mason." My chin trembled again.

"I want Mason, too," I cried. "But I don't know either of them. I don't know you! How can I want you when I don't fucking know you?" He opened his mouth, then paused. I wiped roughly at my eyes as he stared down at me.

"You don't, do you?" he said quietly. "You don't know me." My heart sank further when he took a step back. "Fuck. I'm an idiot."

"Mason—"

"Wait." He held his hand up. "I've been...." He hesitated as he stared at me. "I've been watching you for the last fifteen years. Not every day, but I was able to get out one day every year, and I spent that day with you. I've been with you every day for the last six months. I know you, Raven. I fucking know you. The only thing you need to know about me is that I'm fucking obsessed with you. I live and breathe to be around you. I *survive* to be with you. I haven't found a way to end my fucking existence because of you, because you're my fucking soul. The little shreds of it I have left," he rubbed his chest, "they're yours. My sole reason to exist is you."

My mouth opened and closed a few times, the words completely lost. No one had ever said anything like that to me, and I didn't know what to say. I didn't know what to think or feel; I just stared at him, waiting for him to continue, but he didn't. He stared back; it was my turn to speak.

"I don't know what to say," I replied lamely. He blinked at me, then let out a breathy laugh.

"Anything. Say anything." I shook my head, words still not coming.

"Come with me." He held his hand out again. "I need to show you something. I can't explain it. You won't believe me if I try."

"What?" I asked. I didn't move to take his hand. Instead, I waited. "Try to explain it."

"It's a lot," he sighed. "Just come with me."

"Will there be more Reapers?" I asked, and he nodded. "Will they kill me?" His head reared back.

"Why the fuck would they kill you?" He looked genuinely confused. "No, Raven, they won't kill you. We can't just kill mortals because we want to. Their time has to be up."

"But you killed—"

"Your stepfather," he finished, and I nodded. "I was punished for that."

"Punished?" I gasped.

"I'll explain another time," he said, exasperated. "Please, just come on." He shook his still-extended hand slightly. "Please." I hesitated.

I didn't know if I totally believed him, not after everything, but I slid my hand into his, and when his room began to fade, I squeezed his hand a little tighter.

25

RAVEN

PRESENT

I fell to my hands and knees, the food I'd eaten earlier spewing from my mouth and landing on the soft grass beneath me. Mason kneeled beside me, his big, cold hand rubbing up and down my back as his other one gently gathered my hair away from my face. I blindly swatted at him.

"Get away," I groaned as I closed my eyes. This was the second time this happened, although the first time, I hadn't thrown up. This was embarrassing. "I'm gross."

"I've seen grosser things," he murmured. "I've got you."

"You're the reason for this," I grumbled, then gagged again. My body was still trying to piece itself together. He laughed softly but didn't say anything. "Don't you have a car or something?" I glared at him over my shoulder. The sun was high, the sky was abnormally blue behind him. In the daylight, he was...breathtaking. I'd only seen him in dim lighting and at night—or with his mask on—but now, with the bright sun and no harsh shadows covering his features, he was the most beautiful man I'd ever seen.

I already knew he was attractive, that he was sell-my-left-tit-to-have-him-look-in-my-direction hot, but this was different altogether. He was more than just hot. He was just *more*.

His black hair was still short and spiky from where he constantly ran his fingers through it, and his beard was a little longer than it had been when we hooked up on my birthday, but his eyes are what held me captive. The gentle way he was looking at me made my heart stutter.

This was *not* good.

"What?" he asked, his hand stilling. His eyes searched mine, a soft look on his face that I'd never seen before. "What is it?" I sat back from him, resting my arms on my knees as I stared.

"Are all Reapers like you?" I waved my hand at him, and he tilted his head to the side.

"Like me?" He stayed on one knee, his forearms crossed over it as he watched me.

"You know," I sighed, rolling my eyes. He shook his head, looking confused. "Hot." An arrogant smile slowly spread across his face, and he ran his teeth across his bottom lip.

"You think I'm hot, little bird?" He rubbed his hand over his jaw, the corners of his eyes still crinkled with his smile.

"Shut up," I muttered. My body wasn't aching nearly as much, and in its place was a throbbing between my legs I couldn't ignore. Unfortunately, I had to. I needed to keep my head on straight; no matter how hot Mason—Grim—was, he still lied to me. I don't like being lied to.

I looked around, noticing the giant house behind him. It was a deep red brick with white windows and shutters. Vines grew along one side, crawling up the walls. Colorful flowers grew in beds below the windows, and butterflies and bees buzzed around them. I blinked a few times as I scanned the seemingly ordinary house again.

"Where are we?" I asked quietly. Mason rubbed the back of his neck, looking uncomfortable. He pushed to his feet and held his hand out for me.

"At a friend's place," he said.

"We had to come here so they could tell me what's going on?" I questioned. I squinted up at him, the sun blinding me. "Instead of you just telling me?" He let out a long breath.

"I don't know how."

"You can try," I snapped. His eyes found mine, and he dropped his hand to his side.

"You're right," he agreed. "Fine. Get up. I'm not going to talk down to you."

"What stopped you in the past?" I mumbled as I clamored to my feet. Without warning, he grabbed my jaw and tipped my head back.

"What was that?" he hissed, his coal-black eyes fiery.

"Nothing," I breathed. I gulped as I wrapped my hands around his thick wrist.

"You think I talk down to you?" I shook my head, my eyes widening.

"No," I said quietly. "Please let me go." He lowered his eyes to his hand on my jaw, then let go and took a large step away. I rubbed my jaw, my eyes locked with his as he scrubbed his hands up and down his thighs.

"Come on," he said gruffly, turning his back to me. This man gave me fucking whiplash. How could he be so sweet one moment and like this the next? I followed after him as he led me toward a small gate. He pushed it open, letting me enter first.

A stone footpath wound toward the center of the yard, a giant pond in the middle, stone benches surrounding it with more plants and shrubbery. Large bushes had been cut into random shapes, most of them geometric, but one looked like an elephant, which I thought was odd.

I blindly walked toward the pond. Mason's eyes stabbed into the back of my head, but I tried to ignore him as I crouched and ran my fingers through the water. The water was icy cold—impossibly cold for a warm day like today. It was deep, but I could see small fish swimming below.

"Don't get too close," he warned. I glanced over my shoulder at him, his face tight. "The creatures here aren't like ones in the Mortal Realm." My brows knitted together as I jerked my hand from the water.

"What does that mean?" I looked back down, seeing a giant shadow swim by far, far under the surface. I stumbled back, landing on my ass at Mason's feet.

"I won't let anything harm you," he said quietly. I looked up at him; I wanted to believe him, but could I? After lying about who he was, could I really trust him to keep me safe? He didn't do anything to Eddy.

He just helped me escape. Did it make me a terrible person to want Eddy dead, or at least severely injured for what he'd tried to do?

Mason ran his fingers gently through my hair. It would be so easy to give in to him. The pull I felt was intense, and every touch, every soft look, every sweet word was making it easier to forget his lies. I needed to be strong. Even if I knew I'd give into him eventually, I needed to be strong for now. I couldn't give in to him so easily. He needed to work for it, for me. He had to know he couldn't lie to me and get away with it, that I wasn't happy.

I jerked my head away and crawled onto a bench. Glaring up at him, I waited for him to speak. He stared at me like I'd wounded him, truly hurt him, and maybe I had, but he'd hurt me, too. The pain in the center of my chest worsened, and I rubbed it again, my throat tight.

"Explain," was the only word I could say. He hesitated before he took a few steps back and ran his fingers through his short hair, gently tugging on the ends before looking at me.

"I've been a Reaper for over eight hundred years," he began. I inhaled sharply, my eyes widening. "I've never come across your soul before. I would've felt it. I would've known you before that night. I would've turned you a long fucking time ago." He said the last words so quietly, I almost didn't hear him.

"You're eight hundred years old?" I whispered, and his mouth tucked up in the corner.

"I hope you like older men," he said with a small laugh. I couldn't laugh, though, not when my mind was still reeling over the fact that Mason—Grim, whatever—was eight hundred fucking years old. "Technically, I'm eight-hundred-and-thirty-four. My vessel," he waved his hand at his body, "died at thirty-four."

"Vessel?" I rasped. I wrapped my arms around myself, suddenly feeling cold. What the fuck was happening?

"Body." He shrugged. "When a Reaper dies for the last time, their last vessel is the one they take with them."

"Lucky that's how you looked, then," I muttered mindlessly, and he smirked.

"You have to stop saying shit like that," he groaned, and I blinked at him. "It's giving me a big head."

"You already have a giant fucking head." He laughed, some of the tension in his face and shoulders dissipating. He hesitated before moving to the bench to sit beside me, pressing his thigh against mine.

"I was the first of my brothers to go," he said as he rubbed his hands together, looking down. "I'd already died a few times, mostly in wars, a few times as a sick child. Once, I'd been murdered. Another time, I killed myself." I inhaled sharply.

"You remember all the times you died?" I whispered, my chest aching. He put his hand on his chest and slowly turned to look at me.

"That makes you sad," he said. It wasn't a question. I wiped at my face, nodding. "Don't be sad for me, little bird. It was a long, long time ago."

"Was it painful? Death?" He smiled sadly.

"Leaving behind the ones I loved was the worst part," he admitted, looking away from me.

"Did you have families? Wives? Children of your own?" I didn't know if I wanted to know, but I asked anyway. He sighed softly.

"Sometimes," he whispered. "I've never come across their souls again." He sounded so sad, so fucking broken, that a sob left me. He snapped his head to me, tears welling in his eyes. "Please don't cry again."

"But you lost them," I cried, unable to stop the tears from flowing. "You lost all of them over and over, and you've never found them again. How is that possible?" He shook his head, then gently took my face in his hands. He rested his forehead against mine and closed his eyes as he breathed in deeply.

"I never searched for them," he whispered. "I never knew it, but I've spent my entire existence searching for you." He opened his eyes, the whites of them red and glossy. "I don't think I ever cared enough to look because I knew your soul was coming for me. Because I knew you were out there."

"But—"

"No buts," he said. "When I was a mortal, I loved them, but if I was supposed to find their souls again, I would have by now. I've found yours, though. That means something, don't you think?" I flicked my eyes between his, and his hands tightened around my head.

"You've found billions of souls in your time, I'm sure," I said, pulling away slightly to wipe my face. "Why am I any different?" He dropped his hands and rested them in my lap.

"Because their souls weren't tied to mine," he answered. "They were just another soul to me. You're not. You're something more." I stared at him, my heart racing. I wrapped my hands around his giant ones, and he squeezed them tight. "Because none of them were my soulmate."

26

GRIM

PRESENT

The words hung in the air. Raven stared at me, her eyes wide and chest barely moving. I didn't think she was breathing. Her hands began to tremble, the only sign she was still alive.

"Little bird?" I whispered. She didn't react. I think she was broken. "Raven?"

"Soulmate?" she croaked. "Soulmate." She untangled her hands from mine and got to her feet. Her knees were shaky as she paced, her arms wrapped tightly around herself. "He thinks I'm his soulmate. A Reaper thinks I'm his soulmate."

I covered my mouth to hide my laugh as I watched her meltdown. I didn't want her to think I was laughing at her, but I was. She was fucking dramatic. Adorable as shit, but dramatic.

"Soulmate," she muttered again, then abruptly stopped. "Souls aren't even real." I barked a laugh.

"What do you think we help cross realms?" I asked. "We don't help *mortals* cross realms. We don't help their vessels. We help their souls."

"But souls aren't real," she said again. "They're just made-up."

"I can assure you, they're not made-up," I said as I tapped my fingers on my knees. "Sit down." She looked at the bench, then began to pace again.

"Tell me how you figured out—" She waved her hand between us. "This is fucking crazy," she muttered under her breath.

"Well," I sighed, and she stopped to stare at me. "When I killed your stepfather, I was sent away."

"Away," she repeated, her brows knitted tightly together. "You said that earlier."

"I was punished for it. There's somewhere called the In-Between, kind of like Purgatory. It's where souls go when they're being punished, kind of like prison," I explained. She nodded, her eyes narrowing slightly.

"You went to prison for saving me," she said slowly. I shifted uncomfortably but nodded. She let out a hard breath and ran her hands through her hair. "Fuck."

"We had a free day every year to do as we pleased," I continued. "We could come back, go to the Mortal Realm, whatever. I chose to find you."

"Every year," she repeated quietly. "You found me every year." I nodded, and she took a deep breath, then released it slowly. "Okay. Fuck. Okay."

"Does that make you uncomfortable?" I asked warily, eyeing her. Her arms were still wrapped tightly around her, but she was facing me head-on now. She didn't look entirely uncomfortable, just a little shocked.

"I don't know," she admitted. "Keep going."

"I just got out a few months ago," I said. "I'll be honest." I lowered my head, not wanting to look at her for this part. "I hated you for a long time." She inhaled sharply. "I thought you were throwing your life away. I thought I'd been sent away, lost the respect of my peers, my standing in the Council, fifteen years with my brothers, all for nothing. You were always trying to die. It pissed me off."

"I was trying to find you again," she said, her voice thick, and I nodded.

"I understand that now," I sighed, scrubbing my hand over my face. "I watched you for a couple of months. Then you went to that roof and tried to fucking jump off. I don't know, something snapped inside me that night. The thought of you dying made me irrationally fucking mad. I didn't want you to die, but I wanted to reap you. I wanted to turn you. I—I don't know."

"Turn me?" She stepped closer, and I looked up at her. She didn't look nearly as scared as she should've been.

"Turn you into one of us," I whispered. "A Reaper." Her eyes widened.

"That's an option?"

"You sound too fucking excited about that," I groaned, dropping my head back. She sank onto the bench beside me.

"You can turn me into a Reaper?"

"Raven," I warned. "That's not happening."

"But—"

"No," I snapped, looking down at her. "I don't want this for you." I shifted my eyes between hers, willing her to understand this wasn't some rash decision she could make. This was a big fucking deal. This would be her life for eternity, and it wasn't an easy one.

"Is this why I've always wanted to find you again?" she asked as she rested her hand on my chest. She narrowed her eyes slightly as she stared at my chest, like she was trying to see into my soul, to see where our souls joined. "Because you're my soulmate?" I clenched my jaw tightly as I nodded. "That's why I trusted Mason?" I nodded again. "And Grim?" Again, I nodded, not trusting myself to speak. "I don't know if I believe this."

I let out a hard breath. Yeah, it was hard for me to believe still, and I'd had weeks to process it. She was adjusting remarkably well, quickly, but it made me suspicious. Would this all come crashing down once reality set in?

"There's a test they can do," I said, nodding toward Wes' house. I knew he was aware we were here; he knew the moment we appeared on his front lawn. Him being him, he'd given us privacy. I was surprised Wolfe hadn't stormed out and demanded we stop wasting his time, though.

"Your friend," she murmured as she looked over her shoulder. She studied the house again. "It doesn't look like a place I'd expect a Reaper to live."

"What did you expect?"

"I don't know," she said. "A cave." I choked on a laugh, and she looked at me, a coy smile on her face.

"A cave?"

"Something dark and scary." She shrugged as she stood. "Something creepy for creepy Reapers." She wiggled her fingers, and I laughed.

"Creepy Reapers, huh?" I stood; I wanted to grab her and fucking kiss her, but I refrained. Barely.

She nodded, smiling wider. Something was lingering in my chest, and I knew it was the anxiety she felt. She was putting on a brave face, for herself or for me, I didn't know, but it was commendable. She was trying to pretend like she wasn't fazed by any of this, even though she so clearly was.

"I think you're the creepiest of them all," she teased, then took off in a full sprint toward the house. I faded and appeared on the porch in front of her. She ran into my chest and nearly fell backward before I caught her. "What the fuck?" she shrieked. "How did you—" She looked behind her at where I'd been a second ago, then glared up at me. "That wasn't fair."

I shrugged. "I don't play fair, little bird. Come on."

27

RAVEN

PRESENT

"Hello." A man stepped out from nowhere, and I shrunk behind Mason. The man straightened slightly. "I'm Wesley. Welcome to my home." Wesley didn't seem to notice or care about my reaction. There was a coldness to him that was unmistakable. *Reaper*. Strangely enough, he didn't seem unkind.

"This is Raven," Mason said gruffly. He wrapped his hand around mine, squeezing tightly.

Wesley tipped his head toward me, a small smile on his face. He was handsome, with a strong, prominent nose and piercing blue eyes. His jaw and cheekbones were sharp, his brows highly arched. His dark curly hair was pushed away from his face and brushed his shoulders. The sleeves of his black dress shirt were rolled up to the elbows, and, despite the coldness radiating from him, he seemed friendly enough.

"Please," he said, waving behind him. "The others are in the sitting room." There was the softest English accent to his voice that made me smile.

"Others?" I whispered as I looked up at Mason.

"They have a little club," he said, and Wesley laughed under his breath.

"I'd say it's a little more important than a club," he said. "Do you

146

want a drink? I have water and tea. Stronger spirits are in the sitting room." He winked at me, and Mason growled. Like actually growled. I stared up at him in shock.

"Did you just growl?" I whispered.

"He did," Wesley laughed. "I'm afraid we Reapers are a bit possessive of our mates." I blinked at him.

"You have one too?" I asked as I stepped out from behind Mason. I wanted to move closer, but his hand tightened around mine in warning. "Are they mortal?" I looked around the house. Maybe that's why it seemed so normal, because he wanted his mate to feel at home. That was sweet. When I looked back at Wesley, the sad look on his face gutted me.

"I'm afraid she's gone," he said quietly. My heart hurt for him. Mason looked down at me, his brows bunched tightly together.

"You're sad," he whispered.

"I'm sorry, Wesley," I said, and he waved me off. I ignored Mason staring at me in worry.

"Oh, don't fret about it," he said. "Come." He turned on his heel and moved back the way he'd come.

"You're sad," Mason whispered again. "Why?" I blinked up at him.

"Did you not hear him say his mate was gone?" I said. "That's sad."

"But why are *you* sad about it?" He looked genuinely confused. "It doesn't affect you. You don't even know him."

"Mason," I breathed, shaking my head. "Empathy. Did you lose yours when you became this?" I waved my hand at him, and his jaw tensed.

"This," he gritted out, "is who I am." Guilt twisted in my stomach, and I stepped closer to him.

"I know," I said. "I didn't mean it like that."

His eyes flicked between mine. He opened his mouth to say something, but another voice barked from the other room. "Are you two coming, or are you going to waste more of my time?" Mason closed his eyes as he took a deep breath, and when he opened them, he nodded once toward the archway leading to what I assumed was the sitting room.

I steeled my spine as I walked forward, my hand still wrapped tightly in Mason's. A man was standing by the window, a deep scowl on his face as he stared outside. His hair was buzzed close to his head, his skin deep olive gold. Two more sat on a sofa, watching me curiously.

One had short dark hair and was covered in tattoos—every visible inch of his skin. His face was kind, but something lingered in his eyes, the same emotion that lingered in all of them. *Reaper.* The one next to him had a square jaw and dark eyes, darker than Mason's, with the fullest lips I'd ever seen. I glanced up at Mason, waiting for him to introduce us, but it was Wesley who spoke first.

"This is Raven," he said, gesturing to me. "Mason's mate." I blushed slightly as Mason tensed. He glanced down at me, then glared at the men in the room.

"Don't look at her," he growled. "We're only here because you think we need to be." He glared at Wesley harder, his jaw tensing so hard, I swore I could hear his teeth crack.

"For the test," Wesley said with a nod.

"Why do we need a test?" I murmured to Mason.

"To make sure you're actually mates," the man by the window answered, his voice like gravel. "This could've been over half an hour ago, but you two wanted to fuck around by the pond."

"Fuck off, Wolfe," Mason snapped.

"I thought you said we are," I said, stepping closer to Mason. He gripped my hand tighter.

"We are," he reassured me. "Don't listen to him. They just want to see if their test works." I eyed him warily; I didn't believe him. Wesley cleared his throat, then stepped to the back of the room where a bar cart sat.

"Would you like a drink, Raven? You look like you could use one," he said, smiling gently.

"Please," I muttered. I tried to move toward him, but Mason's grip on my hand tightened even more, if possible.

"Scotch okay?" Wesley asked as he turned around.

"Sure." I glanced up at Mason, finding him watching me carefully. He dipped down, pressing his lips to my ear.

"If this is all too much, we don't have to do this," he whispered. "I'll take you home." My heart both warmed and sank at the thought. Home? My home, or his? Why did I want to go back to his more than

148

mine? Why did he feel more like home than anywhere I'd ever been before?

Honestly, I was curious about this test. A small part of me wondered if Mason and I really were soulmates. It was crazy, wasn't it? This was all crazy. Then again, so was standing in a room full of Reapers. I wouldn't have believed this was even possible, but here I was. Why couldn't soulmates be real? Why couldn't Mason be mine?

"I'm okay," I assured him. He hesitated before pressing his lips to my temple and pulling away.

"Say the word, and I'll get you out of here," he promised, pulling me closer to his side. I nodded, feeling protected for the first time in my life. He gave me a strange look, like he was trying to figure me out, then squeezed my hand again.

"Are you going to introduce us?" one of the men on the couch asked. Mason closed his eyes and took a deep breath. These were his friends? I'd hate to see how he acted around people he really didn't like.

"Little bird, this is Malik." He pointed to the one with tattoos. "That's Damon." He gestured to the other one.

"Little bird?" Damon said, his eyes roaming over me. "Cute."

"Don't," Mason growled. Damon winked at me, and I folded my lips between my teeth to hide my laugh.

"Here you are, my dear," Wesley said, handing me a glass. Mason made a sound deep in his throat, and I glanced up at him. Wesley laughed as he shoved a glass in Mason's hand. "You could use one, too. Take the edge off." Mason glared as he threw the entire drink back; I stared at him in shock. "Show off," Wesley laughed, taking the glass from Mason. He set it down on his way to the bookshelf in the back of the room.

"Can we get this over with?" Wolfe groaned. He sank into a chair, and I shifted uncomfortably.

"I'm sorry," I said, wincing slightly.

"Don't apologize," Mason said. "You've done nothing. He's just an asshole." I winced at his words, not wanting to insult a literal stranger.

"He's right. We should do this," Malik sighed as he stood. Slowly, Damon followed, then Wolfe. I stared up at them, not liking the feeling of being towered over. I was used to being the tallest around and was

149

barely used to Mason. Having five men hovering over me made me uneasy.

"Sit on the floor," Wesley instructed as he walked toward us carrying a book. "Facing one another." Mason and I glanced at each other, then moved to the center of the room. I slowly sank to the floor, expecting him to let go of my hand, but he didn't. He held on tight as he plopped to the floor in front of me, wincing slightly.

"Bull in a china cabinet, this one," Malik muttered, and I cleared my throat to keep from laughing. Mason squeezed my hand again, but his lips twitched.

With his head bowed over the book, Wesley positioned himself beside us. I stared up at him, Mason's hand still wrapped tightly around mine. Wesley's lips moved as he silently read a passage, then he lifted his eyes and stared down at us.

"Are you ready?" he asked, flicking his eyes between us. We glanced at each other, and I swallowed hard. Mason's gaze was unwavering, his grip tight. A calmness settled in my chest, and I let out a long breath.

I could do this—whatever this was, I could do it. With him.

"Yes," I murmured, still looking at Mason.

His lips barely moved before he cleared his throat. "Let's do it."

28

RAVEN

PRESENT

While Malik closed the curtains, Damon turned the light off, bathing the room in darkness. My heart raced, but every time I shifted my eyes, trying to adjust, Mason moved his head, forcing himself into my line of sight.

"Stay with me," he whispered. "Right here." He pointed at his eyes, and I looked directly at him. "Breathe, little bird."

"You're safe," Wesley reassured me, although his reassurance wasn't nearly as comforting as Mason's presence. He looked at the book again as the men began to surround us. Panic rose in my chest. Why were they doing this? Standing around us, trapping me.

"It's okay," Mason soothed. He scooted closer, pressing his knees against mine. "I've got you."

I tipped my head back and stared up at Wolfe's scowling face. Gently, Mason's fingers latched onto my chin, and he tugged my head back down.

"Look at me, Raven." He rested his hand on my chest and took a deep breath. Mindlessly, I followed his instruction and breathed with him. Slowly, my panic began to subside, and he lowered his hand to my lap. "I won't let anything happen to you." I nodded, my throat still too tight to speak.

"Are we ready to begin?" Wesley asked gently.

"Will this hurt?" I croaked. "Is my soul—" My voice broke, and I pressed my knees harder against Mason. "Are you going to do something to my soul?" Wesley crouched; at least, he tried to. His height impeded him a bit.

"It won't hurt. I won't touch your soul. You and Mason will concentrate on each other and recite a few words, then you'll feel a tugging in your chest. It won't hurt," he rushed out when I opened my mouth. "It'll feel like this." He gently tugged on my arm. "Not so bad, right?"

"What if we don't feel it?" I whispered, looking at Mason. A silence fell over the room, and Damon shifted uncomfortably.

"Then we're not mates," Mason answered quietly.

I stared at him, my heart dipping. A whirlwind of emotions roared through me. I didn't know if I wanted to be his mate or what that would entail, but I wanted to find out. If I wasn't his mate...

He leaned closer and wrapped his hand around the back of my neck, tugging me closer until his forehead pressed against mine.

"For the record, even if we're not soulmates, you're still mine. You'll always be mine," he said.

Tears stung the backs of my eyes, and I nodded, my forehead rubbing against his. He kissed me gently, his lips lingering before he pulled away.

"Ready?" he asked. I straightened my spine as I nodded, then wiped at my face, not realizing my cheeks were wet. "That's my girl." Mason winked, and pride filled me.

I was his girl.

I could do this.

Wesley patted my shoulder as he stood, then flipped the book back open and stared down at the pages. He took a deep breath as his eyes flitted over the words. Nervousness swirled in my belly, but I kept my eyes locked with Mason's. His thumb stroked the back of my hand, over and over, reassuring me.

"Do they have to stand around us?" I whispered as I leaned inwards. His lips tucked up in the corner as he nodded.

"They're here to make sure nothing goes wrong," he replied. "They need to be close enough to get to you, in case something happens to me." Fear ripped through me.

"What is going to happen to you?"

"Nothing," he said with a slight shrug. "Just a precaution." I snapped my head up to Wesley, my eyes narrowing.

"How many times have you done this test?" I asked. His eyes lifted from the page, and I knew his answer before he said it.

"You're the first," he said with a smile. "Aren't you honored?" I glared at him. I most certainly did *not* feel honored. "Ready?" I didn't reply. I just glared, letting him know I wasn't happy with this new information.

Mason chuckled, which lightened some of my anger and fear, but not enough for me to not glare at Wesley. He cleared his throat and shifted uncomfortably on his feet as he looked back at the book.

"Seems mortals are just as protective of their mates," Damon mused.

"Look at each other and concentrate," Wesley instructed.

"Concentrate on what?" I asked as I looked at Mason.

We stared at each other, and I felt like I was falling into his depthless black eyes. It was the same way I'd felt the first time our eyes had met before he'd killed my stepfather. I'd felt it when I met his gaze across the club when he was just Mason. He always held me captive—Mason or Grim, it didn't matter. It was still him.

"Feeling each other," Wesley said in a low voice. "Feel each other's souls." Mason nodded, and I found myself mimicking his movements. Something small began to move in my chest—a barely there shift. Excitement flooded me. His lips curved, and I knew he could feel it, too.

"You felt it?" I whispered, and he nodded.

"Hush," he said, grinning. "Concentrate." I listened to him, trying to get back into it, but I was too giddy now. I'd felt the tug, or at least the start of it. Was that all Wesley had been talking about? That wasn't so bad.

"Repeat after me," Wesley said. We waited as he cleared his throat and moved his feet apart. The men shifted around us, and I tried to ignore them. I needed to just focus on Mason.

"Fire and warmth," Wesley said.

"Fire and warmth," we repeated together. A slight wind ghosted through the room, and goosebumps rippled across my skin.

"Two eternal souls."

"Two eternal souls."

The wind blew the curtains, allowing some sunlight to peek into the dim room, momentarily blinding me. A howl sounded, whistling like a wind tunnel, and my grip on Mason's hand tightened. The strain in my chest grew stronger, less like a tugging and more like a ripping—a shredding.

"A promised fate," Wesley said, his voice growing louder over the howl of wind.

"A promised fate." My eyes widened as Mason's eyes rolled back. His hand on mine went slack, and panic shot through my chest. What was happening?

"Keep going," Wolfe barked. "Don't stop."

"One soul finding another," Wesley shouted. The wind was becoming louder and faster with each phrase. My hair whipped against my face, sticking to my lips as I stared at Mason, who'd started to shake slightly. My lungs seized, my throat beginning to close.

"Keep going!" Wolfe shouted.

"One soul," I croaked, "finding another." I screamed as something clawed through my chest, ripping me apart from the inside, trying to get free. Mason fell backward, and his back bowed off the floor as he let out an agonized scream. I kept my hand wrapped tightly around his, the pain in my chest almost too much to bear.

"Two becoming one," Wesley continued, his voice barely audible over the wind surrounding us. Books, paintings, glasses—everything flew from their spots and crashed to the floor. I didn't want to keep going. I wanted to check on Mason. He made another heart wrenching sound as he clawed at his throat with his free hand.

Fire erupted in my chest, and that tugging feeling began. I moved instinctively toward Mason and hovered my body over his. I didn't know what I was doing or why, but I pressed my body to his as I said the words.

"Two becoming one." He mumbled them back to me, and tears

pricked at my eyes. I squeezed them shut, forcing myself to be strong, to fight through whatever this was, for him.

"Fire and warmth," Wesley shouted. He stumbled back a step, and Malik caught him, righting him on his feet again. I opened my mouth, ready to speak, when Mason screamed again. I fell to the floor beside him, my chest ripping open as I screamed with him.

"Say it!" Damon shouted. He ducked, barely missing a book as it soared through the air. "Raven, say it!" I clutched at my fiery chest, trying to keep it together, but it was too late.

I felt it.

I was being torn apart.

"Say it!" Wolfe screamed.

"Fire," I cried, my voice barely audible, "and warmth." Tears streamed down my face as I clutched my chest with one hand and held onto Mason's tighter with the other.

"One eternal soul!" Wesley finished. The wind picked up speed, and the men stumbled in the blistering gust. They held onto each other, screaming at me to say the final three words.

Mason let out another roar as he banged his hand on his chest. I couldn't breathe, speak, think—I couldn't do anything except feel my body shred itself from the inside out. I screamed again as more tears streamed down my face. Mason's back bowed again, and I looked at his face, finding it even more screwed up in pain than it had been moments ago.

Chaos erupted around us, not slowing down enough for me to catch a breath and say the final words. I opened my mouth to take a breath, to scream at them to end this when Mason shot upright, his eyes snapping open. He looked frantically around the room, then down at me. His eyes were different. They were still like coal, but they had a fire behind them I'd never seen before.

"One eternal soul," he breathed, staring at me.

Everything dropped to the floor, and the wind immediately died. The pain in my chest loosened, but there was another feeling there, one I couldn't place. It felt like I was being crowded, like I was sharing my body with someone else. I blinked a few times, realizing it was *Mason's soul*. I felt him.

I felt him.

Wesley fell onto a chair and let out a long breath, his arms flung over the sides as he slouched, his hair wild. He looked wrecked. The book dangled from his fingertips as he breathed heavily. I looked at the three men, then back to Mason. He was staring at me like he'd never seen me before.

"It's true," he whispered, then lifted his eyes to Wesley. "It's all true."

"I told you," Wesley said, still breathing heavily.

"You didn't think this was true?" I asked. I was still lying on my back, too exhausted and weak to sit up. He looked back at me, his eyes softer this time.

"I knew you were mine, always mine," he murmured. "But I never thought Reapers could have a soul. When he told me...." He trailed off as he stared back at Wesley.

"He thought we were crazy," Malik finished for him. "You know we're not full of shit now, yeah?"

"Yeah," Mason agreed. He looked down at me, still utterly shocked.

"I fucking told you," Wesley groaned.

29

GRIM

PRESENT

Raven collapsed on the bed as soon as we returned to my bedroom. Her arms were outstretched, her eyes closed, feet planted on the floor. She looked wrecked.

Guilt twisted inside me for lying to her about the test. Okay, it hadn't been a *total* lie—I didn't know exactly what was going to happen, but Wesley warned me that I might have a reaction to it. I'd never felt that amount of pain in my entire fucking existence.

My soul was not only coming back to life, being reclaimed after centuries of disuse, but Raven's soul was attaching itself to mine. Hers was well-used and well-loved. It was painful, feeling every emotion she had. How did she live that way? Is that how all mortals lived? I couldn't remember ever feeling anything that deeply, but my little bird was different, wasn't she? She pretended to not care, to be heartless, like nothing bothered her, but she felt everything.

Now, I felt everything.

I laid beside her and rolled onto my side. Resting my hand on her chest, I closed my eyes and let myself feel the steadiness of her heart beating under my palm. Mindlessly, she put her hand over mine, almost reflexively. It grounded something inside me, some anxiety I didn't know I had.

"I'm still mad at you for lying to me," she whispered, and I stiffened. I knew that was a possibility but figured she'd get over it. I thought she'd realize Mason and Grim were one and the same and give herself entirely to me. I should've known my stubborn girl better than that.

"Why?" I asked, and her eyes peaked open. The red lights reflected off them, dimming some of their hazel color.

"You're seriously asking me that?" She lifted up on her elbows and stared down at me. I blinked at her, waiting for her answer. She laughed humorlessly as she shook her head. "Mason, you lied to me."

"But you're over it," I said, pressing on her chest, trying to get her to lie back again. "You're my soulmate. What does it matter?"

"Because if you lied about this, what else are you lying about? What else *will* you lie about?" Her eyes flicked to mine, and I pressed harder on her chest, shoving her down. I rolled over her, hovering my face above hers.

"I didn't lie to you because I wanted to," I growled. "I lied because I didn't have a choice." She rolled her eyes and turned her face away from me. Gripping her jaw, I roughly yanked her head straight, forcing her to look at me again. "You will look at me when I speak to you."

"I will do whatever the fuck I want," she snapped, shoving at my chest. "Get off me, Grim." I smirked at her.

"Oh, now you want Grim?" I asked, dropping my voice. I pressed my body harder onto hers and forced my thigh between her legs, pressing it firmly against her pussy.

"Not now," she said, shoving me harder. She squirmed, trying to get out from under me.

"That's it, baby. Fight me. You know it turns me on." I dipped down, pressing my lips to her neck. Her body trembled as she bunched my shirt tightly in her fists. "Come on, push me off. You can do it, can't you?" She tried, her elbows shaking with the effort. I laughed huskily in her ear before pressing my thigh against her pussy again, grinding against her. She whimpered, and I grinned against her skin.

"Get off." Her voice was weak, just like her effort. "Please, Grim."

"Uh-uh," I chided. "What do you call me?" I dragged my tongue along her throat, and her eyes rolled back. Her lips parted, and a small

158

breath left her. She needed a distraction, a way to forget about everything that happened today, since she'd come to this realm. I could give it to her. "Raven, what do you call me?"

"Master," she gritted out, her jaw clenching.

"Good girl," I purred. She melted under me at that, her legs widening slightly. Oh, she liked praise, my little bird. I ran my hand along her thigh, pushing her t-shirt up as I went, bunching it around her hips. She gripped my hand, her eyes locking with mine.

"I'm still mad at you," she said. I lifted my head and grinned.

"So, fuck me until you're not mad anymore." Her hand tightened on mine, but I easily pushed my fingers under her panties, finding her wet.

"I'm serious," she whimpered as I dragged my finger along her slit. She tried to keep her face blank, but I could see the way her lips parted as I brushed my fingertip lightly over her clit, barely teasing her.

"I am, too." I lowered my mouth to hers slowly, giving her plenty of time to turn away. She didn't. I pressed my lips to hers, kissing her languidly, deeply, our tongues pressing together as I stroked her swollen clit.

Her thighs trembled as her pleasure rose, but I wasn't ready to let her come. I wanted her a dripping, crying mess, begging for me. I wanted to feel her come on my cock, fucking explode on it, squeeze me until I couldn't move inside her anymore.

"More," she whimpered when I pulled my hand away. I ignored her as I roughly shoved two fingers into her mouth, gagging her. Her eyes widened slightly, tears already forming in the corners.

"Take it," I growled, thrusting my fingers in and out of her mouth, pressing them into the back of her throat. "Think you can take my cock down your throat, little bird? Or am I too big for you?"

Her eyes narrowed at the challenge, and I pressed my fingers deeper. If my dick was in her mouth, I wouldn't be gentle, and she needed to know that. I would take everything from her, just like I took her ass and pussy. I needed to claim her throat.

I removed my fingers and wiped them across her face. She squeezed her eyes shut, letting me do it as she breathed deeply. I knew if I touched her cunt, I'd find her soaked. I kept my hands and legs far away from her, not wanting her to find any relief.

Pushing to my feet, I pulled my shirt off. She watched me, her eyes hooded as they roamed over my chest and abs. I couldn't help but flex for her, show her what she owned. I opened my belt, whipping it off in a fluid motion. Her eyes flared with heat, and I smirked at her.

"On your knees," I said as I snapped my fingers and pointed to the floor. She hesitated before sliding from the bed. She stared up at me, her big eyes full of trust, even if she was still pissed at me. She'd get over it. I looped my belt lightly around her neck and gave it a gentle tug. "Crawl."

She dropped onto her hands and followed me further back from the bed on her makeshift leash. A sick, fucked up part of me was rock hard at making her do this—crawl for me like a fucking dog. Fuck, it was hot. Her on her knees, a belt around her little throat...fuck.

I crouched and gripped the neck of her t-shirt, easily ripping it in half. She gasped, her eyes wide as she stared down at her now-exposed body. I yanked her bra down, letting her breasts spill out. Groping them roughly, I tweaked her nipples until she cried out.

"You're going to suck my cock like a good little slut, right? No teeth?" I asked, digging my nails into her skin. Her chest rose and fell rapidly as she tried to breathe through the pain.

"Yes, Master," she cried.

"Use teeth, and what will I do?" I asked, twisting her nipples further. She hissed and arched her back, wincing slightly.

"What?" she whispered.

"Knock them out of your pretty fucking head," I said before pressing my lips roughly to hers and pushing to my feet. She gaped up at me. I wouldn't hurt her unless I was fucking her. She knew that, but the threat still lingered in the air, making my dick that much fucking harder.

It was fucked—*I* was fucked—but I never claimed to be a good man.

"Keep your legs spread," I said, shoving my booted foot between her thighs. She slowly widened them, her hands on her thighs as she peered up at me. The red LED light glowed on her creamy skin, illuminating

160

her. "Open your mouth, little bird." I gripped the belt in my hand, wrapping it around my knuckles and tugging roughly. She jerked forward and tipped her head back more, keeping her eyes locked on mine.

I bent slightly, and I knew she didn't know what was coming. When I spat in her mouth, her eyes flared, and I swear I saw a smirk form on her open mouth. "Swallow," I commanded, and she did. *Instantly.* Fuck, she was killing me. "Good little whore." I patted her cheek as I stood again, moving my hand to the top of my jeans.

She waited eagerly, licking her lips as I slowly unbuttoned them and lowered my zipper. Her eyes dropped, and I jerked the belt, forcing her back to me. I wanted all of her attention on me. I wanted to see her face, her eyes, her mouth—I wanted to watch her when I shoved my dick down her throat.

I shoved the waistband of my boxers down just enough to grip my dick and pull it out. I rubbed the tip against her cheek, precum leaking and smearing along her skin. She stared up at me, not moving or saying a word—I wasn't sure she was even breathing.

"Is this what you want?" I muttered. She barely nodded as she licked her lips again. "Come get it." Her mouth opened wide, and, using the belt, I guided her to my cock. She sucked my head into her hot, wet mouth and moaned, her eyes rolling back. "That good, baby? You like how your Master's cock tastes?" She nodded around me, her eyes never leaving mine.

She couldn't get much more than my head into her mouth, but it felt so fucking good, I didn't care. Her tongue lapped at me, flicking over my slit and making my grip on the belt tighten.

"Eyes on me," I grunted, thrusting my hips forward. "Open your mouth. I need down your throat." Tears streamed from her eyes as she tried to widen her mouth. Her teeth scraped along my dick, making me groan at the sharp bite. Fuck. My head probed the back of her mouth, barely touching her throat, making her gag. "That's it. Take it, little bird."

Her legs drifted closed, and I shoved my foot between them, forcing them back open. She whimpered as she pressed her pussy against my boot. Her hips rolled as she humped it, chasing her pleasure as I fucked her mouth.

"Dirty fucking bitch," I laughed. I tangled my other hand in her hair and pulled her head back, angling her so I could slide my cock in deeper. "Humping my shoe like a fucking whore." Her brows tightened as she moved her hips faster, her nails digging into her thighs as I used her mouth. Saliva and tears dripped from her face, sliding down her body. "Relax your throat. That's it. That's fucking it." I slid in deeper, feeling her throat stretch around my thick cock. It tightened as she gagged, trying to push me out, but I held myself there, forcing her to take it.

She wrapped her hands around my leg, her fingers digging into my skin as she rode my shoe faster. "Don't you dare fucking come." I gripped her hair tighter. "Dirty sluts don't get to come." I pulled my cock out slightly, skull-fucking her faster and harder. She didn't have any choice but to take it, and the stinging bite of her nails digging into my skin urged me on.

A part of me worried I was being too rough. I worried I should ease up and let her get used to having a cock my size in her mouth, but the way her eyes shone, how her pussy leaked all over my fucking shoe—she didn't need *easy*. She needed rough. Animalistic.

Without warning, I pulled my dick from her mouth and threw her back on the floor. She landed with a hard thud as she gasped for air. Her legs fell open as she tried to slide her fingers under the belt around her neck, but I yanked on it, tightening it, forcing her to let out a panicked gasp.

Kneeling in front of her, I forced her legs open wider and grabbed her panties. Pushing them to the side, I leaned over her, and without warning, shoved inside her. She screamed, her voice raspy from the brutal throat fucking she'd just had.

I fucked her into the floor as she clawed at my back. Her pussy clamped around my dick, and I pulled out before she could come. She cried out in protest, and when I slapped her across the face, her eyes widened in shock.

"I said you can't come," I growled as I slammed back inside her. "If you do," I pulled almost all the way out, "you won't sit for a month. I'll blister your ass." I bottomed out and she screamed, her back arching up into me.

Tightening the belt around her throat, her face and chest started to turn red. Saliva poured from her mouth as she silently screamed. I fucked her harder, watching her eyes go bloodshot.

"Pass out," I grunted. "Let me use your unconscious body." She turned wide-eyed to me with a look on her face I couldn't totally decipher. I leaned back on my knees and wrapped both hands around her throat, squeezing.

Her body bucked under me as she clawed at my hands. "Grim," she croaked, her voice barely a breath. I squeezed harder, watching her eyes turn unfocused. Her pussy tightened around my cock as I slowly slid in and out of her. My hands shook as I choked her, waiting for her eyes to close.

She looked at me again, a slight grin on her face before her eyes rolled back. Her body went limp, and I immediately removed my hands from her throat. I checked her pulse, finding her heart beating fast under my fingers. A twinge of guilt twisted inside me, but it was quickly overpowered by the need to defile her helpless body.

Throwing her legs over my arms, I held them out and watched my cock slide in and out of her sloppy, swollen cunt. She was still squeezing around me, even in her unconscious state. Her tits bounced with each hard thrust, my dick hitting all the way inside her. She was going to be sore when she woke up. I'd never been this deep inside her, but fuck, it felt good. I'd get her an ice pack or whatever the fuck she needed for letting me do this later. Right now, I needed to fuck her until I filled her with my cum. I wanted her to be full forever.

Pulling out, I stood and lifted her hips with me. I balanced her on her neck and shoulders, keeping her lower body in the air as I drove my cock deep inside her. My eyes rolled back at the new angle. My thumb found her clit, and I began to stroke. I didn't know if she'd come like this, but I wanted to find out.

My thighs burned with my movements, thrusting in and out of her tight pussy, but I wouldn't give up this position if my fucking life depended on it. Her body was pliable, and I could hold her and use her however I wanted. She looked so fucking helpless, laying there with her tits crowding her face, pussy abused by my big cock, that I started to swell.

I stroked her clit faster and her pussy spasmed around me, not strong like her usual orgasms, but I was betting it was at least a small one. I couldn't hold back much longer, so I'd fucking take it. Gripping her legs, I lifted her more, practically off the ground, holding her upside down as I rammed my dick inside her.

"Fuck, yeah," I grunted, watching her pussy stretch around me. Her arms lay behind her, moving with every thrust, her tits bouncing and hitting her chin. Her mouth hung open, her eyes fluttering as I pounded into her. My fingers gripped her soft thighs as my cock thickened. I slammed into her a few more times, then stilled as I came with a low growl.

My cum overflowed around my cock, making her little pussy even sloppier than before. I stared down at her used body, her shirt torn open, the belt slack around her neck, and hair fanned out around her. My dick twitched inside her, ready for more.

Slowly, I pulled out and watched more cum spill down her legs. Carefully, I lifted her into my arms and carried her to my bed. I grabbed my shirt from the floor and used it to clean up the best I could, then removed her tattered clothing and wrapped the blankets tightly around her chilled body.

I removed my boots and jeans, leaving my boxers on, and slid into bed behind her. I held her tightly to my chest, keeping my arms wrapped around her body. Her chest rose and fell in steady breaths, and some of that lingering guilt began to seep away. I wanted to feel worse about using her, but I didn't. I squeezed her tighter, anchoring her body to mine, inhaling her familiar, safe scent, and closed my eyes.

I felt grounded for the first time.

She shifted slightly and rested her hand over mine on her belly. I stroked my thumb back and forth, trying to chase away the wishes of wanting to watch it grow with my child. It was impossible, and I knew that. Reapers couldn't have kids, and even if they could, I wouldn't want to bring one into this fucked up world. Even though it was wishful thinking, I wanted to share that with her, to have something purely her and me mixed forever.

She sighed and settled deeper into the crook of my arm, and I held her tighter, letting her feel the safety of my body around hers. Even if I'd just fucked her senseless, I'd take care of her—she knew that. I pressed a kiss to the back of her neck and let myself drift to sleep.

30

RAVEN

PRESENT

My pussy fucking hurt. Not just my pussy, my entire body. My neck was stiff, my shoulders ached, my thighs were sore, and I felt like I'd done a million crunches. I groaned as I tried to move, but a heavy weight kept me down.

"Don't move." Mason's gravely morning voice hit me, and I paused. My eyes flew open, memories of last night flooding me.

"What the fuck happened?" I asked, pushing at his arm. He left it draped over my waist and curled his body tighter around mine. "Did I pass out?"

"Yeah," he grumbled, nestling his face into my neck.

"And did you—" I hesitated. I knew the answer before he said it.

"Keep fucking you? Yeah, I did." He didn't sound apologetic in the least as he snuggled closer. "Filled you with my cum, too."

"Mason!" I realized I was naked, pressing against his mostly naked body. "I can't believe you did that."

"You didn't want it?" He pushed himself up on his elbow and gently moved my hair from my face. Peering down at me, he looked worried. His eyes were gentle, his touch on my face soft, but his expression was worried. I shrugged.

"Was it hot?" I asked, and he laughed.

"Hottest fucking thing I've ever done," he said as he kissed my forehead. "And I'm ancient." He plopped back down with a sigh and gathered me back in his arms. He tensed for a moment. "You're really okay with it? Probably should've had this conversation beforehand. I just assumed; all the times I'd said something about it, you looked like you'd want it. If I crossed a line—"

"It's okay," I said softly as I stroked his arm. "I'm a bit sore." I glared at him over my shoulder. "Next time, be a little gentler, yeah?" He kissed the back of my head, holding his lips there for a long moment, then pulled away.

"Sorry," he mumbled. "This mean you're not mad at me anymore?" My heart dipped. I'd forgotten I was mad at him.

"Mason," I sighed as I rolled onto my back. My breasts were fully exposed, and I lifted the blanket to cover them. I thought better of it and began to move, then winced when my entire body protested.

"Don't move, little bird," he said again, his arms tightening around me. "Let me serve you today. You're on bed rest." I glanced at him again. Did he feel guilty?

"I need to go home," I said. "Kali is probably losing her fucking mind." The thought of my best friend sent a bolt of panic through me. What if Eddy went looking for me? What if he'd done something to her? What if that serial killer got to her? Fuck. I needed to see her. *Now.*

I ignored my muscles' protests as I slid out of Mason's arms and scooted across his large bed. "I sent Caden to check on her." Mason stared at me from where he reclined, one arm behind his head, the other still outstretched from where I'd been laying on it.

"She doesn't know Caden," I snapped. "How do I get home?" He shrugged, looking arrogant. Picking up the pillow I'd been laying on, I threw it at his face. He swatted it to the floor and glared at me.

"Don't throw shit at me," he growled.

"Then tell me how the fuck I get home," I demanded as I stood. I looked around his semi-destroyed room, trying to find the clothes I'd discarded days ago. "Where are my clothes?" I mumbled as I hobbled around the bed.

"Lay the fuck down, Raven," he barked.

"Mason—"

"Stop calling me that!"

"It's your fucking name!" I shouted. "Take me home!"

"No!" He pushed himself out of bed, his chest heaving. "You're staying here with me." I opened my mouth, then closed it.

"I want to go home," I said, and he shrugged. He fucking shrugged like it wasn't a big deal. I felt ridiculous arguing with him while I was naked, but I didn't know where my clothes were, and I would feel more ridiculous trying to cover myself while arguing.

"Get back in bed." He jerked his head, and I folded my arms over my chest. His eyes immediately dropped to my tits, and I let out a laugh.

"Reaper or mortal, you're all the same, huh?" His eyes lifted to mine, a stupid smirk on his face.

"Not my fault you have nice tits," he said, taking a step toward me. "Come on, baby. Get back in bed. Let me take care of you today."

"How about you take me home?" I demanded. He took a deep breath, his hands clenching into fists at his sides.

"Raven."

"Mason," I growled, stepping toward him. "Kali is probably losing her shit, if she's not dead—" My voice broke, and his face softened in understanding.

"Oh, little bird," he cooed. "She's not dead. I told you Caden is with her." I shook my head as I roughly swiped at my cheek.

"I'm supposed to be with her," I said. "Please, Mason. Please just take me home." I felt the resignation before he answered.

"Alright," he sighed. "But I'm staying with you."

"Whatever," I said, my shoulders slumping. I didn't care, as long as I could see Kali. "By home, I mean her place. Can you—" I waved my hand around the room. "Evaporate us there, or whatever the hell you do?" He laughed as he wrapped his arms around my waist and pulled me to him. Gently, he pressed a kiss to my forehead.

"Are you going to puke everywhere again?" he teased. I swatted at his bare chest, and he kissed my forehead again. "Get dressed. Just wear something of mine. I'll evaporate us to her place when you're ready." He rolled his eyes at the word *evaporate*, but what else could I call it?

Mason chose to shower with me "to save time and water." I was surprised he didn't try anything, even with a hard-on. He washed my hair and body, then his, and helped dry me off. He didn't let his hands or eyes linger.

I hadn't fully believed him when he said he wanted to take care of me today. Honestly, I didn't fully know how I felt about it. I'd never had anyone take care of me, and to think this giant, scary Reaper was going to be the one to do it? Yeah, I didn't believe it.

He gave me his clothes to wear again, and I didn't miss the possessive, cocky way he looked at me in them. A twisted part of me liked wearing his clothes. Maybe I was just as much of a caveman as he was.

"Ready?" he asked as he wrapped his arm around me. "I can't promise this time will be any better." I nodded a few times and swallowed hard.

"This is the only way back home, right? We can't take a cab?" I laughed nervously, and his arm tightened.

"Afraid not." He sounded genuinely sympathetic, which I appreciated. I didn't know what I'd do if he mocked me or made me feel stupid for not enjoying his preferred form of travel.

"We're still going to talk about you lying," I said, and he nodded a few times before kissing my temple.

"I know I fucked up, Raven," he muttered. "I promise it wasn't malicious. I just saw you that night, and after what happened at that building...." He trailed off as he shook his head. "Maybe I am a monster, but I wasn't going to let you leave that club with anyone else. By the time I had you, I needed to be inside you. I needed to claim you. I needed to make you mine. I won't apologize for that." I flicked my eyes to his.

"Why didn't you tell me? The second time you came as Mason? The times you came as Grim? You could've told me," I said softly, resting my hand on his chest. He wrapped his other arm around my waist, holding me tightly, like he was afraid I'd disappear. He hesitated, then let out a long breath.

"I was scared," he whispered, so softly I almost didn't hear him. "I was scared I'd lose you." My chest ached. It wasn't my ache, though. It was his. I pressed harder against him, wanting to be absorbed into him.

"I wouldn't have gone anywhere," I whispered. "I'd tried to get you back for so long. I just wanted you, Grim." He closed his eyes and breathed deeply. "It hurts that you didn't tell me the truth. It hurts that I found out the way I did." He nodded a few times, and when he opened his eyes, the look in them gutted me.

"I know I fucked up," he said. His face turned fierce. "I promise to make it up to you. I know words don't mean shit, but I'll never lie to you again." I searched his eyes, to sense if he was lying, but his gaze was unwavering.

"Don't let me down, Mason." He lowered his mouth and kissed me hard.

"Never," he muttered, pressing his forehead to mine. "If I ever do, you have full permission to choke me until I pass out."

"Will your dick stay hard?" I asked, and he choked on a laugh as he pulled away.

"We'll figure out a way." He tucked my hair behind my ear, his eyes soft as he smiled down at me. "Am I forgiven?" I patted his firm chest as I sighed.

"For now," I said. "Now, let's evaporate to Kali's and hope she hasn't killed Caden." He chuckled and kissed me again as the world began to fade.

31

GRIM

PRESENT

Evaporating was a good word to describe what happened. We disappeared and reappeared somewhere else, evaporating into thin air. I'd long since gotten used to the side effects, but Raven was still getting used to it. I felt terrible doing this to her, but it was the only way we could move between realms, and it was the fastest way to travel.

Maybe I needed to just walk or buy a fucking car for her realm so she'd stop getting sick. She was clutching my shirt in her trembling fists, her eyes squeezed shut as she tried to breathe through her nausea. I soothingly rubbed her back, trying to comfort her through it. At least she didn't vomit this time. That was progress.

"You're alright, baby," I murmured. She shook her head, grumbling something under her breath. I tried not to laugh. She was such a grumpy little bird.

Suddenly, a scream ripped from behind Kali's door. Raven's body tensed, her rolling nausea and lingering pain forgotten as she lept from my arms and wrapped her hand around the doorknob. I yanked her back, pushing her behind me.

"Do not—" I pointed at her, "ever do that again." Her eyes were wide, and her chest heaved as she gaped at me. Then, Kali screamed again, and Raven snapped out of it. She tried to move forward, but I pushed her back, pinning her to the opposite wall. "Stay there. I'll check it out."

"But—"

"Raven, I'm not risking your life. You're staying right there." She clenched her jaw as she glared at me. That was fine. She could be pissed at me, but at least she'd be safe. "Stay there. I mean it." I shoved off the wall and moved toward the door.

Glass crashed, and Raven inhaled sharply. Fuck. With a quick glance at her, I found her eyes wide. Her fear was hot in my chest, making my heart beat wildly. I needed to calm myself; I wasn't used to feeling like this. I took a deep breath, lifted my boot, and kicked the center of Kali's door.

The wood splintered as the door flew open, and the commotion immediately stopped. I stormed in, ready to grab Kali and Raven and get us the fuck out of there, but I froze and took in what was happening.

"What the fuck are you doing?" I barked as I stomped toward Caden. He had his hands up, his back pressed to the wall, and his eyes wide as he stared down at Kali. It should've been comical, a seven-foot Reaper looking terrified of a five-foot-something girl throwing shit at him, but Raven was scared, and that pissed me off.

"Who are you?" she screamed, her entire body shaking as she watched me. I ignored her as I gripped his shirt and hauled him away from the wall.

"Leave," I growled.

"You told me to keep an eye on her!" he said, throwing his arm toward Kali.

"Yeah, not to scare her!" I shook him roughly, and he shoved at my arm.

"I didn't mean to!"

"Why did you take your glamour off?" I snapped, and he shoved me again.

"Mason?" Kali said in a small voice.

"Raven!" I called over my shoulder, not looking to see if she was coming. "Come get your friend." There was a shuffling, and the girls' voices wound through the apartment. When a door closed, I shoved Caden against the wall. "Why did you melt your glamour?"

"I didn't," he said, smoothing his shirt out, looking as cocky as ever.

"Then how did she see you?" I threw my arm behind me, my blood boiling. "You were just supposed to make sure she was safe!"

"I didn't take my glamour off!" he shouted as he pushed me again. "It just—" He shrugged and waved his hands around, looking flustered, his usual cool demeanor slipping. "I don't fucking know! It just melted."

"Melted?" I repeated in a low voice. "What do you mean it just melted? That's impossible." He shrugged. "Caden."

"I don't know, Mase," he sighed. "I was sitting on her couch while she watched TV. One second, I was invisible and laughing at the stupid fucking movie. The next, she was screaming and throwing a lamp at me."

I began to pace, the glass crunching under my boots. Holding my fist to my mouth, I scrunched my eyebrows as my mind raced. Would Wesley know why this happened?

"What else were you doing?" I asked, looking at him. He shrugged and ran his hands through his hair.

"Nothing," he said.

"Was that the first time you sat beside her?" I turned fully toward him and folded my arms over my chest. He shook his head and rubbed the back of his neck, looking chagrined. "Caden, what the fuck did you do?" I groaned as I dropped my head back.

"I've been sleeping beside her," he muttered, his face bright red. "I'm pretty much always right next to her." I scrubbed my hand over my face.

"You've been sleeping with her," I repeated. "Why?"

"I don't know," he said, turning his back to me. "I just can't leave her alone. It's killing me that she's in that room without me." I glanced over my shoulder. Yeah, I understood. I didn't like that Raven was in there alone without me, either. But—

"You think she's—"

"My soulmate," he breathed. He turned toward me and nodded. "Yeah."

173

"Caden, that's fucking insane." I shook my head and let out a long breath. "Do you know how insane that is?"

"Why?" he snapped. "You have one. Why can't I?"

"What're the odds that yours is Raven's best friend?" I said gently. "Come on, man."

"Fuck you." He started for the bedroom door, and I grabbed his arm. "She's mine."

"She's not yours," I said. He tried to shove me off, but I gripped his arm tighter. "Caden, I'm serious. Leave her alone. I shouldn't have sent you."

"She's *mine*." He turned toward me and stepped closer, getting up as close as he could. "Let me go, brother." I rolled my head once, letting my neck crack. Things with Caden were never easy, and if he had it in his fucking head that Kali was somehow his soulmate, then there was no going back for him. Even if he did the fucking test Raven and I did, and it said they weren't connected, he'd refuse to believe it. He'd probably kidnap the poor girl. Fuck.

"I can't let you scare Raven's best friend," I said in a low voice.

"I'm not going to scare her," he growled, shoving me again.

"Cade—"

"Mason." He shoved me harder, forcing me back a step. "I'm going to hit you." I sighed, trying to rein in some of my anger.

"Just head home," I sighed. "Let Raven talk to her." Some of his anger seeped from him as he glanced at the closed bedroom door.

"I fucked up," he whispered. I clapped him on the shoulder but didn't agree or disagree. Yeah, he kind of fucked up, but whatever. We all had at one point or another. "I need to make sure she's okay."

"She's probably scared shitless," I said as he scowled at me. "She didn't recognize you. I thought you two hooked up." He shook his head.

"We just had a drink, then she went home." I narrowed my eyes at him as he shrugged. "I was worried about Brody. I wasn't interested in chasing tail." Letting out a long breath, I nodded.

I'd forgotten about Brody. Well, I hadn't forgotten about him, but he hadn't been at the forefront of my mind, not with everything happening. Shit. I needed to find him.

174

"You know where he is?" I asked, and he shrugged.

"No fucking idea."

The bedroom door opened, and we turned our attention to the girls as they emerged. Kali's face was red and blotchy, her blonde hair twisted into a messy bun. Raven gave me a weak smile, then her eyes traveled to Caden and she scowled. I rubbed my hand over my mouth to hide my grin.

"Caden," Kali said in a small voice. She was tucked into Raven's side, looking tiny beside her. Raven was fiercely protective of her friend, and maybe it made me a fucked up perv to find that so hot, but the intense glare she had on her face made me want to bend her over and fuck her.

"Hey, Kali," Caden said, taking a small step forward. Red crept up his neck as he considered her. She tried to step back, but Raven kept her still.

"He won't hurt you. Right?" She glared at my brother. I was shocked at her bravery, but I shouldn't have been. This was Raven. I didn't know if she felt braver because I was there and she knew I'd protect her, or if she really didn't give a fuck. Probably the latter.

Caden sent her an alarmed look, then stared at Kali. "Of course, I won't hurt you."

"How did you—" She glanced over her shoulder at Raven and sighed. "You're not...human?" She looked up at me, but I kept my face blank. I didn't know what all Raven had told her, and I didn't know how to navigate this. Caden and I glanced at each other. We'd never told mortals who we were and let them live.

"They're Reapers," Raven said softly. Their hands were clutched tightly together, and a surge of possessiveness shot through me. Yeah, I knew Kali was her best friend, but Raven was mine, and I didn't want anyone touching her. From the way Caden bristled beside me, I thought he was feeling the same way.

"Reapers," Kali repeated. "You're going to kill us." Tears welled in her eyes, and Caden stiffened.

"Shit." He took a step forward, but I gripped his elbow, keeping him beside me. This was so fucking awkward, standing on opposite sides of the apartment from each other. "We're not going to kill you."

Her trembling was a normal reaction, a reaction I knew Caden was used to, but I knew he didn't want to see her have it. Shit, she didn't mean anything to me, and it still upset me that she was reacting like this.

"They're good guys," Raven said, her eyes clashing with mine. Something swirled in my chest, an emotion I couldn't decipher, and I pushed my brows together. Her eyes fell away, and coldness bloomed through my body. Did she not believe we were good guys?

Kali gave us a shy look, her eyes lingering on Caden. "You've been here...spying on me?" He stiffened.

"Not spying," he said. "Just watching." She paled further, and when she stepped back, Raven let her. I let out a long breath, trying to calm myself.

"Maybe you should go," Raven said. I thought she was talking to Caden, but when her eyes didn't leave mine, my anger snapped.

"No."

"Mason, I need to be with my friend. Go home."

Caden's head swiveled between us, his eyes wide as he waited for my reaction. She didn't want me here. What the fuck had changed in the fifteen minutes we'd been here? Was she ashamed of me? Of us? I didn't know what I'd do if that was the case. If she didn't want me. I wouldn't let her go.

"Raven," I said in warning. She sighed tiredly, then glanced at Kali, her shoulders slumping slightly.

"Please?" Her eyes searched mine. I didn't know what she was looking for, but I'd give her whatever it was. Whatever would make her feel sure about us, I'd give her. "Just go."

"I'm coming back in an hour," I said. She rubbed her forehead.

"Come to my place tonight." I shook my head.

"You're not leaving here without me." Caden shuffled his feet, his eyes locked on Kali.

"I can stay if you two need to work this out," he offered. Kali took a step back, her eyes wide.

"No," Raven and I snapped at the same time. Caden lifted his hands placatingly.

"Just an offer, fuck," he muttered.

176

"Go home, Caden," I grumbled, my eyes staying on Raven.

"You should go, too," she said softly. "Please, Mason." I glared at her, but she stared impassively back. Did she not care about being away from me? Did it not bother her like it bothered me? I roughly cleared my throat, not wanting to argue with her in front of an audience.

"Fine," I ground out. "I'll be at your place in two hours."

"Three," she said, and I let out a hard breath.

"Two and a half." She narrowed her eyes. A challenge. Then she sighed.

"Two and a half," she repeated. I grabbed Caden's arm, and before he could protest, we disappeared.

32
RAVEN
PRESENT

"I can't believe this," Kali said as she paced. She ran her fingers through her hair and tugged lightly on it. "Mason is—is—the fucking Grim Reaper?"

"Well," I sighed, "a Reaper. There are multiple." She blanched. "And Caden..."

"Is really his brother," I said hurriedly. "And also a Reaper."

"You don't think they'll kill us?" She turned, giving me a bewildered look. "You get yourself into some shit, girl. I swear." We stared at each other for a moment, then laughed. Our laughter carried on until we were rolling around on her bed, tears leaking from our eyes.

It wasn't because we thought the situation was funny—far from it. But with every emotion fighting inside me, inside both of us, it was either crying or laughing to let them out.

"They're not going to hurt us," I confirmed, rolling onto my side. "They're—Mason—" I didn't know how to explain or where to start. What could I say? That we were soulmates? She'd think I'd really lost my mind. I was there, and I still barely believed it.

"What?" She rested her head on her bent arm as she stared at me. "Mason, what?"

"He's kind of my soulmate." I winced as the words left my mouth.

She blinked at me. I was throwing a lot of information at her, and she was handling it surprisingly well.

"Soulmate," she said slowly, drawing the word out. "You think your soulmate is The Grim Reaper."

"He's not The Grim Reaper," I grumbled. "He's a Reaper."

"Same difference." She pushed to her feet and strode to the door. "I need something to drink." I followed her to the kitchen, watching her as she padded around, grabbing wine glasses from the cabinet and a cheap bottle from the fridge. "Explain." I waited until she was done pouring so she wouldn't drop the bottle.

I told her everything—how Mason killed my stepfather, how he came back into my life a few months ago, how Mason and Grim were the same person. I told her about the test and everything he'd told me. It felt good to finally talk about Grim. Even if she knew about Mason, she didn't know everything. Now, she did, and she was staring at me like I'd lost my mind.

Maybe I had, but I don't think I cared.

I WAS RUNNING LATE AND MASON WAS GOING TO BE PISSED. It had taken longer to convince Kali everything was fine and that she didn't need to be scared of Caden than I thought it would. She ended up drinking most of the bottle of wine herself, and after tucking her into bed, I quickly cleaned up the broken lamp and left.

Now, I was hauling ass to my apartment. Kail lived close but not close enough to get there before Mason. I glanced at my phone, seeing it was fifteen minutes past when I said I'd meet him. Shit.

He could just evaporate here, couldn't he? I didn't know how his Spidey-Senses worked or how he knew where to find me. Surely, he could evaporate from my apartment and appear beside me, right? He could find me.

I hurried down the sidewalk, feeling ridiculous walking the streets in Mason's t-shirt as a dress. My heels clacked against the pavement, and I wrapped my arms tighter around myself. The weather was starting to get cooler, and I really needed my coat, but I'd left it in Reaper World.

Kali had taken everything surprisingly well. By well, I meant she hadn't tried to call the psych ward, so she was either too drunk to do it, or she actually believed me. If Caden hadn't magically appeared beside her, I don't think she would've been so easy to convince, but she seemed to believe me, even if she thought it was a little weird that I was choosing to hang around Reapers.

It wasn't that I was choosing to hang around them. Okay, I was, but Mason was my soulmate, so it's not like I had a lot of choice in the matter. I had to be with him, and he was a Reaper. Reapers tended to hang around other Reapers so...

A gloved hand landed over my mouth, and I stifled a scream. I was pulled back, my heels dragging along the pavement as my attacker shoved me face-first against an alley wall. It took my brain a moment to realize what the fuck was happening, and I began to swing blindly backward, hoping to hit something.

"Stop." The voice was one I recognized, but it didn't belong to who I wanted it to belong to. Instead of stopping, more panic rose in my chest, and I began fighting harder. My face scraped against the brick, and I squeezed my eyes shut, trying to hold in whatever sound of pain was about to escape me.

"Get. Off. Me." I tried to push myself off the wall, but he pinned me harder against it, his hand tight around the back of my neck.

"Stop moving." I glanced over my shoulder, finding my assailant with his hood up and face mostly covered. I could feel his eyes on me. "It'll be easier for us both if you stop moving." His voice was low, menacing, but I shook off my fear. I needed Mason.

"Fuck you," I spat. I kicked back, landing a hit to some part of his leg. He grunted and his grip tightened, his hand reaching up to pin my shoulder.

"I said stop!" His spit hit the side of my face, and I squeezed my eyes and mouth shut. It was disgusting. He was disgusting. Fuck. Where was Mason?

My phone. It was still clutched tightly in my hand. He wouldn't let me use it, though. We were too close for me to do it discreetly, but I'd have to try. I dropped my arm between me and the wall and, as quickly as I could, found Mason's name.

"Hey!" He reached for my phone, but I jerked it out of the way. My hand shook as I pressed the call button, then the phone fell to the ground. Eddy's foot landed on top of it, the sickening sound of glass crunching making my stomach twist. Had Mason gotten the call? Probably not. Shit. Shit, shit, shit.

"Please," I pleaded, tears pricking my eyes. His foot landed on the phone again and the alley went dark.

There was really no way out of this. I was stuck in a random part of town, pinned to a dirty wall, alone with fucking Eddy. I was going to die. This was how I was going to die.

I just hoped Mason could find my soul again.

33

GRIM

PRESENT

Where the fuck was she? She was supposed to be here twenty minutes ago, and I was starting to get pissed. Well, I was more worried than pissed, but pissed was still an emotion I felt toward her at the moment.

I stomped back and forth across her tiny apartment, my hand clutched in front of my face. Maybe I should just go to Kali's place. She was probably still there and lost track of time. My phone vibrated, and a strange mix of relief and annoyance flooded me.

"Little bird," I growled. There was a shuffling and my stomach immediately twisted. Something was wrong.

"Hey!"

Fuck.

That voice.

I knew that voice.

"Please." Her voice shredded me, fucking shredded me, then enraged me.

There was more shuffling, then a crunching sound before the line went dead. Shit. What the fuck? How the hell had she ended up with Eddy? I knew I shouldn't have left her. I knew I should've sent Caden home on his own and stayed. Even if she was going to be pissed, she would've been safe. Fuck.

After tonight, she was never leaving my sight again.

It took me longer than I'd wanted to find her. I could feel her, but I couldn't find her. Her emotions were all over the place, so it made mine just as erratic. When I finally calmed down enough to concentrate, I ended up on a dark street.

Fucking Raven.

Didn't she know not to walk alone at night? I should've met her at Kali's apartment. I'd made so many mistakes in my time, but this had to be the biggest and worst fucking one. I sent Caden a text, telling him and Rage to meet me, then searched the street again.

"Raven," I called, my voice too loud. There was more shuffling, and my heart twisted. Fear shot through me—mine or hers, or a weird combination of both, I didn't know.

Fuck. Fuck, fuck, fuck. Please let her be alright.

Dread coursed through me as I moved toward the alley. Faintly, I was aware of Caden and Rage appearing behind me, but they stayed back, letting me go after my girl alone.

I didn't want to know what was happening to her. I knew that if she was harmed, I was going to rip this motherfucker's head from his body, and I couldn't do that. I couldn't be sent away again. I couldn't leave her for another fifteen years, maybe longer, but I couldn't let him touch my girl and go on breathing, either.

Turning down the alley, I paused, not fully prepared for what I saw: Raven pinned face-first to the wall. She reared her foot back but didn't hit anything. It was her voice, though, that made me move.

"Let me go," she cried.

That was it.

Those three words were enough to make me want to burn the fucking planet.

I could hear the tears in them, feel her fear and pain in my chest, and I wanted to rip that fucking monster apart with my bare hands. I'd never felt so much rage in my existence, as mortal or Reaper, and in that moment, there was nothing I wanted more than to end every life to protect her from them all.

I stormed toward them, not caring about the sound I made. Maybe I should've so I could've snuck up on him, but I couldn't force myself to be quiet. I couldn't force myself to move slowly.

She cried out, the sound echoing around us. It was full of pain, and I saw fucking red.

Grabbing his shoulder, I yanked him away from her, and she fell to her knees. I didn't have time to check on her. This fucking guy was going to die. I didn't care anymore. I would spend the rest of forever running from the Council if it meant I could kill him.

I shoved him to the ground, his hood falling from his head, but he didn't look afraid of me, not like he should have. Instead, he grinned, a wicked, cold grin that, if I was a lesser man, would've made me second guess myself. But I was a Reaper, and he'd messed with my girl, and now he had to die.

"Mase." Caden's voice hit me, reminding me he and Rage were here too. I didn't look at him. I couldn't take my eyes off the slimy fucker on the ground, still staring at me like he'd somehow won.

Then a cold feeling crept up my spine, and I slowly glanced over my shoulder.

"No," I breathed. "Fuck, no."

Caden was kneeling beside Raven, her body in his arms. Blood was staining his skin—her blood. Too much of it. Too much fucking blood. Her eyes were open but unfocused, her full lips parted slightly, trickles of blood at the corners.

"No," I whispered, moving slowly toward her. Faintly, I felt her drifting from me. I rubbed the center of my chest, trying to grab hold of her, but I couldn't. She was slipping through my fingers, her soul fading with each passing second.

I dropped to my knees, not feeling the concrete bite into them at the impact. This wasn't happening. Her eyes stayed staring ahead, straight up at the starless sky. Couldn't the Universe give her some fucking stars to look at while she died? Couldn't it give her something beautiful for once in her life?

"Little bird," I whispered, my throat tight. A small breath left her open mouth, but her body stayed limp, her eyes unfocused. "Please don't fucking die."

"You need to do it," Rage ordered. "Do it before it's too late."

"I—I can't." My chest was too tight. My throat and body were cramped with pent-up emotion. Eddy was completely forgotten, and if he was still there, I didn't care, not with Raven taking her final breaths, her heart beating for the last time. Not when she was dying. "I can't do it."

"I'll do it," Caden said softly. "I did it for Brody. I can do it now." I shook my head, tears blurring my vision. I didn't want her to go. I didn't know if I'd ever find her soul again.

"Let him." Rage's hand landed on my shoulder, squeezing until the pain forced me to focus. "We'll go home—"

"No," I said abruptly. "She can't travel like this. She—she hates traveling. Just do it here." My brother's exchanged a look, one that pissed me off. "I'll do it." I reached for her, but Caden pulled her away. "Give. Her. To. Me."

The temperature around us dropped, prickling my skin as I glared at my brother. Maybe I couldn't kill him, but I could sure as fuck hurt him. If he pulled my mate away from me again, he would end up limbless.

Death was in the air, lingering close to us. We had to take her soon; if we didn't, her soul would be lost to the In-Between forever. We needed to act quickly. Now. We needed to act now.

"Cade," I growled. "Give her to me."

"I'll do it," he said quickly. "It'll take too much out of you."

"She's mine." I reached for her again, clenching my jaw when I felt how cold her skin was. "I will do it." Again, they shared a look.

I wrenched her from Caden's grasp and held her in my lap. I knew she'd said she wanted to be a Reaper, but that was when she was still a mortal and thought she had a choice. Now she was dying, and her choice was ripped away from her. She might feel differently when she woke and found out she not only could never die, but now had to reap souls. She was going to be the bad guy now.

I stared down at her, feeling torn for the second time in my life. I

185

hated it. I hated feeling unsure. I hated not knowing my next move, not knowing what was coming next. I needed to know. But now, I wasn't worried about my future. I was worried about hers, ours.

What was she going to think? What was she going to feel? Would she hate me for this? At least she'd be alive to hate me. I would have eternity to beg her forgiveness.

"You need to do it now," Rage said again, his voice low.

I laid my hand on her chest, feeling the slow, erratic thump of her heart. It was almost done, only a few more in her before she was gone. Before my little bird was no more. Before she was just another lost soul.

"Now," Rage barked.

Closing my eyes, I focused on her, on her soul—our soul. I didn't know how this would work, turning her while she was my mate, but I was about to find out. Maybe I should've called Wesley. He would've known. The bastard knew everything.

Power surged into my hand as I pressed it harder against her chest. She wasn't strong enough to cry out at the pain, but I knew she felt it. Her face barely twitched in a grimace, her hand lifting then falling limply back to her side.

"I know it hurts, baby," I whispered, "but it has to be done. I'm sorry. I'm so fucking sorry." More power left my body, and she finally grunted, the first sign she was coming back to me.

Tears spilled from the corners of her eyes, some life finally re-entering them. I pressed on her chest harder, feeling a stirring in mine, and nearly sobbed. I was draining fast, but I needed to finish it. I needed to make sure she was one of us.

Her body bucked, her hand lifting and weakly shoving at mine. I held firmly against her, forcing her soul into darkness. I hated to do it, hated doing this to her, but it was the only way. Maybe it was for my own selfish reasons that I wanted to save her, so I could have her forever, but she was mine, dammit, and I needed her.

"Stop!" she screamed, her voice raw and raspy. "Please stop!" It shredded me to hear her scream, to hear her beg like that. I could feel her pain, and I hated being the one causing it. I knew this was why Caden wanted to do it, but she wasn't his. It had to be me.

"Almost done," I gritted out, feeling my energy draining fast. "So close, little bird. Then you'll be one of us."

"No!" Her head thrashed back and forth, but I didn't have the strength to keep her still. I just pressed harder, pouring the last bit of energy I had into her, giving her my power.

She was so close. So fucking close.

Then Caden's hands were on her shoulders, holding her still while Rage soothingly, if not a bit awkwardly, stroked her bloody, sweaty hair. I should've been furious that other men were touching her, but I wasn't. Not at that moment. All I cared about was finishing and letting her heal.

Her body bowed off the ground in a deep bend, her eyes squeezed shut as she let out an ear-piercing howl. Her blood had stopped, and her skin wasn't as deathly pale anymore, but she was still ice cold. Finally, she fell back to the ground, landing roughly on my lap, and let out a long breath.

I felt a shift in my chest, and something I didn't recognize wedged itself in there. A feeling I didn't understand or want to acknowledge, cold and hard and full of pain. But she was alive.

She was a Reaper.

34

RAVEN

PRESENT

"You found him?"

I could barely make out the words, but the voices were clear. My mind was taking too long to decipher what they were saying and who was speaking.

"Yeah, he was at some cabin in fucking Canada," another voice grumbled. "Said he won't come home."

"Fuck."

I groaned, and every cell in my body protested.

"Whoa, little bird." Mason. Grim. He was here. I cracked my eyes open and stared up at the industrial-looking ceiling. The lights were too bright and they seared my eyes. I hissed and tried to lift my arm to cover them, but it felt too heavy. "You're okay."

"I'm okay," I repeated. He chuckled softly before pressing his lips to my forehead. "Where am I?"

"Home," he murmured, his lips still on my skin. "How do you feel?" He pulled away, his brows drawn, and his face etched with worry, more than I'd ever seen.

"I'm fine," I said again. I looked around, finding Caden and another man sitting in chairs across the coffee table from us. "Who are you?" The big tattooed one's face barely shifted.

"Rage."

"That's your name?" I asked. My head was throbbing, and the room was spinning. What happened? How drunk did I get last night?

"Yep," was all he said.

"My other brother," Mason filled in. "You've met him before. You don't remember?" I shook my head, then winced when it felt like my brain bounced off my skull. "It was brief." I closed my eyes, needing the dark.

"What's going on?" I croaked. Mason's hand cupped my face, and I leaned into his cold touch. No, not cold: normal. My eyes snapped open. "You're warm." His eyebrows shot up, and he glanced at his brothers.

"Warm?" he asked cautiously.

"Well, not cold," I shrugged, pressing my cheek harder against his palm. He was always so icy, but his coldness brought me comfort. Where did it go? "You're not as cold as usual."

"What else is different?"

I glanced around the room and paused. Everything was...brighter. The colors were more saturated, the blacks richer. Was that a normal symptom of migraines? Then there was the sound. I could hear...something. It was faint, like a hummingbird whizzing past my head, but constant.

"What's that sound?" I asked, glancing at Mason. His eyes were narrowed as he watched me.

"What sound, little bird? There are lots of them." His mouth tucked up at the corner when I scowled at him.

"The...humming." The guys glanced at each other again, then Caden cleared his throat.

"That'd be our blood."

I snapped my head to him. What the fuck?

"Your blood," I repeated slowly. I was still dreaming, that's what this was. There was absolutely no fucking way I was able to hear someone's blood.

"Yep," he said as he leaned back in the chair. "You can hear it pumping, though our hearts don't beat as much as mortals do. You'll learn that. It's weird at first, but you get used to it." I blinked at him.

"Caden," Mason growled.

"I'll get used to it?" I muttered, then turned toward Mason. His jaw was tense as he glared at Caden. In his defense, he didn't look scared in the slightest, just as arrogant as ever. "Mason..."

"This isn't the way I wanted to tell you," he said under his breath. "What's the last thing you remember?"

I closed my eyes and thought back. What was the last thing I remembered?

Caden in Kali's apartment. Telling Kali. Walking home to meet Mason. Getting pinned to the brick wall. Calling Mason. A searing pain in my neck, then hot blood pouring down my body.

My eyes snapped open, and I stared at him.

"What did you do?" I murmured. He winced, looking like I'd slapped him. "What happened?" I looked at Rage and Caden, waiting for someone to tell me something, anything. When no one immediately offered up information, a sinking feeling stirred in my gut.

"At least you don't remember the pain," Caden said unhelpfully. "I remember the pain. It was the worse part—fuck!" He glared at Rage, who'd just smacked the back of his head hard enough to make me wince for him.

"What's he talking about, Grim?" I asked. His face softened by a fraction, then he rested his hand over mine, squeezing gently.

"Remember how you said you wanted to become a Reaper?" he asked quietly, almost like he was afraid of the answer. "Well, you got your wish." I stared at him. I didn't breathe, or blink, or think. I just stared.

Well, you got your wish.

Did that mean I was a Reaper?

I slid my hands out from under his and patted my neck, looking for the wound I knew was there last night. Nothing. There was nothing but smooth, unblemished skin. I looked down at myself, seeing I was in a clean t-shirt of Mason's, and gently ran my hands over my body. Everything was as it was supposed to be. Normal.

"I'm a Reaper?" I whispered, staring down at myself in a strange mix of excitement and horror. When he didn't answer, I looked up at him. He was bent over, the heels of his hands digging into his eyes. Caden and Rage were nowhere to be found. I hadn't even known they'd left. "Mason?"

He let out a soft, broken sob, and my chest ripped in half. I felt like I was being torn apart from the inside as I watched this giant, strong man cry, full body sobs that shook me to my core.

"I know you hate me," he said, his voice choked. "I fucking hate me. I didn't want to do this to you, but you were dying, Raven. I could feel it." He put his hand on his chest and rubbed it in a circle. Finally, he looked up at me. His eyes were wet, his cheeks blotchy and red. I'd never seen anyone so torn up about anything before. "I could feel you drifting away, your soul leaving your body. I had to decide; I could either escort you to the other side, or I could turn you. I was a selfish bastard." He slid onto his knees beside me, his face inches from mine. "I was selfish because I want you. I need you. I couldn't give you up. I couldn't let you go."

My mind was reeling, and I could feel every broken emotion sitting in his chest. I wanted to reassure him, but when I opened my mouth, nothing came out. Maybe this was shock. I'd never been in shock before. I wasn't sure if it was the fact that I was now a Reaper or because Mason was crying. Over me.

"I'm sorry," he said, wiping his face roughly. "I can find you somewhere to live. It's safer for Reapers to live in this realm than in the Mortal Realm, but I'll help you find somewhere. I'll earn your forgiveness. I have eternity to prove myself to you, Raven, and I won't give up. I'm so fucking sorry."

I stared at him, confused.

"Why?" I muttered. His body went stiff, and he blinked at me.

"Why? Why, what?" He pinched the bridge of his nose, wiping the last of his tears away.

"Why are you sorry?" I asked. I pushed myself up, and he immediately kneeled, bringing us to eye level again. Resting his hands on either side of my hips on the couch, he bunched them into tight fists, like he was forcing himself not to touch me.

"Because I made you a monster," he said quietly. He dropped his eyes. It was the only time I'd ever seen him do that, and it made my stomach drop. He really believed I was disgusted with him.

"You think I'm a monster?" I whispered. His head snapped up, his eyes wide.

"No," he said, shaking his head firmly. "But you do." I lifted my brows.

"I do?" His eyes flicked between mine.

"Don't you?"

"No." I rested my hand on his shoulder. He tensed, like he was anticipating a blow, but I just kept it there until he relaxed. "I don't think you're a monster, either. I never have." It was his turn to be stunned into silence.

"You don't?" he breathed, and I shook my head. Slowly, I cupped his face and gently pressed my lips to his.

"Never," I whispered as I pressed my forehead to his. "I don't hate you. I don't think we're monsters. I love you." He inhaled sharply and moved his hands to my hips.

"You love me?" He sounded genuinely shocked. I pulled away to look at him, a soft smile on my face.

"We're soulmates; shouldn't I love you?" I asked with a small laugh. He shook his head.

"Love is earned," he said quietly. "It's not something to be given out freely, even to your mate." My smile fell, his words settling deep. "You mean it?" I nodded without hesitation.

"I think I fell in love with you the moment you killed my stepfather," I said honestly.

"I fell in love with you when I saw you ride your dildo while you choked yourself with a scarf," he said seriously. My mouth fell open, then I threw my head back and laughed.

"What the fuck? You saw that?" I shook my head. "That can't be the moment. Choose a different one."

"Nope," he said, grinning. "That's the moment. I saw you make yourself come, and I thought, 'yeah, that's the girl I'm going to marry one day."

I went quiet at that. "Do Reapers get married?" I asked, tilting my head to the side, and he shrugged.

"Who says we can't?" He pressed his lips to mine again, softer than he ever had. "Is that something you'd want?"

"I've never thought much about marriage," I said honestly. "I think I'd want it with you." He kissed me again. "Is this your way of proposing?" I narrowed my eyes at him.

"If it is?"

"I'll say no," I said, leaning away from him. He laughed, a giant smile spreading across his face.

"Why?"

"This was the shittiest proposal in the world," I scoffed. "Do better." He laughed again, then nodded.

"Alright," he said, shaking his head. "Anything for you, little bird."

35

RAVEN
PRESENT

My eyes fluttered open as Mason pressed his lips to my neck again. Neck kisses from him were the best way to wake up, I'd decided. I smiled to myself as he kissed me again.

I didn't know if I should've felt so...free after finding out I'd died and become a Reaper, but that's how I felt. I wasn't upset with Mason for turning me, even though a part of me felt like I should've been. No matter how hard I tried, I couldn't make myself mad at him.

He'd saved me.

Again.

"Good morning," I murmured as I rolled over. He smiled lazily at me, his eyes soft.

"We don't technically have time here."

"But the sun—"

"Is always out." He pressed his lips to mine, smiling as he did. "That's why I don't have windows. I like it dark."

"Because you're a creepy Reaper," I teased, pressing my body further into his.

"And now you're a creepy Reaper, too." Something passed over his face, and his regret bloomed in my chest. He was having a hard time with my change, and I knew he didn't believe I wasn't upset. I didn't think I was a monster, and I didn't think he was, either. "There are a few things we need to do today."

"Can't we just stay in bed?" I nestled my head into his chest as he wrapped his arms tightly around me. Now that I wasn't mortal, he didn't feel so cold anymore. Oddly enough, I missed it.

"We need to get you registered, and you have to take the oath," he said, rubbing his hand up and down my back. "I'll see if I can train you. That's what I did before...." He trailed off, and I closed my eyes. *Before he was sent away.* "We can find our own place, too, if you don't want to live with my brothers."

"We have time," I muttered. "I don't mind. They're quiet."

"That's because Brody hasn't been here. When he and Caden get together, they're way too loud," he grumbled, and I smiled.

"I never had a family," I whispered. "I wouldn't mind living with yours." He paused, then pressed his lips to the top of my head.

"They're your family now, too, little bird," he said softly. Tears stung my eyes, and I nestled deeper against him. "We should probably see Wesley, too. See if this changes anything about our connection." I reared my head back to stare at him, my lips parting. "Settle down," he growled, "I don't think it has."

"But you're worried about it," I muttered. He tucked a strand of hair behind my ear and shrugged.

"Until a few weeks ago, I thought our souls died when we became Reapers. I just want to make sure yours is okay." He searched my eyes as he spoke. He was trying to keep his voice soft, but I couldn't help the surge of panic that shot through me. He moved his hand to his chest, feeling what I felt, and sighed. "Little bird, everything's okay."

"But—"

"But nothing," he said. "I shouldn't have said anything." He shook his head, rubbing his chest as he turned his head away. "You still feel me, right?"

"Yes," I said immediately. He slid his eyes to me and lifted his brow.

"As strongly as before?" I nodded quickly, and he sighed.

"Please don't make me do that test again," I whispered. "I can't see you like that." He tugged me back down to his chest, wrapping his arms tightly around me.

"You'll tell me if you start feeling different," he said in a low voice. "You'll tell me if you start feeling disconnected or if you think something might be wrong with your soul." Relief flooded me, and I nodded.

"You're very bossy," I muttered, and he laughed, the sound vibrating against my cheek.

"It's one of my best qualities." He tilted my head back and kissed me again. "My number one best quality is my ability to make you come so hard you see stars, though, isn't it?" His voice dipped, and goosebumps rippled across my skin.

"You think so highly of yourself," I breathed, and his eyes heated.

"Do I need to remind you of what I can do?" he growled. "How I can make you putty in my hands?"

He rolled me onto my back and hovered above me, his face shadowed in the red lighting of his room. I didn't know why he never changed the color, but it didn't bother me much. Sometimes, I'd have liked to see more of his face, that's all.

His lips were soft against mine. It was the gentlest kiss he'd ever given me, and it stole the breath from my lungs. Slowly, he trailed kisses down my jaw and neck, pausing to slide my shirt off and toss it to the floor. I kept my eyes trained on him as he slowly worked his way down my body, stopping to suck on my nipples until I was moaning and silently begging for more.

Then he was between my legs, his face inches from my pussy. His eyes met mine, a wicked glint in them that made me squirm. He wrapped his fingers around my thighs and gently pried them apart, pinning them to the bed so I was spread wide for him.

"You smell delicious," he groaned before pressing a kiss to the top of my slit, right above my clit. Lightly, he tapped my clit with the tip of his tongue, and I inhaled sharply.

"Grim," I gasped, lifting my hips.

"I like when you call me that," he admitted quietly.

"More than Master?" I teased. My eyes rolled back as he ran his tongue through my pussy, then swirled it around my clit.

"Master Grim has a nice ring to it."

"Whatever you want," I said breathlessly. He chuckled as he licked me slowly again. He was moving at an agonizingly slow pace, and it was killing me. Even though it felt amazing, I needed more. "Please." My voice was a soft whimper, one I didn't recognize, and he lifted his eyes to mine.

"What was that, baby?" He grinned at me, his lips glistening in the dim lighting. "Were you begging?" I nodded, and he laughed again, then roughly sucked my clit into his mouth, making me scream. "I'm not ready for you to come yet." He pulled away, and I groaned, long and loud and irritated. "Keep the attitude, and you won't come at all, little bird."

He shoved his boxers down and kissed his way back up my body. When he got to my lips, I didn't hesitate to press my tongue into his mouth, knowing he loved when I tasted myself on him. His cock nudged at my entrance, and I spread my legs wider, inviting him in. Finally, he began to press inside, and I moaned into his mouth.

"Fuck, you're tight," he breathed, dropping his forehead to mine. Slowly, he surged forward, taking his time, letting me feel every thick inch of him as he went. "Does that feel good, baby? My cock stretching your tight little cunt?" I could barely breathe, so I just nodded, my eyes still locked with his.

He kissed me again, sealing his lips to mine until he bottomed out, and then he stilled. He'd never taken his time or let me slowly adjust to his size, and I'd never wanted him to. I always wanted it hard and fast, the rougher the better, but something about him taking his time and being gentle made me wet for an entirely different reason.

The rough sex we always had was hot and special, but this was love. This is what people wrote poems and songs about. This is what people did to express how they felt because words could never be enough. What we were doing was more than sex, more than claiming me and making me his.

He slowly dragged his cock out, letting me feel every agonizing inch. My back arched, and his lips lowered to my nipple to gently suck it into his mouth. He moved languidly, pushing and pulling, shoving me to the edge and keeping me there. My body was tight with the need to come, but I wanted to ride that edge forever if it meant he could stay inside me.

"I love you, little bird," he whispered as he buried his face in my neck. Finally, he slammed into me with full force, making me cry out. "That's it. Let me hear you." He fucked me harder, and I clawed at his back and arms, feeling every nerve in my body light on fire.

"Choke me," I whimpered, and he shook his head.

"Not this time," he said as he pulled back. He gently stroked my hair from my face, his eyes soft.

"Please." I tightened my legs around his waist as he fucked me into the bed. My pussy clamped around him, and I knew I was close. "Please, Grim."

"No, baby. Now, be my good little bird and come on my cock." He rested his hand on my throat, not squeezing or tightening, just holding me. That sent me over the edge.

I tightened around him, my entire body tense as I screamed his name. It was the first time I'd come without depriving myself of oxygen, and after I came down from the best orgasm of my life, I stared up at him wide-eyed.

He fucked me faster and harder, making my sensitive pussy flutter around him with every stroke. Finally, his hips stuttered, and with a deep groan, he came, filling me completely. I kissed him softly, loving that he could do what no one else could: make me feel safe and normal and seen. Loved.

So fucking loved.

36

RAVEN

PRESENT

"So," Caden said, grinning at me from around his beer bottle. "How does it feel to officially be a Reaper?" I shrugged and snuggled closer to Mason on the couch.

"Fine," I said, and he snorted.

"Bullshit. No one is fine with being a Reaper." He reclined on the opposite sofa, an ankle propped on his knee. "Almost everyone I've ever met hates it."

"I'm not everyone." I shrugged and twirled my bottle. Mason's arm tightened around my shoulder as he pressed his lips to my temple. "They didn't have a reason to be excited for eternity." I glanced up at him, smiling shyly.

"You mean, you're excited to be with this asshole forever?" Caden stared at me with wide eyes. "I think something is seriously wrong with you." Mason threw a pillow at him and I laughed.

"Probably," I agreed, and Mason grumbled something under his breath.

"You did the oath and everything?" Rage asked gruffly. He stood against the wall in the back, his arms folded over his thick chest as he watched us. I cleared my throat, feeling uncomfortable under his full attention.

"Yeah," I said, shifting closer to Mason. "It was...interesting."

"She means it was a waste of time," Mason grumbled again. "It's gotten worse. They fucking changed it. Have you heard it?" They both shook their heads. "They're making them swear total allegiance. If they veer off the beaten path, they can be sent to the In-Between."

"Really?" Caden shook his head as he took another pull of his drink. "We just had to promise to help souls when they crossed and be a safe place for them to mourn. We didn't have to pledge allegiance to anyone."

"It's fucking Thomas," Mason growled. "He's ruining everything."

"It could be because you really shook shit up when you saved her," Caden suggested, using his head to point at me, and my stomach dropped. "He can't have a bunch of Reapers going rogue, which is what was going to happen if he didn't do something to control them."

"Well, maybe someone needs to go rogue," I said, and everyone looked at me. "Someone needs to show this Thomas guy he isn't God."

"Don't even think about doing anything stupid, little bird," Mason said darkly.

"I wasn't." I shrugged as I took a small sip of my beer. Caden gave me a knowing grin and shook his head.

"She's more like you than I thought," he muttered, his eyes sliding to Mason. "You're gonna have your hands full."

"Or, if we're not careful, they're going to take over the fucking realm," Rage said seriously. "Fuck. If you do decide to go rogue, at least let someone know beforehand, yeah? Not like fuckface did. We don't want to be caught by surprise again." Mason tensed beside me and something thick swelled in my chest, an emotion I didn't understand and couldn't decipher.

"You saved me because you were going rogue?" I asked. I didn't know why that hurt. I thought he'd saved me for me, but maybe it was just a statement to the Reapers in charge here.

"No," he said, glaring at Rage. "I saved you because you were being abused and were going to die that night." His face softened as he turned toward me. "I had no intention of ever doing anything like that, but I didn't hesitate when it came to saving you."

"Gross," Caden said, then gagged. "Is this what we have to look forward to? Lovey-dovey mushy shit all the time?"

It was my turn to throw a pillow at him.

———

"I NEED TO TELL KALI," I SAID, NOT LOOKING AT MASON. I felt his eyes on me, but I stayed looking at my lap. We were sitting on his bed; he was reading, and I was lost in my thoughts. I didn't know how I was going to tell my best friend, who was the most dramatic person I knew, that I was technically dead and a Reaper.

She wasn't going to freak out or anything.

"Alright," he said slowly, then roughly cleared his throat. "Why?" I finally turned toward him, giving him an exasperated look.

"She'll know something's wrong when she's fifty and I still look twenty-five," I deadpanned. "I need to tell her sooner than later. I can't lie to her."

"It's not lying—"

"It's lying by omission," I said, glaring at him. "Did you learn nothing?" He sighed and closed his book before turning fully toward me.

"That's not what I meant." He rested a hand on my knee, his eyes soft as they searched mine. "I just meant it's not lying if you choose to keep this from her until you've come to terms with it all. It's not lying if you wait to tell her." I shook my head as he spoke.

"I don't need to come to terms with anything," I muttered.

"You're handling all of this awfully well," he said slowly. "It's worrying me." I narrowed my eyes at him.

"Why? Because I'm not reacting like you think I should?"

"I think you're ignoring your feelings and it's going to bite you in the ass later," he said dryly. "But if you want to avoid how you feel, fine. I'll be here when you're ready to open up and face them."

"I told you, I'd looked for you since the night you killed him," I said quietly. "I knew what that meant. I knew finding you meant I would die. I accepted it when I was ten years old, Mason. I don't need to mourn my mortal life. I already did that."

Finally, understanding bloomed on his face. I wasn't avoiding my feelings or pretending like everything was fine. It wasn't. I knew there would be struggles I would face now that I was a Reaper, but dying and being with him forever? It was what I'd always wanted. I'd known that from the second I saw him at ten. I didn't need time to freak out because I'd already accepted it long before he'd ever come back into my life.

I'd resigned myself into knowing that I would die one day for the sole reason of being with Grim again. If that meant killing myself or begging him to kill me, then that's what I would do. I always knew he was it for me. I just never thought I'd be it for him.

"Alright, little bird," he murmured as he tucked my hair behind my ear. "We'll go talk to her." I opened my mouth to protest, to tell him it should be just me, but he leveled me with a firm look. "Together."

Beggars couldn't be choosers. I nodded, feeling a little better about it.

She was going to absolutely lose her fucking mind when I told her. Only a few nights ago, she learned that Reapers were a thing, and now, I was going to tell her I was one. Yeah, she wasn't going to take it well.

"What's going to happen to Eddy?" I asked suddenly. His brows furrowed as he dropped his hand back to my knee.

"What do you mean, what's going to happen to him? Nothing." My head reared back. What the fuck?

"He's just going to get away with killing me? He won't be punished? That's hardly fair." Mason sighed tiredly and rubbed his forehead.

"I didn't say it was fair, Raven, but it's what happens. He did a bad thing. Lots of mortals do, and nothing happens to them. We don't get to play God. We don't get to pick and choose which mortals live and which ones die. We just accompany their souls. That's it." He studied me like he was trying to see if I understood his words. I did understand them; I just thought they were fucking stupid.

"That's ridiculous," I scoffed. "If he's done this to me, how many other people has he terrorized? He shouldn't be alive." Mason shrugged, but his face looked pained.

"I'm not disagreeing with you," he said softly. "But it's Reaper Law. You learned about it earlier. If you reap his soul, you'll be punished. You'll be sent away, like I was." His face darkened at his words and my chest tightened, but it wasn't from my emotions – it was from his. He didn't like the thought of me sent away. "Don't do anything stupid, Raven. Please."

I flicked my eyes between his. I couldn't promise him that; I wouldn't promise him that. Eddy was a fucking creep. A loser. If he'd tried to lure me back to his apartment, he was bound to have done it to other women.

I was in a position of power now. I could punish him. I could kill him. He should be punished. He should be killed.

"Nothing stupid," I repeated as I crossed my fingers behind my back. "I won't do anything stupid."

I wouldn't.

Killing Eddy would be the very opposite of stupid.

37

GRIM

PRESENT

I knew she was lying. I didn't know what she was conjuring up in that beautiful head of hers, but she'd lied to me. She said she wouldn't do anything stupid, but I saw how her eyes lowered from mine and how she shifted uncomfortably. Maybe she wanted to mean it, but she didn't. Not really.

She was going to do something stupid, and I knew what that something stupid was going to be.

She was going to reap Eddy.

Honestly, if she wouldn't get in trouble for it, I wouldn't try to stop her. I didn't give a shit about that fucking piece of shit mortal. After all the women he'd killed, all the victims I'd had to reap, Raven reaping him would be the least he deserved. She would get sent away for it too, and I couldn't let that happen. Not because I didn't think she'd survive it. I knew she would, she was a fighter. No, I was a selfish prick, and I wanted every second of her time to be mine.

I hadn't let her out of my sight for two days, much to her annoyance. She may not realize it, but I was doing this for her own good. And in a few decades, when he was dead and gone and we were still here, he'd be a faint memory. He'd be nothing but someone for her to look back

204

on with annoyance, but he wouldn't be able to hurt her. He wouldn't be able to hurt anyone anymore.

But she was new to the whole Reaper thing, and patience wasn't her strong suit.

"Can we go see Kali?" Raven asked for the millionth time. I rolled my eyes. She wanted to see her friend, and I understood the urge, but she couldn't just pop in whenever she wanted. Well, she could, but, again, I'm a selfish fucking asshole and I wanted her all to myself.

"Soon," I said, shrugging. She glared at me over the rim of her coffee mug. I tried to ignore it, but my cock hardened at the fiery look.

"You wanna fix your face?" I asked in a low voice. Her eyes narrowed further.

"Or what?" she challenged. Slowly, I pushed off the counter and stalked toward her. Resting my hands on either side of hips, caging her in, I leaned forward, our lips almost touching, my breath mixing with hers.

"Or I'll shove my dick down your throat. Now that you're a Reaper, I don't have to pull out to give you air." Her eyes widened comically, and I pressed a quick kiss to her lips. "Now, I can be as rough as I want with you and won't have to worry about killing you."

"Like that ever stopped you before," she said. I grinned at her and leaned closer, letting her scent surround me. Fuck, she was potent.

"That was me holding back, little bird. Imagine the fun we can have now."

"Will you two stop?" Caden grumbled as he walked into the kitchen. "We just woke up, for fucks sake." He didn't have a shirt on, but Raven's eyes didn't linger on his sculpted, tattooed torso, which only turned me on further. She truly was my mate. Caden's hair was sticking up in every direction, and he still looked half asleep as he poured a cup of coffee.

"What does just waking up have to do with anything?" I asked as I slid onto the barstool beside her. She had a soft smile on her face as she flicked her eyes between us.

"I don't want to witness my brother and his girl fucking on the kitchen counter first thing," he said, and I snorted.

"We weren't fucking," I laughed.

"Close enough."

Raven shook her head as she took a sip of her coffee, clutching the mug tightly in her hands. She slid her eyes to me and gave me a coy grin before turning her attention to Caden. Sitting up straighter, she smiled brightly at him. He looked utterly confused.

"So," she said, drawing the word out. "Have you been back to see Kali?" Oh, the little brat. I wrapped my hand around her thigh in warning, but she just grinned wider.

"No," he said slowly. "Why?" He looked between us, clearly sensing something was off. She shrugged and took another sip, her eyes twinkling with mischief.

"Wanna go with me? I'm going to see her today." I squeezed her thigh harder, but she didn't react. She didn't even flinch. Caden's head reared back.

"You want me to go with you?" he repeated. He was staring at her like she'd lost her mind. She apparently had, if she thought I was going to let her and Caden go to the Mortal Realm without me. She shrugged and glanced at me again, that shit-eating grin still on her face.

"Sure," she said. "Now that Kali knows who you are, maybe she won't throw a lamp at you again." He laughed breathily, but I could see the giddiness forming on his face at the idea of seeing her.

Fucking hell.

This girl.

"I told you no," I said in a low voice.

"I didn't realize you were the boss of me." She narrowed her eyes, challenging me. Caden waited with bated breath, no doubt enjoying the show.

"You know I am." I smirked at her. "What is it you call me again?" I tapped my chin, then snapped my fingers. "Oh, yeah. Master, right?" Caden choked on his coffee, then hissed as it spilled down the front of his bare chest.

"Mason," Raven hissed, hitting my thigh with the side of her fist. Her eyes darted to Caden, but he was too busy cleaning up his mess and sputtering to pay attention to her.

"I'd say that makes me the boss of you, little bird." I smiled triumphantly. Folding her arms under her breasts, she glared so hard at me, I thought she was going to pop a blood vessel.

She leaned forward and dropped her voice into a whisper. "If you ever want to hear me call you that again, or if you ever want to come near any of my fucking holes again, then we're going to see Kali."

"Oh, my sweet little Raven." I stroked her cheek with my thumb. "You're saying that like you have a choice." Her eyes flared and she shoved my hand away.

"Fuck off, Grim. We're going." She scowled at me, and it made my dick rock fucking hard.

"What kind of shit are you two into?" Caden asked, breathless from his coughing fit. His chest and stomach had a giant red burn from his hot coffee, his eyes watery, but he looked amused. I opened my mouth, and he held his hand up. "Never mind. I don't want to know. When are we leaving?"

I sighed. When I turned toward Raven, she was giving me her best puppy dog eyes, and I groaned. *Fuck.* Fuck both of them, honestly. She couldn't manipulate me by pouting or using my brother as leverage.

But when she stuck her bottom lip out, I broke.

"Fine," I groaned. "Fine, but we're going and coming straight back. No leaving her apartment. Understand?" Raven and Caden were already across the kitchen before the words were fully out of my mouth. I shook my head but couldn't help the small chuckle that left me.

When was the last time I'd felt this happy?

38

RAVEN

PRESENT

I shoved Caden out of the way and stepped in front of him. He made an annoyed huffing sound that had me biting my lip to keep from laughing as he tried to push me behind him. Mason rested his hand on my lower back and urged me toward Kali's door, muttering something to Caden I couldn't hear. I didn't know Rage well, but Caden and I were becoming fast friends.

Knocking on Kali's door, we waited for her to answer. Nothing. Caden and I glanced at each other, and I quickly knocked again, then waited. Again, nothing. Unease began to stir in my stomach as I lifted my hand to knock again.

"I don't think she's home," Caden said quietly. He rested his hand on his chest, tapping his fingers against it. "I think something's wrong." I turned toward him, my eyes narrowed.

"How would you know?" I asked, and Mason cleared his throat.

"He thinks they're mates," he mumbled, and I threw my head up to look him.

"That would've been nice to know," I snapped, then sighed. "Whatever. Now isn't the time." I stooped and flipped her welcome mat over, snatching the spare key. Quickly, I unlocked the door, and we slowly cracked it open.

208

"Maybe we should have our glamours on," Caden said. I scanned the disheveled, upturned apartment. My knees grew shaky, and my breathing turned ragged. Her couch was flipped, the cushions shredded. Her barstools were toppled over, paintings on the floor with holes punched through the canvases, glass shattered everywhere.

This was *not* good.

Shit.

"No one can hurt us." I stepped further into the apartment and Mason latched his hand around my wrist.

"Just because they can't hurt us doesn't mean we shouldn't be careful," he said, his voice low. I tried to shake his hand off, but his grip tightened. "Little bird."

"I need to make sure she's okay," I snapped, almost in tears.

"Stay here." Caden waved at us as he stepped forward, glass crunching under his boots.

"Cade," Mason growled, but he ignored us.

"She might be hurt," he said, not looking at us.

"She's not here." He ignored me as he searched the apartment, carefully looking around. When he turned toward us, his face was devastated.

"She's not here," he repeated, and I nodded. Obviously. "Where is she?" I glanced at the clock on the wall. It was well past the time she would be off work, so unless she had a date, she'd be home. Maybe she'd gone by my place? Why would she? She knew I was with Mason. Why was her place a wreck? I didn't like this. This wasn't right.

"I don't know," I sighed.

"Can you feel her?" Mason asked, taking a step forward. "If you think she's your mate, you should be able to feel her. You should know where she is." I glanced up at him.

"That's how you always knew where I was?" I asked incredulously, and he shrugged.

"I can't really explain it," he said. "It's almost like I subconsciously know where you are at all times. I mean, you're a part of me, so I should know where you are, but..." He trailed off and shook his head. "You should be able to feel her." We looked to Caden, finding him with his eyes closed and lips pressed tightly together.

"There's...something," he muttered as he put his hand to his chest. "It's tight. My chest is tight." Mason and I glanced at each other. "Fear. I think it's fear." Caden's eyes snapped open. "She's scared."

———

"Are you sure this is the right place?" I asked as I gripped Mason's hand tighter. Caden's shoulders were thrown back as he stomped up the steps of Eddy's building. Fury was rippling off him in waves like I'd never felt, and I glanced up at Mason, finding him shocked.

"She's here," Caden growled. "Fucker has her."

I was a Reaper. There was no reason for me to be scared anymore, but the thought of facing Eddy again had my body trembling. I was scared. *Of him.* I was afraid of Eddy, which was ridiculous. He wasn't intimidating, or big, or scary. He shouldn't frighten me, but there was something in his eyes, something cold, something that told me he was a monster, and I couldn't shake that slimy feeling I got when he looked at me. There was something lurking under the surface, ready to attack. Even though I couldn't be killed, whatever bit of my mortality I had left was terrified.

"You still feel her, though?" I asked warily as we walked into the dingy lobby. He nodded stiffly, his footsteps thundering in front of us.

Mason and I glanced at each other. Gone was the fun-loving Caden. This Caden was all murder, and we'd need to hold him back. He couldn't get sent away like Mason had. I knew that's what most of my anxiety was—it was Mason's. He was worried about Caden. I was, too, but we needed to make sure Kali was safe before we worried about his brother. He couldn't die, but she could.

Caden didn't knock or hesitate. He just rammed his foot into the center of Eddy's door and sent it flying open. A muffled scream had true terror rippling through me. I tried to run forward, but Mason's grip on my hand tightened, holding me back. Caden stormed inside, his head frantically swiveling around as he searched for her.

We saw her at the same time.

"Kali!" I wrenched my wrist free and sprinted toward my best friend. She was tied to a chair in the middle of Eddy's sparse living room, a dirty rag tied around her mouth as a make-shift gag. Her clothes were torn and dirty, her hair plastered to her sweat-soaked skin, her eyes wider than I'd ever seen.

"We're here," Caden said as he dropped to his knees beside her. "I'm here." Tears streamed down her cheeks as she cried behind the gag. My hands shook as I tried to untie it.

"Shit. Hold on," I muttered as I worked on her bindings, forcing my nails between the tight knots. I pried them apart as Caden snapped the rope holding her wrists together. Mason was watching the door; it seemed Eddy was gone for the moment.

Finally, the gag fell away, and she let out a loud sob before slumping forward. Caden caught her, his arms tight around her as she rested her head on his broad shoulder. He stared up at me with wide, shocked eyes. I didn't have time to console him, to let him know it was fine. I kneeled beside her, rubbing my hand up and down her back to try to calm her down.

Poor Kali. As shitty as my life had been, hers wasn't. She'd had a good childhood with a loving family, a safe upbringing. She didn't deserve this.

"Raven," she cried as she pulled her head from Caden to look at me. "He—he's coming back."

"We need to go," I said to no one in particular.

"Did he hurt you?" Caden asked, his voice low. He scanned her body, his eyes latching on her torn shirt. His jaw flexed, and a murderous look fell over his face. "Did he touch you?" She let out another sob, and I froze. Caden and I glanced at each other before he shot to his feet, his body vibrating. "Gonna kill that fucker."

"You can't," I rasped. He couldn't leave her. She'd need someone, but I could kill him. I could kill Eddy. Fifteen years was nothing when you're immortal. "Don't do anything to get sent away, Cade." He stared down at me, his face like thunder, then he flicked his eyes to Kali.

She'd shrunk in on herself, her face swollen, eyes red from sobbing. He heard my unspoken words and nodded once, then kneeled beside her again.

"I'll take you home with me," he said gently, and she shook her head.

"I want my mom," she sobbed. "I just want my mom. Please." He glanced at me, and I nodded. Her mom was wonderful and would look after her.

"Alright, princess. I'll take you home." He hesitated before setting his hand on her thigh. She jolted at his touch but didn't try to push him away.

"He'll take care of you," I whispered, still rubbing her back. I'd never seen her so broken before, and I hated it. Kali was strong, stronger than anyone I'd ever known, and it was killing me to see her crying. "Trust him." She didn't say anything, and let Caden lift her into his arms. She looked so tiny in comparison, fragile.

It pissed me off. That's not who she was. She wasn't fragile. She wasn't weak.

"Traveling doesn't feel too good," he warned her gently. "But this is the fastest way to get you there." She nodded tiredly and gave me one last, sorrowful look before they began to evaporate.

Mason and I stood alone in the apartment for a moment, the silence deafening around us. He moved to me, his big hand landing on the small of my back.

"We need to go before he comes back," he murmured, and I shook my head as I took a step away.

"I'm waiting for him." He dipped his chin forward and glared at me.

"You're not doing that," he growled. "That's fucking ridiculous and dangerous and—"

"He hurt my best friend, Mason. That won't go unpunished." He took a deep breath, trying to calm down, but I could feel his fear and anger building in my chest.

"I understand you're upset—"

"Upset doesn't even begin to cover it."

"If you reap him, you'll get sent away, and I can't let that happen," he said, his voice pleading.

"It's only for fifteen years, right?" I said quietly. "What's fifteen years when we have eternity together?" He opened his mouth to argue, but before he could, the broken door swung open, slamming against the wall, and Eddy walked in, splintered wood crunching under his shoes.

"I thought I killed you," he said, and I turned my glare to him. "Whatever. I can do it now." He looked around me, and his face shifted. "Where the fuck is she?" I shrugged and took a step forward.

"Raven," Mason growled. "Don't." I gave him a long look, hoping he could feel and see my apology, and took another step toward Eddy.

39

GRIM

PRESENT

"Raven. Don't," I growled. Our eyes met, and I could see her intent before she moved. As if in slow motion, she turned toward Eddy and closed the distance between them. I couldn't move. My feet were rooted to the spot, watching as she gripped his shirt.

"You hurt my friend," she snarled. Her voice broke whatever shock I was in, and I quickly moved to her, wrapping my arm around her waist and pulling her back. "You're fucking dead!" Eddy looked smugly back at her as he straightened his shirt, then pushed his greasy hair away from his face.

"I didn't hurt her," he scoffed. "She loved it. She was nice and tight, much tighter than you ever were." My body stiffened as Raven lurched forward, trying to break free. Now that she was a Reaper, she was stronger than she had been as a mortal, and it wasn't something either of us was used to yet.

"What the fuck does that mean?" she shouted. "You never fucked me!" He laughed, cold and cruel, and my arms locked tighter around her.

"You really don't remember, do you?" She finally froze, her body going rigid against me. "We fucked, Raven. We fucked when we were

214

kids. Remember the Robinsons? You lived with them for a short time—"

"Holy shit," she breathed. "No fucking way." She shook her head frantically. "Declan?"

"So, you do remember me," he sneered. His eyes roamed over her and it took all I had not to kill him on the spot.

"What you did to me—that wasn't—that wasn't fucking. That was —" I squeezed my eyes shut, not wanting to know or hear the rest of her words. "That was assault." He threw his head back and laughed.

"You came every fucking time," he mocked. I squeezed her until her breath left her, trying to calm her, but I felt her anxiety, her fear, build higher.

"How many times did he touch you?" I growled in her ear. She shook her head, her eyes still trained on him. She looked terrified, and my girl never looked terrified.

"You didn't go by Eddy back then," she said, her voice trembling.

"Edward is my middle name." He shrugged. "Honestly, it hurts that you didn't recognize me. I recognized you immediately." She let out a shuddering breath. "All the times we've met, I kept thinking you'd realize who I was, but you never did. Always up here." He tapped the side of his head. "Always living in your head, never aware of who surrounded you." I heard her swallow, and I glanced at her. Her face was deathly pale, her eyes wide.

"That's it, we're done." I hauled her tighter back against me, ready to leave. I wasn't expecting it, so I couldn't catch her. She threw herself down, landing on her feet. Without hesitating, she charged Eddy and tackled him to the floor. "Raven!"

She didn't listen as she wrapped her hands around his neck. I rushed to her, grabbing her around the waist as she tried to straddle him.

"How do I do it?" she screamed, her voice thick with tears. "How the fuck do I reap him?" She was wrestling me, fighting me to get to him. He lay on the floor, staring up at her in shock. It was the first time he'd seemed anything other than smug. "Grim, let me go! I need to kill him!"

"Raven, calm down." She jerked her elbow back, hitting me square in the chest and knocking the air from my lungs. Her legs flailed, kicking

215

mine as she tried to scramble toward him again. It was impossible to hold her when she was hysterical like this.

"How do I do it?!" she screamed again. I didn't say anything. I couldn't. She clawed at my forearms until the skin ripped open, and her body thrashed until she finally slid free and lurched forward again. Dropping to her knees, she straddled Eddy and pressed her hands to his chest.

"Raven, wait!" But it was too late. She tipped her head back, an agonized look on her face as she poured her power into him. I felt it in my chest–her power leaving her. "That's enough!" I grabbed her, pulling her off him.

Her chest heaved as we stared at Eddy's lifeless body. She'd done more than just reap him. She'd fucking obliterated him. His eyes were burned from his skull, his flesh bubbling as steaming blood and slime oozed from his nose and ears. I'd never seen a Reaper do that, but with so much emotion and power behind her reaping, it shouldn't have been a shock. It still was, though, a huge fucking shock.

"We need to get out of here," I gasped, grabbing her hand. Her breath was ragged as she stared at him.

"I killed him," she breathed.

"Congrats," I said dryly. "Now we need to leave before any other Reapers turn up and find us here." She nodded a few times and let me help her to her feet. She clung to me as I wrapped my arm around her waist. "Stop looking at him, little bird." She didn't. She stared at him until we disappeared and reappeared in my bedroom.

"I can't believe I did that," she said shakily. She wasn't getting sick after traveling anymore, not since she'd turned. She began to pace and shoved her fingers through her hair. "I killed him. Mason. I killed him."

"You did." I folded my arms over my chest. I needed to calm down before I freaked the fuck out on her, but she didn't listen to me, and now we were in a world of fucking trouble. How the fuck were we going to explain this?

They were going to come for her. It was only a matter of time, and I had to protect her. Maybe we could go on the run, but where the fuck could we hide where they couldn't find us? We'd have to keep running and never stop. That was no way for us to live. Shit. What the fuck was I supposed to do?

"But he touched Kali. He—he touched me." She let out a broken-sounding sob, and I squeezed my eyes shut.

"You knew him?" I asked, and she nodded a few times, still pacing.

"I didn't recognize him, not until he told us who he was. I lived with a foster family after you—after my stepfather died. I was seventeen, almost out of the system. I was only with them for a few months; they were my last family. He was their biological son, and he was a total fucking creep, always staring at me or finding an excuse to touch or sit next to me." She took a deep breath and turned to face me.

"What happened?" I asked quietly. I didn't know if I wanted to know, but she was on a roll, and she needed to get it out.

"One night, he snuck into my room. I shared it with his little sister, but she was at a sleepover, so I was alone. He—he—please don't make me say it, Mason." Tears streamed down her face. I'd never seen her look so fucking broken.

I moved to her, wrapping her up in my arms as she sobbed against my chest. Rage boiled inside me. If she hadn't killed him, I probably would've gone back to do it myself. She cried until she was too exhausted to stand. Finally, she sat on the bed and looked up at me as she wiped her face.

"He snuck into my room every weekend," she continued, her voice small, broken. "His sister was never home, so I was always alone. When I tried telling his mom about it, she accused me of lying and kicked me out. It was a few months before my eighteenth birthday, so I said fuck it and just left. I traveled around for a bit, and that's how I met Kali. I moved to New York, and a year later, she called me and said she was moving there, and we've been best friends ever since."

"You didn't recognize him? How?" I asked, and she shrugged.

"I blocked out most of my time as a foster kid." She looked down at her hands. "It wasn't that bad at first, but as I got older, it got worse. He looked different back then. He was chubbier and shorter and didn't look as gross."

"He was the one killing the girls in your neighborhood," I said, and her head snapped to me. "It makes sense why he was targeting ones who looked like you." She shook her head.

"You're saying he's the killer?" I nodded. "How?"

"I helped a few of his victims cross," I muttered, and she blinked at me. "I didn't know how to tell you without scaring you, so I just didn't say anything. I know I fucked up. I should've told you, but—"

"You did tell me," she said, shocking me. I was sure she was about to rip into me for lying again. "You told me to stay away from him, but I didn't know you meant *him*."

Something crashed downstairs, and we turned our heads toward the bedroom door. "Get behind me and stay there," I said, giving her my hand. "Do everything I say, Raven. I mean it." She swallowed heavily and slipped her hand into mine as the door burst open.

40

RAVEN

PRESENT

I clung to the back of Mason's shirt, my head barely peeking out from behind him to stare at the Reapers filing into his bedroom. Holy fuck. They were there because of fucking *Eddy*?

"I thought you would've learned after last time," the one at the front of the formation said, smiling smugly at Mason. My stomach dropped. *Shit*. They thought it was him? With a deep breath, I let go of his shirt and took a step back. His shoulders bunched tightly, his body vibrating with his anger.

"He touched my girl and her best friend. What did you expect me to do?" I paused. No. He couldn't be doing this. He couldn't be taking the blame.

"Mason," I hissed, but he reached behind him, his hand finding mine.

"That so?" the same Reaper drawled. He eyed me, and Mason stepped in front of me again, blocking me from view.

"Yeah," he growled. "I'd do it again." I inhaled sharply. *Stop*. I wanted him to stop talking. He should've turned me over. I could've handled whatever they threw at me.

"I think you might be lying," the Reaper said. I gripped Mason's hand tighter. "Is he lying, Raven?" I swallowed hard. I couldn't stand

219

this. I couldn't let him take the blame, but he'd fucking kill me if I told the truth. So, I stayed silent. The Reaper laughed coldly. "Like that, is it? Alright. We can take you both in."

"Do not fucking touch her," Mason snarled. "I'll rip your fucking throat out." It wasn't an idle threat, I knew that, and I fucking hoped they did, too. Even if Reapers couldn't kill other Reapers, we could still injure them, and Grim was about to injure the fuck out of these guys.

Not that I blamed him. The one in the front looked like a fucking prick.

His smug smile never fell as he stared up at Grim, his eyebrow arched slightly. It made me bristle, the way he seemed to be looking down on Grim. On us both. I knew I wasn't good enough to be here, good enough to be with him, but this asshole had no right to look at my Grim like he was nothing. He wasn't. Grim was something. He was special and brave and amazing. He was self-sacrificing and everything good in the world.

"Is that any way to speak to me?" he drawled. I ground my teeth together, knowing Grim hated his condescending tone more than anything else at the moment.

"I'll say a lot fucking more," Grim growled. "I swear, if you come near her, I'll fucking—"

"What?" the other man mocked. "What can you possibly do?" Grim's mouth snapped shut.

Nothing.

There was nothing he could do. Not really.

"Whatever," he sighed. "Since you're not being helpful and telling me the truth—"

"I did," Mason snapped. "I was the one who reaped him." I bit my tongue. He knew this was killing me, not telling them the truth and not protecting him. I knew he could feel my emotions as much as I felt his.

"Fine," he said, rubbing his forehead. "Grab him. Leave the girl."

"Wait!" I cried as I gripped Mason's hand tighter. "Please don't take him. It wasn't—"

"Raven," he said quietly. A warning. "Stay with Rage. He'll know what to do."

"I don't want to leave you," I said, tears welling in my eyes. "I don't want them to hurt you."

"I'll be fine, little bird." He tucked my hair behind my ear. "Just stay with my brother and let him protect you until I can get out, alright?"

"Oh, you're not getting out," the Reaper said from the door, morbid amusement in his tone. "Reaping an innocent is a deadly offense now. You'll be executed."

My stomach dropped.

"No," I whispered. "No. Please, Mason." I side-stepped him, and when he reached for me, I moved out of his grasp. "It was me. I killed Eddy. I did it. Take me. Mason is innocent."

"Raven!" Mason shouted, but I ignored him.

"Take me." I held my hands out, expecting him to cuff me like mortal cops did. He just grinned at me.

"Isn't this interesting? Who are we to believe, boys?" He glanced at the few Reapers surrounding us, and I swallowed hard.

"We could take them both," one of them suggested.

"Perhaps." The Reaper stroked his chin as he looked me up and down. "You're a new Reaper, haven't even had your first day on the job, and you're telling me you reaped that soul? That you mutilated the vessel?" Bile rose in my throat, and I nodded stiffly.

"I did," I said, my voice hoarse. "Mason tried to stop me, but it was me."

"Was it now?" He grinned at me, then flicked his eyes up to Mason. "I think you're just covering for him." I took a step forward, and Mason's hand latched around my wrist.

"Stop," he pleaded.

"No," I said, shaking my head. "It was me. Please. Leave him alone. He had nothing to do with it." The Reaper waved dismissively at me.

"Grab him, leave her."

"But I just told you it was me!" I shouted, yanking my hand free from Mason's grip. I moved toward the Reaper, and he straightened his shoulders. "Leave him alone!"

One of the Reapers grabbed my arm and pulled me away from his boss. Mason's roar nearly ruptured my eardrums. It echoed off the walls of his room, the fury in his voice sending a cold shiver through my body.

"Don't fucking touch her!" He lurched forward, grabbed the man by the throat, and hauled him away from me. His hold hadn't hurt me. I'd barely even realized he'd touched me, but Mason had him pinned against the wall, his chest heaving as he glared down at the Reaper.

"Don't just stand there! Do something!" the main Reaper shouted.

"Wait!" I ran forward, trying to put myself between the Reapers gathering around Mason. One of them shoved me back, and I fell to the floor, landing painfully on my ass.

Mason whirled around, his eyes wild. When our eyes locked, he turned toward the nearest man, reared his fist back, and slammed it into the middle of his face before turning and doing the same to the next. Over and over, he punched the few Reapers moving toward him. To their credit, they never stopped. They just kept going after him.

I finally shook myself enough to get to my feet and try to move forward.

"Raven," a deep voice called me from the doorway, but I ignored it as I fought my way toward Mason. "Raven!" I pulled Reapers away from him, forcing them to stumble back a few steps.

I stood in front of Mason, my shaky hands outstretched as I scanned the room. Rage was in the doorway, looking torn about what to do next. I felt his pain. I was fucking lost, too. All I knew was that I had to protect Mason.

"I said it was me," I said, breathing hard. "Take me."

"They don't want you," Mason growled. "They've been waiting for me to fuck up again. They want me."

"But you didn't do anything!" I couldn't look at him like I wanted to. I didn't want to risk being blindsided, but I couldn't keep the desperation out of my voice. He was innocent.

This was all my fault. Why hadn't I just listened to him? I'd fucked everything up.

"Raven, let me go." His voice was resigned, and it made me hate him. I fucking hated him for giving up so easily. Is this who he really was? I thought he was a fighter, like me. I thought he'd never give up, but here he was... "Please."

"No," I cried. "I'm not—"

"We'll remove you," the main Reaper drawled. He stood beside Rage, who was vibrating with anger. "We'll exterminate you right now."

"Raven, please," Mason said again, his voice low. "We'll figure something out." I shook my head. He sighed, then gently kissed the top of my head before easily stepping around me. I couldn't stop him, I knew that. He was too big, too strong, but I still latched onto his arm.

"Don't." I stared up at him, his face blurry from my tears. "Just stay."

"Call Wes, alright? He'll know what to do," he said quietly. I took a deep breath.

Okay, I could do that. Maybe he was forming a plan. If he was, I could help him. If Wesley was part of that plan, then I'd get on my knees and beg him to help Mason. I'd do anything to protect him.

"Okay," I breathed but still didn't let go.

"We don't have time for this. You have five seconds."

"Love you, little bird," Mason said quickly. "Stay with Rage and Wesley, okay? I'll see you again soon."

"I love you—"

Before the words could leave me, the main Reaper grabbed Mason and hauled him back, evaporating without a trace.

41

RAVEN

PRESENT

I banged on Wesley's front door, ignoring Rage's grumbling behind me. If Wesley wasn't home, I'd hunt him down and force him to help. If he was home...I'd still figure out a way to force him to help me.

"Wesley!" I shouted, banging my fist on the wood again, the brass Reaper knocker hitting the door. "Can you break the door down or something?" I turned toward Rage. His arms were folded over his chest, his face blank. If it weren't for the firm set of his jaw and the tenseness of his shoulders, I'd think he was unaffected by Mason being taken, but I knew he was just as upset about it as I was.

"I don't think he'd appreciate that," he said dryly.

"What if he's asleep and can't hear us knocking?" I let out a hard breath when Rage leveled me with a look. Yeah, that sounded stupid, even to me. "Maybe he's in the garden." I stepped down, ready to sprint around the house, when the door swung open.

"What—oh, Raven." Wesley cleared his throat, his eyes flicking momentarily to Rage behind me.

"You're home," I breathed. "Thank God. I need your help."

"Is everything okay?" He smoothed his wrinkled shirt over his stomach, looking uncomfortable. I eyed him warily.

"Do you know?" I asked quietly. His brows bunched together.

"Know what?" He looked to Rage again. "What's happened?" He stepped out onto the porch and closed the door behind him. Something was off.

"Why can't we come inside?" I asked, glaring at him. If he was playing Mason, I'd fucking kill him.

"Raven," Rage said in a low voice. He didn't sound nearly as suspicious as I felt.

"Um." Wesley rubbed the back of his neck. "I have someone inside."

"I gathered that," I said. "Who?" I took a step forward, and Rage caught my wrist.

"I'm assuming a woman," he hissed in my ear. I paused. Wesley had a woman...fuck. Of course, he did.

"What is it you need help with, Raven?" Wesley said politely, still looking uncomfortable.

"Do you have a woman in there?" I asked, jerking my chin at the door. Rage groaned and let go of my wrist. Wesley cleared his throat and squared his shoulders.

"Who I choose to entertain is none of your business," he said in that oh-so-proper English accent of his, and I grinned at him. The last thing I felt like doing was smiling, but he was funny.

"Are we cockblocking you, Wes?" I teased. He sighed tiredly.

"A bit," he said dryly. I laughed, then glanced at Rage's very serious face. Right. There was a reason we were here.

"I need your help," I said, dropping my head forward. He stared at me for a long time, waiting. "They took him."

"Reaper Police took Mase. They're accusing him of reaping an innocent," Rage explained.

"Did he?" Wesley asked as he took another step down. I shook my head and wiped roughly at my face.

"It was me," I croaked. "I did it, and he's taking the blame for it. They said they're going to execute him."

"Did you tell them it was you?" he asked, and I nodded frantically.

"It was Seth," Rage said, and Wesley inhaled sharply.

"Fuck," he muttered. I wiped at my face again. If Wesley was freaking out, and this was as close to a freak out I'd ever seen from him, then things weren't good. "It'll be okay, dear. Why did you reap the soul? What was the reason?" I glanced at Rage, and he barely nodded.

I explained my connection to Eddy. I told them everything, from meeting him at the party, Mason saving me, taking Kali, and who he was in my past. When I got to the part about him killing me and Mason turning me into a Reaper, Wesley paused.

"He was the one who killed you? You're sure?" he asked, bouncing on the balls of his feet. I nodded a few times.

"I was there," Rage said. "He stabbed her in the neck. She died quickly, but Mase turned her before she was fully gone." Wesley began to pace on the top step, his hands rubbing together in front of him.

"I need to call the guys," he said. Rage and I looked at each other again. "We need Wolfe."

"Wolfe?" I repeated, and he nodded.

"He's an asshole, but he's the best at what he does. He can help us."

I wasn't so sure about that.

"Go over it again," Malik said, rubbing his forehead.

"How many more times?" I groaned. "I've told you the same story a million times; nothing will change."

"You said he's the one who killed you," Damen said, and I nodded. "And you reaped him for...." I groaned again.

"For hurting my friend," I replied. "For everything he'd done to me. For being a general asshole. For killing me. Do I need more of a reason than that?" I put my hands on my hips to glare at him. He shrugged as he reclined back on the sofa.

"Just making sure that was your real motive," he said.

"Does my motive matter?" I asked, and he shrugged again.

"It doesn't, dear," Wes answered tiredly. He had to kick his lady-friend out, which he wasn't thrilled about. She wasn't either, but they'd get over it. Once Mason was safe and freed, they could fuck like rabbits for all I cared. But that was *after* we saved Mason.

"Do we know when the execution is?" Wolfe asked from his corner of the room. My stomach twisted. I hated knowing that was what loomed over us if we fucked this up. Mason's execution.

"Likely a few days," Rage said. "Thomas probably wants it done quickly and quietly."

"Why quietly?" I asked.

"If he makes noise about it, there might be some push back from not only the Council, but the public. If it's already said and done, he can ask for forgiveness and move on," he explained. "He can feign ignorance and pretend he was doing his job, even though no Reaper has ever been executed for reaping a soul before."

"He has a personal vendetta against Mason," Wes grumbled. "It's bullshit. He doesn't like that Mase was going to take his spot on the High Council." My brows shot up. This was the first I'd heard of that. I knew Mason was involved in politics before getting sent away, but I hadn't realized he'd been that important.

"Now that Mase is back, some Reapers want him to take over again," Damen added. I nodded a few times, the pieces all falling into place.

"So, if we get Thomas kicked off the Council before the execution, will Mason be safe?" I asked, and Wolfe shook his head.

"Probably not," he said. "We need to get you in front of a High Reaper."

"Me?" I croaked. Everyone turned to look at him.

"We need to make it known that Mason is innocent and taking the fall for you," he said. "It's your word against his. He'll need to go against you and say you did it, which—"

"Which he'd never do," I said, and Wolfe nodded a few times. "What else?"

"We could break him out," Rage suggested, but Wes shook his head.

"That would only put a bandaid on things. They'd still come after him," he said. "We need to have Raven take his place."

"Why?" I asked, my stomach twisting. "I'll be the one executed." Wolfe shook his head as I spoke.

"No, there's an old law that'll protect you, but it won't protect Mason. We just need to convince someone more powerful than Thomas to release Mason in exchange for you," Wolfe said simply and glanced at Wes. I swallowed hard.

"Will?" Wesley thought for a moment, tapping his finger against his chin before nodding. Wolfe looked back at me, seeming sympathetic to our plight for the first time. "You okay with this? You might have to be in a cell for a few days." I nodded a few times. I could do that for Mason. He'd done it for me, twice. I could do this for him.

If I ended up executed instead, then so be it. Mason would be safe.

42

GRIM

PRESENT

"You have a visitor," the guard grumbled. I barely lifted my head as the cell door opened. Seth and his cronies had done a number on me. I was healing, but not fast enough. It had only been two days since I got here, but it felt like I'd been stuck in this cell for a century.

"You look like shit." I glared up at Wes. He stared at me, his brow arched as he took in my fucked up body and face. "Seth?" He waved his hand at me, and I grunted. "Thought so."

"Raven?" I rasped. I needed to know she was safe. All I'd felt since being here was anxiety, fear, and rage. If I was being totally honest, I couldn't tell if those were my emotions or hers. "Is she okay?"

"Oh, she's fine," he said, waving dismissively. "She's why I'm here to see you." He grinned, then looked around the tiny, dirty cell. Sighing, he moved to the other end of my too-small cot and sat. He looked ridiculous, in his pristine suit and shiny shoes, sitting in a grungy cell on a disgusting mattress.

"Why didn't she come?" I asked as I leaned back against the stone wall.

"She's visiting High Reaper Will," he said, giving me a sly look. I ground my teeth together.

"Why the fuck is she visiting Will?" I growled, my blood heating. He folded one long leg over the other and turned his head to look at me.

"I'll explain, but I need you not to freak out." He stared calmly at me, his face blank. How the fuck was I supposed to respond to that? Not freak out? I couldn't promise anything until I heard what he had to say.

"Talk, Wes," I said, glaring at him.

"We need you to turn Raven in." His words were a slap in the face, and my head reared back.

"What the fuck?" I barked. "Have you lost your fucking mind?" He ran his hands over his thighs, smoothing the fabric of his pants.

"No, I haven't," he replied, calm as ever. "She's talking to Will to explain it was her who reaped Eddy, not you. He'll be calling for you in a few moments, and we need you to turn her over. We need you to say it was her." I shook my head as he spoke.

"You've lost your damn mind if you think I'd ever do that," I snapped. "Are you hearing yourself? I'd never throw my girl under the fucking bus."

"Wolfe has a plan."

I barked a humorless laugh. "Oh, Wolfe has a plan? Excuse me for not trusting him with her fucking life."

"You know he's the best at what he does," he said calmly. "You know he can get her out of this." I shook my head again.

"Not with Thomas involved."

"Oh, I forgot." He tapped his fingers on his leg, a slight grin curving his lips. "Thomas has been removed from his position. Temporarily, at least." I gaped at him, my entire body frozen.

"How the fuck did you manage that?" I asked.

"Told you, Wolfe is good at what he does." He shrugged.

I swallowed hard. Could I really trust fucking Wolfe to save Raven? Protect her? He was a selfish asshole at the best of times. Could I trust that he'd do all he could to keep her from getting executed? I let out a hard breath.

"What do I have to do?" I asked warily. "I'm not agreeing to anything yet," I added in a rush. Wes nodded, like that's what he'd been expecting.

"All you have to do is say Raven was the one who reaped Eddy. It's the truth, right?" I nodded, feeling like I was falling into a trap. "Your stories will match if you tell it exactly as it happened."

"I can't do it," I breathed, dropping my head into my hands. "I can't turn on her."

"It's not turning on her," he said gently. "She's in on it. She knows the risks involved. She wants things to change, maybe more than you did before you got sent away." I nodded a few times as I dug the heels of my palms into my eyes. "She knows the plan and fully trusts Wolfe to get her out of this." I took another deep breath.

"I can't lose her," I finally whispered. "I can't fucking lose her, Wes." I turned to look at him. If anyone knew what it was like losing a mate, it was him. His face tightened with grief, then softened as he nodded.

"I understand," he murmured. Hesitantly, he reached out and set his hand on my shoulder, squeezing gently. "We won't let anything happen to her. We'll keep you together."

There was a knock at the cell door, and I stiffened. His eyes searched mine to make sure I was in. I didn't know if I could fucking do this. Could I? Fuck. I hated this. I hated this so fucking much.

"It's now or never, Mase," he murmured as he got to his feet. "You always wanted things to change, to be better. Well, now's your chance."

WILL'S OFFICE WAS COLD, COLDER THAN THE REST OF THE building, even colder than my cell. I didn't know if it was because he was so much colder than everyone else, or if it was just my imagination.

As soon as I stepped inside, my eyes found Raven. She was sitting in a chair by the window, her back ramrod straight and her dark hair pulled back in a low ponytail. She didn't look like herself—she was too serious. Meek. She wasn't her.

I wanted to go to her, crouch beside her, hold her, but I couldn't. Not yet.

I leaned against the wall beside the door and forced my eyes to stay on Will. He was younger than Thomas and, like me, wanted things to change.

But that was before I got sent away.

I didn't know if he still held the same beliefs. A part of me worried he didn't. How else would he have become a High Reaper, higher than Thomas, if he wasn't willing to play this fucked up game? How could he get to where he was if he was still trying to change things? Help Reapers? He wouldn't. He had to have decided power was more important than what was right.

"Mason," he drawled, his long fingers tapping against his desk. He grinned at me, his dark hair combed neatly to the side and pushed away from his face. Tattoos peeked out from under the collar of his cloak, showing off his life before all of this began.

"Will." I nodded once at him, and his grin broadened.

"I've had the pleasure of meeting your...." He trailed off as he glanced at Raven, his dark eyes taking her in. She shifted uncomfortably, and I narrowed my eyes. "Girlfriend?"

"Wife," I corrected. They snapped their heads to me, but I forced my face to remain relaxed.

"Interesting," he mused. Slowly, he rose to his feet, his eyes sliding back to Raven. It made me bristle. "She's told me an interesting story." He smirked, and my blood began to fucking boil.

I couldn't do this. I couldn't let her take the fall, even if she was the one who technically did it. It was my job to protect her, no matter what. If she got sent to one of the cells here, they'd eat her alive.

A knock at the door made me stiffen, and I glared at Will as I shuffled my stance further apart. He strolled toward me, careful to avoid touching me as he reached around and pulled the door open.

"Wolfe," he greeted, his voice tight.

"Will." Wolfe's voice was brusque, as it always was. "I'm in a hurry. Let's get this over with." I sighed.

"Hey, Wolfe," Raven said quietly. He barely looked at her. I wanted to shove his head to the side, force him to acknowledge her, to say hello. I didn't. I just balled my hands into tighter fists.

"Alright, so she's confessed already, right?" Wolfe asked bluntly. Will rounded his desk and slowly sank into his chair. He let out a long, tired breath, then nodded. "And Mason has admitted—"

"Mason hasn't admitted anything yet," Will said, interrupting him. "We were getting to that part." Was he in on this, too?

I glanced at Raven, finding her looking at me expectantly. She gave me a watery smile, then slightly nodded. I tapped my fingers against my bicep as I thought.

Were they all in on this? The way Wes made it sound, they all knew the plan, but what if I fucked something up? What if I said something wrong, and Raven really was executed?

What if Wolfe couldn't save her?

What if Will turned on us?

"Have a seat." Will waved toward the chair on the other side of his desk. I glanced at Wolfe, and he gave me a hard nod. I ground my teeth together as I forced myself to move to a chair. Gripping the back, I pulled it beside Raven and sank onto it. I wasn't going to be away from her anymore. Will just grinned.

"Tell us the story," Wolfe demanded. "Don't leave anything out." I glanced at Raven again, and she nodded. She rested her hand on mine, squeezing it reassuringly. "Raven, you're going to have to leave for this part."

"She stays," I growled. Both men looked passively back at me, like I was nothing but an inconsequential gnat.

"Sorry, she has to go. We have to make sure she's not influencing you," Will said. "Just wait outside with Wesley and the others, alright, love?" She nodded. Before she could move, I grabbed her hand and pulled her to me as I stood.

I crushed my lips to hers, kissing her hard enough to steal her breath. When I pulled back, she stared up at me with glazed eyes. Suddenly, tears filled them, and all the heat in my blood turned to ice. She pulled me into a tight hug, pushing up on her tip-toes to wrap her arms around my neck.

"Tell the truth," she whispered against my skin. "Trust me. Please." She pulled back before I could reply and quietly moved across the room. With a final look at me, she slipped from the door and out into the lobby. I sank back into the chair, feeling like the air had been knocked out of me.

"Alright," Wolfe said, sounding irritated. "The story."

My stomach churned with unease. She wasn't asking me to trust anyone else but her. I could do that, right? I had to do that. She'd done nothing but trust me, even when I'd broken it a million times. She had no reason to love me or be loyal to me beyond our connection. She could've told me to fuck off, but she chose to love me. She chose to trust me.

I could choose to trust her.

"She reaped him," I said quietly. I leaned forward, resting my forearms on my knees. "She did it." The room was tensely silent for a moment, then Will cleared his throat.

"Why?"

I glanced up at him, my eyes narrowed. Why? Did it really matter why? No one asked me why when I'd reaped her stepfather. They just sent me away. But maybe it did...perhaps this was a part of their plan.

"He'd kidnapped, assaulted, and hurt her best friend," I said. "After, she told me he was a boy at a foster home she lived in when she was a teenager. He—he did terrible things to her." Will nodded a few times and leaned forward, resting his elbows on his desk. "He was killing women who looked like Raven. I think it's because he'd always been obsessed with her, and it was his way of having her again." Both men nodded. "He killed her."

"He did?" Wolfe asked, but he already knew the answer. He knew her story. I glanced at him, my brows furrowed, before looking back at Will. He didn't look shocked by this information, either.

"He stabbed her in the neck, and she bled out. I turned her before her soul was lost," I explained.

"So, she reaped her murderer," Will said. It wasn't a question, and I tilted my head to the side.

"Yes," I answered warily. "She reaped her murderer." I looked at Wolfe. "Why does that matter?" He grinned at me. Wolfe fucking grinned. I'd never seen it before. Truthfully, I hadn't thought he was capable of anything other than scowling. Will scribbled on a piece of paper, then set his pen down.

"You're free to go," Will said as he stood. I blinked at him.

"What?"

"You're innocent. She reaped the soul, not you." Panic filled me. Had I just signed her death warrant?

"She'll be fine," Wolfe reassured me.

"If you fuck this up, I will figure out a way to fucking kill you," I said in a low voice. "Both of you." Will nodded a few times, like he'd expected me to threaten him. Wolfe just looked passively back at me, blinking once.

"Trust us," Will said, his smile wolfish. "She won't be executed."

Fuck, I hoped not.

43
RAVEN
PRESENT

It had been two days since my meeting with Will, but no one had come to get me yet, and I was starting to worry. I hadn't heard from anyone in two days. Two whole days. Four days without Mason, not including the brief moment in Will's office.

I just wanted him.

A knock at my cell door had my spine stiffening. I stared at it as the guard slowly swung it open, not looking at me as he waved his hand toward the dingy hall.

"Come on," he said, his voice gruff. "It's time."

It could only be time for one thing.

Slowly, I rose from the worn cot and rolled my shoulders, readying myself. Maybe Wolfe hadn't been able to save me. My feet were like lead. I couldn't move. I didn't *want* to move.

Moving would mean walking to my death, my execution, and I couldn't do it. I couldn't fucking do it.

"Come on." The guard stepped into my cell, still not looking at me. He grabbed my arm and hauled me from the room. I tried digging my heels into the concrete floor, but they skidded against it. He easily pulled me out, the cell door slamming shut behind us.

Then I was being pushed toward the light at the end of the hallway.

I didn't know what I was expecting, but walking through the Council building in my dirty clothes and smudged face in front of prestigious Reapers wasn't how I thought I'd get to the execution room. I thought it would be off to the side, hidden away like a dirty secret no one talked about.

Maybe they liked to parade prisoners around, show them off like prized cattle before slaughter.

With every step I took on the cold marble floor, my hope of seeing Mason again dwindled. I didn't hold it against Wolfe or the others for being unable to save me. It'd been a stupid idea to think he somehow could. There were too many powerful people at play.

"Can I call Mason?" I asked, emotion thick in my throat. The guard kept his hand tight around my arm, ignoring me. "Please?" He barely lowered his eyes, our gazes clashing.

"No," he finally said. My chin wobbled as tears streamed down my cheeks. No? He couldn't just tell me no, right?

Panic set it, and I jerked on my arm, trying to rip it from his grip. I didn't know what I'd do—make a run for it? Where could I go where they wouldn't find me? They would find me anywhere.

My body flailed as I tried to escape his iron grip. It was no use. He tightened his hold, his thick fingers digging into my flesh.

"Please," I cried again, using my fingers to try to pry his hand off me. "Let me talk to him, just one last time." I wasn't above begging. I'd do it to talk to Mason one more time, just to tell him I loved him.

"Stop it," he snapped, but I didn't. I didn't stop fighting him. I threw my body to the side, but his hold didn't waver. I dangled from his hand, and he sighed. "We're here."

No.

No, no, no.

Please no.

I wasn't ready to die.

There were so many things I hadn't done. I hadn't told Mason I loved him enough times. I hadn't seen enough of the world. I hadn't told Kali how proud of her I was, how much I loved her, how happy and thankful I was that she was my best friend.

"What's going on here?"

I snapped my head around, nearly sobbing when I saw Wolfe striding toward us, his face like thunder.

"She was supposed to be taken to High Reaper Will's courtroom," Wolfe said, glaring at the guard.

"I was told to bring her here," he said. He had the sense to appear frightened, at least. To be fair, Wolfe could be frightening when he wanted to be, which seemed to be all the time.

"I don't give a fuck what you were told," he snarled. "High Reaper Will wants to see her." Wolfe's hand wrapped around my other arm. I looked between the two men, feeling panic and excitement warring in my chest. The guard hesitated.

"She's..." He looked down at me and sighed. "Fine. I'll escort her there."

"That's not necessary," Wolfe ground out. "I can take it from here." He glared at the guard for another moment before jerking on my arm again. Finally, the guard let go, and it felt like a lead weight lifted off my shoulders.

As we walked away, I stared up at Wolfe. "Thank you," I cried softly, subtly wiping my face.

"We're not out of the woods yet," he grumbled. His words echoed around my head as he pulled open a set of giant double doors. I gave him a wary look before side-stepping him and looking into the room.

My eyes immediately found Mason.

He stood at the end of the aisle, his arms folded over his chest. When our eyes met, he didn't hesitate. He jumped over the small partition separating the dais and rows of benches for on-lookers and sprinted for me.

It wasn't sweet, the way he swept me into his arms and crushed me against him. It wasn't a romantic gesture or a gentle, loving hold. It was possessive. It was a promise to never let me go.

"Mason," I cried against his neck. I couldn't help the tears that slid freely from my eyes, and he squeezed me tighter.

"I'm here, little bird," he murmured over and over. He was. He was there. I knew he would be.

My body went stiff as Wolfe's words echoed in my head.

He was here for my execution.

He was here for my death.

He was here to watch me die.

I pulled away from him, horrified that he could even be here to watch. I would've been here for him, of course, but that was different. I'd do anything for him, no matter how much heartache it brought me. I never wanted him to hurt.

"Are you two finished?" Wolfe grumbled, sounding annoyed, as he stormed past us. I stared at Mason, unable to pull my eyes away.

"He's not happy it took you so long," he said.

"The guard wasn't bringing me here," I muttered. "He was taking me—"

"Doesn't matter." He put his hands on either side of my face, his eyes searching mine. "You're here. I have you."

It took me a moment to realize he wasn't hysterical, or bloodthirsty, or ready to blow the realm up.

Maybe I wasn't going to die.

"He did it?" I whispered. His eyes lit up as he nodded.

"He did it, baby." A sob left me, and I wrapped my arms around his waist, burying my face against his chest. "We're not in the clear yet, though. We need to get this done." I nodded, my face sliding against his shirt.

"Come on," Wolfe groaned. "I don't have all day."

Mason gripped my hand tightly and led me down the narrow aisle. He opened the little door for me and let me walk out onto the floor in front of the dais before he followed. I gave everyone gathered a weird look, waiting for someone to explain.

Rage and Caden were there, which surprised me. I thought Caden would never want Kali out of his sight again, and from the tense way he was pacing, I could tell not being with her was stressing him out.

Wesley, Malik, Damen, and, of course, Wolfe were there, too. Wolfe was rummaging around in a little black leather bag sitting on a table. Damen and Malik were talking between themselves as Wesley silently observed. He did that a lot: just sat back and watched.

"Guys, what's going—"

"Hush," Wolfe snapped, holding his finger up. Mason growled, and

I glanced up at him, feeling his hand tighten around mine. "Don't speak until I ask you a question."

"Wolfe," Mason warned. Finally, he looked up, giving Mason an exasperated look.

"Well?" he said, sounding irritated. "Is she supposed to talk?" Mason ground his teeth together, his jaw flexing.

"No," he gritted out.

"Okay, then," Wolfe said reasonably. "Then she doesn't need to speak. No need to go all wildebeest on me." I folded my lips between my teeth to keep from laughing. Wolfe didn't joke. He never joked. That meant he was fucking serious, which made it all that much funnier.

Maybe it was the anxieties of the day that had laughter-induced tears streaming down my face. Yeah, that's what I was going with. They were laughter-induced tears, not stress tears.

Before Mason could ask what was wrong, a door behind the dais opened, and a tall man in a black cloak strolled out. His head was down, his dark hair hiding his face. I glanced around as I shifted uncomfortably on my feet.

He sat in a large, high-backed chair and smiled at me.

"Hello, Raven," Will said. "You look well." I stared at him for a long moment, then cleared my throat.

"As do you, High Reaper," I said politely. Mason snorted beside me, and I snapped my eyes up to him.

"Wolfe, what can I do for you?" Will turned his attention to Wolfe, his casual face hidden behind a serious mask. Wolfe held a small book in his hand as he strolled towards Will.

"As you know, today is Raven's execution day," he began. "She was on her way there before we intercepted her." Will nodded.

My stomach twisted. They'd intercepted me? So if they were only a few minutes later, I could be fucking dead right now? That didn't make me feel panicky or anything. Fuck.

"Well," Wolfe continued. "I won't lie and say she's innocent."

"Shouldn't there be a jury here?" I whispered to Mason. He just shook his head, then jerked his chin at Will. I silently followed his order and looked back at Wolfe pacing in front of Will's chair.

"She did reap that mortal's soul," Wolfe said. I squeezed Mason's hand tighter, feeling uneasy about this. What the fuck was Wolfe doing? Yes, I'd technically already admitted that I was guilty, but to do it officially felt...different. "But she can't be punished for that."

"And why not?" Will drawled. He folded one leg over the other, rested his elbows on the arms of the chair, and locked his fingers together. He grinned down at us like a king on his throne, enjoying the show.

"This law," Wolfe handed him the small book, opened to a page, "says if a Reaper is murdered, they can reap their murderer's soul. That's what Raven did." Will quickly scanned the pages, then reread them and nodded.

"Of course," he said.

I blinked at him.

What the fuck?

It was that easy?

"This law hasn't been used for—"

"Centuries," Wolfe finished. "I know, but it's still valid." Will nodded a few times, a coy grin playing on his lips.

"He's in on this?" I whispered, and Mason nodded.

"I'll need to sign a few things and take official statements." Will looked at the small group of people assembled. "But Raven?" He looked at me pointedly. "You're free to go."

MY MIND WAS STILL REELING WHEN WE GOT HOME SEVERAL hours later. Mason had explained it to me already, but I couldn't comprehend it all.

"So, he's on our side," I said slowly as I sat on the couch. Caden walked past us to the kitchen to rummage around for food.

"He is," Mason said. "I didn't think so at first, but he still holds the same beliefs he always did. He wants to change the realm, and the best way to do that is from the inside. So—"

"He became a High Reaper," I finished. "Fuck." I scrubbed my hand over my face. "That seemed too easy." I looked up at him, and he shrugged. Rage sat on the couch opposite us, not standing against the wall for once.

"He'll probably want a favor at some point," Rage grumbled. "Slimy fuckers like him always do."

"How can he be slimy if he helped us?" I asked as I leaned back. Caden handed out open beers. I smiled my thanks and chugged it. Alcohol didn't have the same effect as it did when I was mortal, but enough of it still got a Reaper drunk.

"You don't become a High Reaper without getting your hands a little dirty," Mason said. "He has a lot of powerful friends, which is how he was able to pull so many strings today. But the shit he did for you, it wasn't out of the kindness of his heart. It was a favor, and he'll cash it in one day." I sighed, feeling heavy.

"Right," I breathed, then took another long drink of the beer. "So he's not entirely a good guy, then."

"None of us are," Caden muttered. He shrugged as he took a sip of his beer. "Any of you disagree?" I swallowed hard.

No.

I couldn't disagree with him.

44

RAVEN

PRESENT

Walking into Mason's room felt weird, like I was seeing it for the first time, but also like I was coming home. I didn't know what to think, seeing the room completely cleaned up, none of the things they'd knocked over during their fight on the floor anymore. It felt like the last week hadn't happened, like I'd dreamed it.

"I'm still waiting for the other shoe to drop," I said, laughing breathily as Mason sat at the edge of the bed. I stood beside his desk, my eyes flitting around the room, never resting on him.

"It's over," he sighed. "For now." That didn't make me feel any better. At all. If anything, it only made me feel worse.

Mason's Reaper mask lay discarded on his desk, and I traced my finger over it. How different would my life have been if I'd never seen this mask? If I'd never felt the connection to the man wearing it? Everything that happened since Mason came back into my life was insane. I hadn't had time to take a breather, and now, it was all catching up with me.

I was technically dead.

I wasn't alive anymore.

I was a fucking Reaper.

My soul almost died today. I almost disappeared from existence forever.

A quiet sob worked its way up my throat. What the fuck was wrong with me? How had I been so calm before? How had I pretended like I wasn't totally freaking the fuck out?

"Raven?" Mason's voice was quiet and unsure, like he didn't know what to do with me, and somehow, that made everything worse. He was supposed to know me better than I knew myself, and yet, he didn't know how to fix me, how to fix whatever spiral I was about to go down.

He got to his feet and moved to me. Without giving me a choice, he pulled me into his arms and held me tightly to his chest. The tears wouldn't come; they stayed lodged in my throat, choking me.

"You're okay," he murmured. "I've got you, and I'm never letting you go." Somewhere deep in my soul, I believed him. I knew he meant it, but his words couldn't make the panicky, overwhelmed feeling disappear. "What can I do?" He pulled away just enough to stare down at me.

"I don't know," I admitted, my breath stuttering out of me in huffs. His dark eyes searched mine.

"Do you still trust me?" he asked quietly, his hands tightening around my shoulders. "You know I'll always protect you." I nodded as he spoke.

That wasn't the problem. I knew him. It was me I didn't know anymore. Did being a Reaper change me? Did it change who I was?

"I don't know what to do with my life anymore," I said quietly. "I searched for Grim for so long, it's all I focused on. Now I have you, and I don't know what to do anymore." He bit his bottom lip, his eyes narrowing slightly. "I think everything is just hitting me now." I smiled tiredly, but my lips wobbled.

"How about you turn your mind off tonight?" he murmured. "Let Grim take care of you." He gripped my chin lightly, forcing me to look at him. It wasn't a request, not entirely. He wouldn't force me to do anything I didn't want to do, I trusted that, but that's what I wanted. I wanted to forget about everything else and focus solely on him, on pleasing him.

So I nodded.

"That's my girl," he said softly before pressing his lips gently to my forehead. "We didn't get to celebrate our anniversary."

"Grim..." I hesitated. It's not something I wanted to celebrate: my stepfather's death, but wasn't that we were celebrating, was it? It was our first meeting: the night that changed our lives.

He ignored me as he grabbed his mask from the desk and his haphazardly discarded cloak from the floor. He turned toward me, an evil glint in his eye. My stomach churned with unease.

Holding his hand out to me, he waited. I slowly slid mine into his, and he pulled me to him. "It's just you and me tonight, little bird. Just you and Grim."

Then, we began to disappear.

THE OLD FARM ROAD LOOKED EXACTLY AS IT HAD THAT night: starless, cold, deserted. I hated it. All that was missing was my blood staining the dirt, my screams echoing through the trees, and my stepfather's evil sneer.

"Hey," Grim said softly. "Just you and me. No ghosts." I nibbled my lips as I scanned the road again, then nodded.

No ghosts.

I could do that.

"I want you to run," he growled suddenly, and I snapped my head to him. "Just like that night, but it'll be me, Grim, who catches you." My heart pounded as I watched him slide his mask over his face, then slowly pull his cloak on. He rolled his shoulders a few times, loosening his muscles. When he looked back at me, he wasn't Mason anymore. Something inside him shifted when that mask was on, and fuck if it didn't turn me on.

"Why?" I breathed. His head tilted to the side, his face hidden. I'd forgotten how terrifying he looked in his mask, and I clenched my thighs together.

"I want to chase you, little bird." His voice was darker, and my mouth went dry. "Don't let me catch you." Without hesitating, I turned, sprinting down the road, away from Grim.

This was so fucked up. So fucking fucked up.

He was making me run from him just like I'd run from my stepfather. He was chasing me. What was going to happen when he caught me?

My feet pounded against the ground, loose gravel sliding under my shoes. These were the wrong fucking shoes for running, but I couldn't stop. I had to keep going. The predator at my back was gaining on me, his ragged breathing and heavy footsteps loud, mocking me.

With each aching breath, my lungs burned. Tears swam in my eyes, blurring my vision. I pumped my arms harder, forcing my body to move faster, away from him. Away, away, away.

I needed to get away.

How close was he?

It felt like he was right on my back, like he was right there, about to reach out and grab me.

I glanced over my shoulder, finding him further away than I'd thought he'd be. My feet slid on a rock, and down I went, landing painfully on my hands and knees. The world spun around me as my breath sawed in and out of my chest. His footsteps slowed, then his presence loomed over me.

I couldn't look up at him, not on my knees like this. I felt weird and panicky, like I was thrown back to that night. When his hand wrapped around the back of my neck, his thumb gently stroking up and down, I let out a long breath. It felt good, like I'd been holding that breath for years, and finally, I could breathe again.

"It's just me, little bird," he rasped, breathing hard. "Your Grim."

My Grim.

"I hated you," I said, tears stinging my closed eyes. My voice was just a whisper, but it was loud in the quiet night. "I hated that you left me here, that you abandoned me after you killed him." His thumb stopped moving, and he stiffened. "You made me think I was fucking crazy, that I'd killed him myself and made you up, but you were real."

I pushed back on my knees and tilted my head up to look at him.

His mask was shadowed, his eyes completely hidden. I wanted to know what he was thinking—I could feel his emotions, but they weren't his thoughts.

"Did you still hate me the night of your birthday?" he asked as he pulled his hand away. He straightened to his full height, his full chest heaving. I shook my head as I stared at him. It was a miracle I'd found him again, that he'd found me, that he'd wanted me.

"No," I whispered. "I stopped hating you almost as soon as I started." His breath stuttered as he dropped his head forward.

"I'm sorry," he finally said. "I didn't think how killing him would affect you. I saw him hurting you and wanted to kill him for it. I wanted to protect you, but I should've thought about *you*. I'm so fucking sorry."

"It was a long time ago," I said quietly. "If you'd left me with him, I would've died eventually. We wouldn't be here now." He nodded a few times. There was tension around us, unwanted and unneeded tension. I let out a tired breath. "Why did you want me to run? I'm too out of shape to do that." I was trying to lighten the mood and it seemed to work, because he straightened again, his hands flexing at his sides.

"I was hoping to get you on your knees like this," he said, using his chin to point at me, and I smirked up at him. "Then get your mouth around my cock."

"You're not choking me until I pass out again," I growled, pointing at him. "At least, not out here. It's fine if we're in private, but I don't want to do that shit in public." His laugh was deep and unexpected. I didn't hear it often, so when I did, it felt like a reward.

"Fine," he said, amusement still clear in his tone. He cleared his throat. "Damn it, Raven. I'm supposed to be serious. Grim is serious." I rolled my eyes. "You're such a fucking brat. Open your mouth."

His hands disappeared under his cloak, and I watched eagerly as he fumbled with his jeans. Licking my lips, I flicked my eyes to his masked face, then back to his crotch, waiting. Finally, he parted his cloak, revealing his thick cock, heavy in his hand. He roughly stroked it, squeezing the base until pre-cum dripped from the tip.

"Lick it," he growled. Lifting my eyes to his, I ran my tongue slowly along his slit, and he groaned. His other hand shot out to my head, and he fisted my hair. Gravel dug into my knees as I bobbed my head back and forth, trying to take more of him in my mouth. "Down your throat." I forced myself to relax and pushed the tip of his cock into my throat. He groaned, his hand tightening in my hair. Suddenly, he shoved me away. "Fuck this. I'm not going to last that long. Take your clothes off."

I blinked at him. He was so abrupt, it took me completely off guard. I slowly stood, kicked my shoes off, and then peeled my jeans down my legs.

"Shirt and bra, too," he said. "I want you naked."

"Are you getting naked, too?" I asked softly as I kicked my panties to the side. He shook his head.

"Only my slut gets naked. Not me."

I squeezed my thighs together as I took my shirt and bra off, throwing them on top of the rest of my clothes. Suddenly, I was standing naked in front of him, in the middle of that dirt fucking road that held so many terrible memories.

He stroked his cock as he watched me, his black eyes glinting in the silver glow of the moon. He stared at me, and I shifted uncomfortably, waiting for him to say something, give me an order, anything. Anything would be better than him silently watching me. Instead, he just stroked his dick and stared.

"Do you like it when I call you my slut?" he asked. I bit my lip as I nodded. "Tell me, then."

"I'm your slut," I breathed. His grip tightened, the head of his cock turning painfully red.

"On your hands and knees, ass in the air," he commanded. It was hard to breathe again, not from running, but from his control. His demands. *Him.*

Slowly, I turned away from him and sank to my knees. I pressed my shoulders into the hard ground as I lifted my ass, spreading my legs wider. He groaned before kneeling behind me, his rough hands gripping my hips painfully.

He rubbed his cock against my sensitive clit, and I moaned, my eyes rolling back at the feeling. I reached toward him blindly, and he bent my arm, pinning it to my lower back before grabbing my other one and holding them in one hand.

"Ready for me to fuck you, little bird?" His hand flexed on my wrists as he positioned his cock against my entrance. I nodded frantically, but he didn't press inside me.

Glancing back, my stomach tightened. His mask was dark, all shadows, barely highlighted with the moonlight. He was terrifying, formidable. My pussy clenched in anticipation.

"You're scared," he breathed. "You get turned on when you're scared." The tip of his cock prodded at me, barely pushing inside, and I groaned. "See that tree over there?" I forced my head to move to look where he gestured with his chin. "That's where I stood that night." He pushed another inch inside me, and I cried out at the feeling of being stretched. "This is where his body fell." Another inch of his cock entered me, and I clenched around him. "This is where I fucking killed him for you."

Without warning, he shoved the rest of the way in. My screams were muffled by the dirt, plumes wafting in the air around my face. I squeezed my eyes shut as he pulled almost all the way out, then slammed back in. My knees and shoulders dug painfully into rocks, my body jerking back and forth with his powerful thrusts. He grunted behind me, fucking me harder than I could have anticipated.

"This is where your soul became mine," he gritted out. "I fucking own you, little bird. I owned you that night, and I've owned you ever since." I nodded frantically, incoherent cries falling from my lips.

His hand slid up my back, his fingers tracing my scythe tattoo before tangling in my hair. He yanked me back, pulling me against his chest as his cock rubbed shallowly inside me. Slowly, he slid his hand from my hair, the other moving up my waist until he cupped my breasts. His mask was cold and hard against my skin, his loud breathing muffled behind it.

Suddenly, he pulled out, and I nearly fell backward. He caught my waist, holding me upright as he sat and turned me toward him. Roughly, he jerked me forward, forcing me to straddle his lap.

"Ride me, baby," he rasped as he pushed my hair from my sweaty face. I shoved at his shoulders, forcing him to lay back. His hands found my hips as I slowly lifted myself up, then dropped back down, taking him in one rough thrust. "Fuck, that's it. My little bird's pussy is magic."

His hand moved to my lower stomach, his thumb finding my clit. He rubbed back and forth, forcing me closer toward that edge. My thighs trembled each time I lifted myself, my body tightening with each stroke of his thumb.

"Grim," I whimpered.

"I know," he said, his dark eyes intense on mine. "Come for me." I bunched his cloak tightly in my hands as I squeezed my eyes shut.

I focused on my impending release. It was right there, *right fucking there*. I was so close. With his cock rubbing me deliciously and his thumb stroking my clit just the right way, I was about to explode.

It wouldn't come.

"Come, slut," he grunted, lifting his hips and forcing his dick deeper.

"Choke me," I pleaded. I slammed myself down, riding him harder as his hand moved from my hip to my throat.

"You're such a dirty, freaky little bird, aren't you?" he gritted out. "Needing to be choked so you can come on your Master's cock." He squeezed my throat, and I smiled brightly at him. I moved faster, my orgasm about to hit me as he squeezed more. "Scream my name. I want everyone to hear who you belong to. Scream for me."

My head fell back as I braced my hands on my thighs, my nails digging into the tops of them until the biting sting urged me forward.

"Grim!" I screamed, my voice nearly inaudible. "Grim, Master, please!"

"Fuck, come on my cock," he groaned. His hand tightened as his thumb flicked my clit faster, harder. "Fuck, I need you to come for me. Now, little bird." I slammed myself down, my scream loud in the dark night. I clenched around his thick cock, milking him as he squeezed my throat harder, his hot cum painting my walls white.

Finally, he let me go, and I inhaled deeply before falling limply to his chest. He grunted out a breath as he wrapped his arms around me, his softening cock still buried inside me. He pressed his lips against my sweaty forehead, basking in our shared pleasure.

As shitty as the night we met had been, this made it worth it. This erased all the pain and memories of that night and all the nights that came after it.

All that was left was Grim—Mason—and me.

Epilogue

GRIM

Leaning against the kitchen counter, I watched as Raven poured coffee into Caden's mug, then her own. She floated around the kitchen like she'd lived here forever. It made my chest warm to know she saw this place as her home—that she saw my brothers as her family.

Even if she didn't know Brody or Rage well, she loved them because they were my brothers. She and Caden became fast friends, which didn't surprise me. They loved to gang up on me and make my life a living hell, not that I was complaining.

As long as she was happy, I was too.

"Still nothing from Kali?" Caden asked, his voice quiet. Raven sighed as she slumped into the chair beside him.

"No," she said regretfully. It was killing them both that Kali wasn't talking to them. They didn't know if she was pissed, or just healing, and Caden was losing his fucking mind. He sighed loudly, but didn't say anything else. After a moment, she turned toward me. "Nothing from Brody, either?"

"Nope," I said. I wasn't too worried about him. If he'd been Exterminated or taken, we would've heard by now. He was still hiding, which was impressive. "I heard there was a Reaper trying to hunt him down,

252

but wherever the fuck he is, it's somewhere Reapers can't find him." She let out a long breath.

"And where the fuck is Rage?" Caden asked. I shrugged.

"No idea," I replied. "He said he needed to go out."

"That was two days ago." Caden took a sip of his coffee, grimacing slightly. "God, I'm sorry, but why does your coffee always suck?"

"It's not that bad," Raven protested, rolling her eyes.

"It's like drinking sludge." My lips twitched. He wasn't wrong. I never drank the coffee she made. I didn't know how she always managed to fuck it up, but she did.

"Just add more sugar, you'll be fine," she said.

"This will burn a hole through my fucking stomach if I finish it," he grumbled as he got to his feet and poured it down the sink unapologetically. Raven didn't take it personally—I think she found it funny. Brat.

"Rage?" She looked at me questioningly. "He was home last night." I nodded and sipped my water.

"He's gone during the day, home at night." I shrugged. "No idea where he's going or what he's doing."

"Have you asked him?" Caden turned toward me, his arms folded over his chest.

"Why the fuck would I ask him?" He lifted his brows expectantly.

"So you can know what he's doing?" he said slowly, like I was stupid.

"I don't care what he's doing," I replied. "It's Rage. He doesn't cause trouble. There's no reason to worry."

There was a beat of silence.

It was true. Rage was the least likely to do anything stupid enough to land him in trouble. Caden nodded a few times, then moved past me and grabbed the coffee pot to pour the rest down the sink, earning a snort from Raven.

"If he wanted us to know, he would've told us," I concluded. He nodded again, keeping his back to me.

"I just think we should know," he said, shrugging slightly, sounding hurt. Finally, he turned to face us again. "I'm going to see her. Fuck it. I'm just going to go see her." Raven and I exchanged a look.

"Cade," she said slowly. "She's not ready—"

"I'll make her ready," he snapped. "I can't stand not being with her." I let out a long breath.

"If she doesn't want you around, you need to accept that," I said, trying to slowly and softly bring him back to reality. He glared at me, his hands shaking. I knew he wanted to argue, but he wouldn't. He couldn't; there was nothing to argue with. If she didn't want him around, he'd have to leave her alone. It wasn't like he could kidnap her and force her to be with him.

He flicked his eyes between us, then stormed from the kitchen. We watched as he disappeared, then she let out a long breath.

"She does this," she said. "When she's struggling, she isolates herself. She doesn't let anyone in. If he thinks he's going to break her of that habit, he's wrong. I've been trying for years." I nodded a few times, but didn't totally agree. Caden, when he wanted to be, was the most stubborn person I knew, even more so than my little bird.

"She'll be okay," I said, and she nodded, clearly trying to trust me, even though she probably didn't believe me, not completely.

"I just hate that she's hurting," she murmured.

"She's strong," I said as I moved to the island. Leaning my forearms on the marble, I brought our faces closer together. "You wouldn't be friends with someone who wasn't." She smirked and dropped her eyes.

"You think he'll leave her alone?" she asked, glancing up at me through her lashes.

"Not a chance," I laughed. She rolled her eyes, smiling wider as she leaned back.

"Yeah, didn't think so." She took a sip of her coffee and tried to hide her grimace. I just shook my head. She'd never admit how much she hated it. She smiled at me brightly, and my breath caught in my chest.

How fucking lucky was I that this girl was mine? That she'd chosen me?

I had something for her in my pocket and it was weighing on me. It'd been weighing me down for days, but I'd been too nervous to give it to her. I didn't think now would be the right time, but with the way the sunlight poured through the window, illuminating her hazel eyes, and making her skin glow, she looked ethereal, and I felt my chest tighten.

"So," I said awkwardly. Her eyes narrowed slightly.

"So, what?" She laughed; she knew something was up.

I hesitated before pulling it from my pocket. Carefully, I set the ring down on the counter and left my hand over it, hiding it from her. Was I really going to do this? It was fucking stupid, but she'd told me I had to do it the 'right way,' so this was me trying to do it the right way, for her.

"A ring doesn't mean shit," I started, then winced; not the best opening for a proposal. "A ring can't show all that I feel for you. It doesn't show how you make me feel." I paused. I wasn't doing this right. There weren't enough words to tell her all I wanted to.

"Are you..." She trailed off as I pulled my hand away, showing her the ring. She stared at it, her mouth opening slightly before she flicked her eyes up to me.

"You told me you wanted a real proposal," I said, and she smiled. Tears swam in her eyes and it killed me. "Don't cry. Fuck. Am I really fucking up that badly?" She laughed as she wiped her cheek.

"You're not fucking up." She smiled, her eyes crinkling. "I thought you were skipping the whole proposal thing since you told Will I was your wife." I rolled my eyes, sighing heavily.

"Those were dire circumstances. I didn't like how he was looking at you and he needed to back the fuck off." I growled the last few words, my blood heating with the memory of his eyes on her, undressing her in his mind. *Fuck.* I wanted to kill him for that. She laughed again, then leaned forward and pressed her lips to mine.

"You're cute when you're all growly and possessive," she teased. I growled, mostly to make her laugh again.

"Are you saying yes, then?" I asked. I didn't know why I felt so nervous about her answer. I thought I already knew it, but giving her the power to say no was making me anxious.

"Am I saying yes?" She tapped her finger on her chin. "Hmmm." She rolled her eyes as she dropped her hand. "Obviously."

She launched herself at me, clutching her arms tightly around my neck as she peppered my face with kisses. I couldn't imagine ever letting her go. In that moment, with her in my arms, everything calmed. Everything, all the bullshit of my eight-hundred years, the last fifteen years, all of it, was worth it for this exact moment.

"Love you, little bird," I murmured, and felt her smile against my skin.

THE END

About Haley Tyler

Haley Tyler is a dark romance author who writes your favorite book boyfriends, and badass, strong heroines. She lives in Texas with her boyfriend and dog, Maverick.

When she's not writing, you can find her reading a dark romance novel, scrolling social media, listening to music, or obsessing about her next book hero.

www.haleytyler.com
Facebook Group

instagram.com/haleytylerthewriter

tiktok.com/@haleytylerthewriter?

facebook.com/Haley-Tyler-109176778467806

goodreads.com/haleytyler

amazon.com/author/haleytyler

bookbub.com/profile/haley-tyler

pinterest.com/haleytylerthewriter

Also by Haley Tyler

The Salvatore Brotherhood MC Series

Killing Calm

Little Bear

Lost and Found

Safe House

A Salvatore Brotherhood MC Short Story

At First Sight

Say I Do

Just One Night

Standalone

Queen of Demons

The Reapers

Calling on the Reaper (Reapers Book One)

Coming soon

Secret Santa

Man Possessed (Salvatore Brotherhood MC 5)

Acknowledgments

Thank you for reading and (hopefully) enjoying *Calling on the Reaper!* This is the start of a new series. I'll be totally honest, I hadn't planned on making this a series. Originally, I thought this was going to be a one-and-done story, but as I began writing, more characters started showing themselves and I realized they had their own stories to tell too. So, here we are.

Brody's book is next! Where is he? Who is he with? Is he really an Exterminator? Did he really save someone and Exterminate another Reaper? Find out in his book. He's so much more than meets the eye.

A quick and GIANT thank you to my amazing editor, Alexa. Grim and Raven's story really came to life after she worked her magic on it. I'm incredibly thankful she was willing to work with me and didn't run when she read the first spicy scene. Thank you a million times over, and I can't wait to work on more books in the future!

Thank you to my Chaos Crew. You keep me grounded and smiling when I feel like I'm spiraling. You remind me who I'm doing this for. I love you guys!

Of course, I always have to thank my friends who help me navigate my chaotic brain. They always know the story I want to tell, and help me achieve it. So, thank you. Seriously. (Especially Melissa on this one!)

My ARC readers!! Omg. Thank you guys so much! I always appreciate you taking the time to read and review my books, especially this one!

Finally, you! My readers! Thank you a million times. I'd never be writing these books without you.

Haley Tyler

Made in the USA
Middletown, DE
31 October 2022

13850728R00152